ODESSA

BEACH

Other books by Robert Leuci:

Blaze
Captain Butterfly
Doyle's Disciples
Double Edge
Fence Jumpers
The Snitch

ODESSA

BEACH

A Novel by

ROBERT LEUCI

MOYER BELL
WAKEFIELD, RHODE ISLAND AND LONDON

Published by Moyer Bell

**LIBRARY OF CONGRESS
CATALOGING-IN-PUBLICATION DATA**

Leuci, Robert, 1940–
Odessa Beach / by Robert Leuci

  p.   cm.

I. Title
PS3562.E85703   1985
813'.54–dc21   85-20716
ISBN 1–55921–242-X   CIP

Printed in the United States of America

Distributed in North America by
Publishers Group West, Publishers Group West,
1700 Fourth Street, Berkeley CA 94710
800-788-3123 (in California 510-528-1444) and
in Europe by Gazelle Book Services Ltd., Falcon
House, Queen Square, Lancaster LA1 1RN
England 524-68765

For Anthony and Santina

A very special thanks to
Anatoly,
"Dneprov" Gross
and Olga Gross.
New and special finds for America.

"The Americans thought they knew him, liked him, had no reason to fear him. He looked as vital, as capable as ever. He was the man who would lead—"

A FLAG FOR SUNRISE
Robert Stone

ODESSA

BEACH

Chapter One

MOSCOW
November, 1980

Nikolai Zoracoff sat comfortably on a bench near the fountain in Pushkin Square. He turned his face toward the sun and relaxed as if he were lounging in the tropics. Bright sun in early November, a rare gift in Moscow. Niki savored it. Still, the air smelled cold, he enjoyed that too. Niki was a true Muscovite.

Nikolai Zoracoff appeared different in every way from the crowd that pressed its way into the park. American jeans, white turtleneck sweater, and short leather jacket gave him the look of a Scandinavian ski instructor, instead of a Russian black marketeer.

He glanced at his watch. It was Swiss, and gold, and cost more than most people in the square earned in a year. He was ten minutes early.

A redheaded woman strolled past him, she stopped and smiled. Out of politeness Niki acknowledged her. He was strikingly handsome. Tall, and blond, blue eyes framed by soft, long feline lashes.

Before his marriage to Katya, Niki had danced in and out of dozens of bedrooms. Nowadays he was selective, but he'd never be monogamous.

He looked past the redheaded woman and past the statue of Pushkin to the Gorky Street entrance, where a crowd of teenagers headed toward the cinema. An opening in the crowd, revealed the waving arm of Viktor Vosk.

Viktor signaled Niki to follow, then turned quickly and walked out of the square toward Kalinin Prospect.

Viktor was twenty years older than Niki, he limped, and slouched. But he moved very quickly.

On the coldest of days, Viktor never buttoned his coat. He said the cold was a friend to be embraced, a great cognac to be sipped slowly and enjoyed. His topcoat flew behind him like a cape.

Niki followed him with long strides, stepping around teenagers in boots and imitation leather jackets, grandmothers with small children who looked like potatoes, in insulated coats and pants; clothing much too warm for this sunny, bright day.

Viktor, the old policeman, moved through the afternoon crowd like a mink.

The warm weather brought the Muscovites out in hordes. They filled the parks and cafés along Gorky Street and Kalinin Prospect. They crowded onto the sidewalks, some moved single-file in the street. Students, clerks, bureaucrats, old and young, showing surprise at the gift of warm sunlight.

Viktor flew past the Café Angara. Niki knew he wouldn't go in there; too full of students. Unruly Bolshevik, throwbacks, Viktor called them. Noisy young people made Viktor cough.

He stopped in front of the Pechora, peered through the window, waved impatiently for Niki to hurry, then sped up the street. He moved like a man in total panic.

At the Café Metelitsa, he stopped, turned toward Niki, then disappeared inside.

He was already seated when Niki walked through the café door. Coughing, his chest heaving, Viktor had the stricken look of an untrained runner. Why the need for this goddamn pursuit, Niki wanted to yell. But, when he saw Viktor's red-rimmed eyes and heard that horrible cough, he felt nothing but pity for his alcoholic friend.

Clearly, Viktor's morning ration of vodka had already taken him off somewhere high, and was now dropping him with stops and starts, and small explosions in his chest.

Niki knew Viktor very well. They had been business partners for almost eight years. A partnership Niki sometimes found hard to understand, at least from Viktor's perspective. As for himself, well, people spoke of him as the Tsar of Gorky Street, the Prince of Pushkin Square. Niki lived a sinfully full bourgeois life.

Viktor Vosk was a captain of the Militia (Moscow city police). A hard man who studied people closely. Niki doubted that Viktor understood how much Niki cared for him. The drinking was killing Viktor. Niki could see it. He could see it in the yellow of Viktor's eyes and the golden tint of his fingers. Viktor had a deadly Russian tan.

"Done, finished, all arranged," Viktor said, "thank God you're a Jew, otherwise I don't know what we would have done."

Niki's life had made him a great believer in luck. He couldn't help a small smile; Viktor smiled back.

"I'm as much a Jew as you are a communist," he said. "I really didn't think you'd be able to do it." Had he forgotten how unique Viktor was. The man was magical.

"For ten thousand American dollars, there is nothing I can't do." Viktor tapped his coat pocket with the flat of his hand, then he dabbed at his eyes with his coat sleeve. "I will suffer more than you, Niki. I'll miss you."

"You'll miss the money, you old bull."

"True enough, but money has limited meaning for me. I can spend only so much. No, Niki," he said, "it's the adventure I'll miss."

Niki laughed and patted his friend's cheek. It was moist, unhealthy feeling. "Viktor, we've had too much adventure. Look where adventure has brought us. I'm lucky I'm not pissing ice cubes. And you, you're—"

Viktor cut him off. "Luck is bullshit," he said, "spirit is what counts. You see all these people"—Viktor waved his arms like a conductor—"they all have secrets in their hearts, dreams, fantasies. But what do they do? They sit on their hands and moan. We have spirit, Niki, we have what it takes. That is what made the revolution! That is what makes the Union great! Spirit!" Viktor shouted and pounded on his chest with his fist. People sitting at other tables stared. As they talked, Niki smoked filtered Dunhill cigarettes. There was no filter between the vodka and Viktor's bloodstream. He drank three before Niki could finish his first.

When Viktor spoke emotionally about the wonders of America, Niki began to feel ill. "I have friends in Cleveland," he said. "Americans that were stationed in Moscow during the war."

"What war?" Niki laughed.

"America is a hustler's paradise. You'll see, you'll be a millionaire and I'll be in snow up to my ass."

"Then come with us, why don't you? We'll put our show on the road like the circus. We have friends in New York; Yuri and Petra and Vasily. They're all there."

"Listen to me and stay away from those clowns. They're small-time crooks. You, on the other hand, have the"—Viktor ran his thumb across the tips of his fingers—"the touch! As for me, even if I had a choice, I would probably stay in Moscow. I'm a Russian. You, you're a Jew. Jews, Niki, were born to emigrate."

4

It had been only two weeks ago that Niki received word from Viktor, the way he always did, through Mikail Yagoda, the jeweler.

"Meet him at the bench in one hour," Mikail whispered in his ear, while standing on tiptoe. Mikail was from Tashkent, small and almost black, he could split a diamond, or a head, with his little chisel and ball hammer.

That day Niki had gone to Pushkin Square unaware that anything special was going on. Maybe Viktor needed some money, it wasn't unusual. Viktor constantly said he didn't need money, but he was always asking for it, with moans and a litany of problems.

Viktor's story stunned Niki.

"It was a simple double murder investigation," Viktor had said, "nothing out of the ordinary. But now it has leaked into an area that is far more dangerous—labor books."

It seemed that a manager of a textile plant, in a drunken rage, had axed his mother-in-law and son. Decapitated one, gutted the other. "Messy, messy," Viktor said, clucking and shaking his head.

"Gruesome, bizarre, he's probably from Georgia," Niki suggested. Then he asked, "What does that have to do with me?"

"It seems that the plant manager's wife blamed vodka for his act of insanity."

"What else, we Russians blamed vodka for Kruschev's magical corn-crop failure."

"The plant manager had more money than he could spend. Frustrated, he turned to vodka. He bought and drank gallons of it, the selfish bastard," Viktor said. "But, that's not the problem."

"Maybe not," Niki remembered saying, "but I wouldn't want his troubles."

"How does a plant manager end up with more money than he can spend? Simple, he collects salaries from workers who are on the payroll, but who do not appear at the plant. Sound familiar?" Viktor asked. Niki remembered beginning to feel nauseated as he sat and listened.

"He kept the workers' labor books, and checked the attendance spaces regularly."

"I know, I know, go on."

"The Militia had turned a simple homicide investigation over to the KGB. The KGB doesn't like the idea that there may be other plants, with other plant managers, with other employees, who turn over their labor books, and don't appear at their jobs.

"While plant managers keep salaries," Viktor continued, "factory workers do other, more lucrative things. And the *other things* workers do, the KGB likes even less.

"Get it, Niki?" Viktor had said. "It's not your forged labor book. No, by the time this investigation is completed you'll be one of hundreds in Moscow alone. But, the KGB is very interested in exactly how these unemployed people are earning a living. You will be forced to explain a lifestyle that puts you somewhere between a Central Committee member and a lead dancer of the Bolshoi. For an unemployed electrical technician, that will not be easy."

Niki hadn't worked in five years. For five years the manager of the electronics plant in Boloshelvo kept his salary, while he did *other things*.

How long would it be before the KGB looked at Nikolai Zoracoff's labor record? A month? Six weeks? Who can tell? In the Soviet Union the wheels of justice turn as unevenly as they do in Manhattan. Eventually they'd catch up to him, that was certain. What would be the worst case scenario?

For a forged labor book? A jail sentence, maybe. For profiteering? A few months at Lubyanka, the KGB prison and interrogation center, then some morning, a walk in the snow, and a bullet in the head. Profiteering is often a capital offense in the Soviet Union.

"You'll have to run," Viktor had said. "You have no options. You're always talking about the West . . ." He remembered Viktor whispering, "If you stay, you're a *goner*." He remembered his friend underlined the word goner.

In the ensuing days there were other meetings.

These were the short-lived, warm days of détente. Emigration, for Russian Jews, had become a reality. By year's end more than fifty thousand would leave the Soviet Union.

"Jews are leaving the country by the thousands," Viktor had said. "The ungrateful bastards are jamming the airports and railroad stations."

There were times Viktor sounded strangely neurotic, as well as anti-Semitic—very Russian.

He explained that the Jews were totally confusing an already screwed up bureaucracy. No one has any idea how long this romance with America will last. Brezhnev was making people very unhappy with his toasts to the American president. Jimmy Carter, most Russians believed, was a closet Zionist, and, therefore, a criminal.

Time was short. Niki and Katya had to get into the stream of emigration.

Russian Jews could emigrate only to Israel. But, they had to have documented proof that they had a blood relative living there.

"It's a ploy," Viktor explained. "The government knows that these people want to go to Israel, as much as I want to spend Christmas in Siberia."

Another meeting . . . "The waiting list is long, the process is slow. You can't wait. For ten thousand American dollars, five thousand for you, five thousand for Katya, I can grease the wheels. Move you and Katya to the head of the line, put air under your arms, get you away."

Viktor told Niki to be ready to leave at a moment's notice. No preparation, no furniture storage. Shipping forms would

7

be checked. "I want one person to look at your papers, and one person only. My contact with emigration—he'll be at the airport the day of your departure."

Now this. Only fourteen days after Viktor had told him of the tragedy concerning the labor books (forget the double murders), he prepared himself to take the news with a smile.

"When?" he asked.

"Tomorrow morning at ten o'clock you fly from Sheremetievo to Vienna."

Niki groaned, sipped a little vodka, and lit a cigarette from the tip of the one he was already smoking. He thought of Katya.

Viktor handed him a small manila envelope. And, he must have been reading his mind, because he said, in that way big-hearted alcoholics do when they mean to be kind, "Your tickets to the Western wonderland. Now all you have to do is tell your wife."

For the past two weeks Niki had sat up nights watching his Katya sleep, rehearsing a short speech. After an hour or two, he'd lie next to her on the bed, but saying nothing. She would ask questions, questions he would be unable to answer. Katya knew nothing of his real business. She had decided, totally on her own, and early on in their relationship, that Niki was a special agent of the KGB. Niki had not dissuaded her. It explained their apartment, their full refrigerator, their theater tickets, Niki's unusual comings and goings, his unique friends.

Katya taught at a middle school. She, like her father, was a member of the party. She thought Niki was a hero of the motherland.

"Well, my good criminal," Viktor asked, "what will you do? You must tell her. There are two tickets in that envelope. Still, if you feel it's not possible to explain your situation to Katya, go by yourself."

"I'm not a criminal," Niki said. "I serve the people, Viktor, I'm a civil servant like you."

"The people of Moscow," Viktor pointed out, "have many problems." Viktor nodded as if he'd said something of historical importance.

"The main problem with this city," Niki said, "is that life here can be boring, but only if you don't know where to find the spice; the simple pleasures."

Viktor continued to nod, he was in total agreement. He swallowed more vodka.

"I put some spice into peoples' lives. That doesn't make me a criminal. I didn't steal, I didn't kill anyone. I was a businessman. I delivered to the people things they truly needed in order to escape the . . ."

"Boredom," Viktor said, then he carefully filled both their glasses with vodka. He poured orange soda into another glass for Niki. Niki found it impossible to drink pints of vodka without washing it down with soda. It went well with the vodka. It dampened the fire in his head and chest, it allowed him to breathe. "Exactly," he said and rubbed the tip of his nose. It was beginning to feel numb. That's the way it went. First the nose, then the arms, and finally, the legs.

"You can try that explanation on Katya," Viktor said mildly. "If it works, why not try it on the KGB. Katya, the rare beauty that she is, will probably understand. The KGB will put you in an asylum, wrap you in a canvas, wet it, and watch your head swell. Then they'll ask you questions, which you, not wanting your head to explode, will answer."

"That's it, isn't it," Niki whispered, "you were afraid that if I ended up in Lubyanka, I'd inform on you."

Viktor's laugh was not convincing.

"I don't know," Viktor said. "To be honest, I never considered the possibility."

"I'm glad, because I wouldn't have."

"People often do what they don't want to do in Lubyanka." Viktor grinned.

"I want to leave now," Niki said.

If it had been another time, he would have turned the entire exchange into a joke—to a fun-filled, vodka-flowing afternoon. But he'd just felt the first punch of the vodka. It ground his teeth, it made him angry.

"I don't want to leave Moscow," he said.

"Then don't."

"You tell me I must. I have no options."

"You'll be dead in six months."

"You really believe that?"

"Well, I don't think it's worth the risk to find out."

Niki could almost feel Viktor thinking about his chances. More vodka gone, more orange soda for Niki. Was there more to this than Viktor was telling?

"Your documents are in perfect order. You leave tomorrow, with or without Katya."

"Just like that."

"Well, stay then," Viktor yelled, but there was fear in his voice. "Damn you, Nikolai Zoracoff, I will miss you." Down went another tumbler of vodka. But, then, as if he'd just seen a photograph of his own death, Viktor got up from the chair and stood over Niki. "My God," he said, "last month, when we were in the baths at Sandune, I remember thinking my Jew friend is not circumcised."

"That's right," Niki said, not looking up. But out of the corner of his eye he saw Viktor grab his forehead.

"What if they check at the airport? What if they look at that hooded prick of yours and think you're not a Jew, but a real Russian trying to escape."

Niki got so angry he didn't know which way to look.

"What do you mean, real Russian. My grandparents were born in Moscow. If I remember correctly, yours were Volga Germans. And besides, what about your contact? You have one, I hope?"

"My contact is with emigration, not customs. Customs checks for little things, like your prick."

"Viktor, please sit down, you're embarrassing me."

Viktor had broken out in a sweat. And then suddenly, as if he realized all at once that people in the café could easily overhear their conversation, Viktor blushed and his eyes widened. He looked nervously around the café. Taking hold of Viktor's elbow, Niki urged him to sit back down.

"Most Jews in the Union of my generation are not circumcised," he said.

Viktor was fifty years old, with heavy creased skin, and a thick drooping mustache. At that moment he looked to Niki like a very tired, very old, worn-out man. He nodded his head, groaned, and pushed himself back up from the table.

Viktor Vosk was tired. He'd already drunk over a liter of vodka, and it was not yet two o'clock in the afternoon. Age was put on his face by a dying liver.

But he was a hard, tough policeman. A man who had been cheating the government since childhood, for the pure adventure of it. He told Niki he would see him at the airport in the morning.

Taking a freshly opened bottle of vodka, Viktor shoved it in his coat pocket. Then he announced to all his intention to go quietly mad, and walked away, leaving Niki to pay the bill.

As he left the café Niki looked skyward and thought that the blowing snow was paying homage to the grandmothers, who wrapped their wards in quilt and down. The temperature had dropped twenty degrees, and there were several inches of snow on the ground. The *babushki* of Moscow knew . . .

He stood in front of the café with his hands in his pockets, and his collar turned up against the howling wind.

Niki decided that he must be straightforward with Katya. That was a joke, he had little choice. The plane for Vienna would leave in sixteen hours, and if Viktor was right, he had to be on it.

Katya, beautiful Katya, with a soul more beautiful than even her face, she'd understand. He'd start from the beginning, tell her everything. How, at twenty-two, his life had been set onto a track going nowhere. He was a small-time street hustler, till Viktor came along. No, he couldn't say that. That was stupid, that was the vodka thinking. Katya would hate him. She despised black marketeers; "a plague on the people," she called them. She was young, still a believer. Niki knew no one who was truly a communist, but Katya came close. She understood nothing of the chess game that was Moscow.

Nikolai Zoracoff was an orphan. He had little education, and before Viktor came into his life, no connections.

He was an electrician's helper, and the chance that he could do more within the Soviet system did not exist. His future would be a never-ending series of crowds and lines.

He was twenty-two years old and supplemented an income of eighty rubles a month by selling records and tapes in Pushkin Square. With the extra money he was able to buy clothes on the black market and an occasional book. The records and tapes he bought from foreign students. They were old and worn, but in great demand.

Viktor Vosk, along with two other policemen, caught him. At the time he was selling two Beatles records and an Elvis Presley tape. The police took him to a satellite station in Gorky Park. It was there they questioned him, and it was there that they beat him.

Friendly at first, in that way policemen are when they know they have you cold, they joked and asked him silly questions.

"Wasn't Presley a homosexual? Didn't the Beatles get the highest medal in Britain? And for that, weren't they allowed to spend a night at Buckingham Palace?"

Niki shrugged his shoulders, he smiled and said, "How would I know?"

Then they really beat him. They punched, slapped, and kicked him. All the while Viktor Vosk watched.

The more they hit him the more Niki smiled. His stance was not heroic, simply a reflex he'd picked up at the orphanage. A response to power, a tranquilizer for fear.

The police bullies broke two of his ribs and scarred his right eye. Niki continued to smile. All at once one of the policemen lifted him off the floor and slammed him against the wall. Niki smiled and noticed that Viktor was smiling, too, as though he understood, like he'd been there. Viktor Vosk smiled and nodded his head, but he didn't stop the beating. Still Niki held to his story. He'd found the records and would have turned them into the police had he had the opportunity to do so. They put him in the hospital for three days, but didn't arrest him.

When he checked out of the hospital Viktor was waiting, and his real life began (he could describe it no other way).

Viktor insisted he go to school nights and learn English. He taught him about icons, real and forged. Niki became an expert on Romanoff art, silver, and gold coins. Viktor brought him to the dark side of Moscow where the *fartsovshchiki* (black marketeers) dealt in money exchanges with foreigners.

Viktor knew scores of foreign students and diplomats for whom Niki would arrange women. And, he delivered packages. It was money, he knew that; he could tell by the weight and feel. Viktor never offered an explanation about the money, and Niki never asked.

Niki became a major hero when he was able to provide, for a substantial charge, *propiskas*. A *propiska* is a blue stamp on the "in Union" passport that allows the bearer to live in Moscow. It was the most sought after visa in the Soviet Union. And Viktor could deliver it.

In time, Niki had his own apartment at the Artist's Building. He'd given his labor book to Viktor. From that day on crowds and lines were a part of his history. He was known as the Tsar of Gorky Street, the Prince of Pushkin Square. All, thanks to Viktor Vosk, a captain of the Militia, who seemed to have the power of a member of the Politburo. Niki never asked questions about business, there never was a reason to.

Then the bottom fell out. Niki would be on his way to exile in America. All this he had to tell Katya, beautiful Katya, with a beautiful soul and a face that was classic Romanoff. Enormous green eyes, white skin like new snow, always cool always fresh. Niki had what all Russians dream of, the love of a beautiful, intelligent woman, and a well-placed friend. But all of that was being ripped from him because of a madman with a hachet, and too much vodka.

Standing on the street in front of the café, Niki heard a car horn and turned. It was a taxi, parked ten meters behind him. Moving carefully, he worked his way, with slips and skids, to the cab's front door and got in.

In Moscow, passengers in taxis sit up front with the driver. To sit in the back would give the impression that you somehow thought of yourself as superior to the driver.

"Five hundred and ten Karetnya Ryat," he said, stamping his feet to get the blood moving, "The Artists' Building."

The driver said, "I know, Mr. Zoracoff," then carefully pulled out from the curb.

For five minutes Niki sat wondering where the driver knew him from. The man's face was slightly familiar, maybe from Luzniky, the beer hall across from the skating rink. He couldn't remember, an afternoon in the arms of vodka will do that to you.

"You know me?" he asked, finally.

"Absolutely," the driver said firmly.

Most people who were serious hustlers Niki knew in varying degrees. Many of the street criminals, muggers, robbers, burglers, and the like, knew him by sight. Niki called them junk people, and kept his distance. With their homemade tattoos, they were targets for the police. Some were Jews, and that embarrassed him. The few that he knew well had already left for America.

"I apologize," Niki said, "but I don't—"

"Pasha Rublev," the driver announced, as if he were a relative. He didn't know him, but the name was famous.

"Are you related to the painter?" he asked, now interested.

"What painter?"

"Andri Rublev, the famous icon artist."

The driver thought for a second, rubbed his chin with a hand that had a tattoo of a tiny bird, then said, "Never heard of him."

"How is it you know me?"

"You bought a piece of antique silver from me last June."

That was it, he did remember him, and it was at the beer hall.

"How much was it?" he asked.

"You gave me a thousand."

"Good, good," Niki said, taking note of the man's even stare. It had been a fair deal.

Then he lit a Dunhill and looked out at the lights of Hermitage Park. He would be home soon, and it was fitting that his last night in Moscow should be spent driving through a new snow, with a *fartsovshchiki* taxi driver who would remember him kindly.

It was just past nine o'clock when Niki strolled into the apartment and saw Katya hunched over the kitchen table, drinking Georgian coffee from a hand-painted espresso cup.

From the hallway where he stood, Katya looked radiant in the soft light of the kitchen. It was the only light in the apartment.

"Hello, stranger," Katya said, and smiled in a way that Niki thought didn't look friendly.

He nodded, still at a loss on how to begin. He wished that he'd told Katya the truth, if not years ago, then certainly when Viktor told him he'd have to emigrate. Emigrate, the word pounded inside his chest, made him dizzy. The thought terrified him. He'd soon be alone, without Viktor, adrift in a world of hustlers. Truth was, Niki felt safe within the quiet orderliness of the Soviet state. He understood all the games, all the moves within the crowds and lines.

"The snow is really coming down," he said.

Katya nodded and said, "It's November, Niki."

With difficulty he resisted an urge to turn and walk out of the apartment. It was too late to tell Katya his life story, too late to tell her the truth, and he wasn't all that sure what the truth was.

Niki walked to the kitchen window. It was large and looked out over Hermitage Park fourteen floors below.

In the window's reflection Niki could see Katya holding a book of poems. She glanced at him, sipped her coffee, and read.

Why did he have to make this so damn difficult?

"Are you all right?" she asked softly.

He nodded and continued to look at the storm as if hypnotized.

"Come, sit down, have some coffee."

He joined her at the table.

Katya never looked better. All her features were exceptional. Her incredible green eyes and high cheekbones were a reflection of Russian history.

"I will have some coffee," he said. Then he saw the other cup.

"Who was here?" he asked.

But Niki already knew, because standing next to the cup was an almost empty bottle of vodka. The same brand of vodka he and Viktor had been drinking earlier in the day. It was a less expensive brand than the one he kept at home.

"Your friend with the watery eyes," Katya answered.

Ignoring her comment, Niki got up from the table. "What did he want?"

Katya smiled and handed him an opened letter. "He left you this," she said.

Niki felt his face redden and quickly pulled the letter from her hand.

"You opened it?"

"Of course," her hand made a little gesture, "he said I could."

Katya poured some of the vodka into her coffee cup. Her hand shook. It was a clumsy move. The liquid ran over the cup, staining the beautiful embroidered tablecloth.

"Wouldn't it be wonderful," she whispered, "if my husband trusted me. Tell me, Niki, were you ever going to tell me, or were you going to leave quietly like a burglar? You were, weren't you? You were going to pack your shirts and sweaters," now she was getting louder, "your black turtleneck that I bought for you. You were going to wait until I was asleep, then write me a long note. Or maybe you've already written it. Do you have a letter for me, Niki? Does it say you love me, that you will always love me? Does it say you'll miss me? Did you tell me to forget you? Did you say, I should go and find a *good* man that will value me?"

She began to cry. "Why didn't you tell me? How could you be so cruel?"

Niki was stunned. Katya knew—she knew everything—even what he was thinking.

He went to her. He hugged her. He tried holding Katya close for a long moment while he thought about an answer. But that didn't work. She pulled free.

"I want to know why," Katya cried. She was no longer able to control herself. She pushed him away when he tried to touch her.

"What it is you want to know?" Niki said softly.

"How could you be involved in such things without talking to me about them? I mean your leaving, not the business about your *business*. About that, I've always known. Did you really think that I believed for more than a day that you worked for the government? You think because I'm a woman I'm stupid? You're a *refusenick*! You have always been."

"I am not," he said flatly.

"Do you listen to yourself? Do you hear the things you say? Of course you're a *refusenick*. And, it's not so bad, I understand why. My God, you're a Jew, you can't help it."

"Now that is stupid," Niki said. He tried to glance at the letter as Katya spoke.

"I don't care about any of that. What I care about is that you would leave, just walk out of our lives without trusting my love for you, without trusting me."

Niki couldn't help himself, he smiled, Katya smiled back. Clearly she felt better. She crossed the room and touched his cheek.

"I love you, you foolish, foolish man. I've always loved you. You're the kindest person I've ever known."

Niki had always thought well on his feet. He began to talk, to explain. Everything he planned to say rolled out just the way he'd hoped it would. His childhood, the loneliness and control of the orphanage. That Viktor was the only family he'd ever known. How frightened he had been to confess the truth about his life. Afraid he'd lose her. He'd waited, afraid she'd judge him. He'd postponed. He would have told her tonight, after lovemaking. He would have said it all.

"I love you," she whispered as he spoke. "Don't you know how much I love you? I don't care about your politics."

He didn't see things in a political way but he knew that she did. He loved her more than he could say.

Niki ended his little speech by leaning one hand on the

table. With the other he caressed Katya's face, her forehead, her sparkling black hair.

"You are the *most* political person I know," she said slowly. "You don't see yourself in that way, but you are. You want to live your life the way you want to." Katya sighed. "Niki, you want freedom. In the Union at this time, you can't have that. It is not possible. It would be like cells running wild, multiplying by the second. It would be a cancer, it would be the end of us."

Niki disagreed. He had beliefs. Of course he had beliefs, but they were not political, had nothing to do with politics. Human beings were meant to be happy. That was all he'd ever wanted, simply to be happy. His search for happiness led to Lubyanka. It was unfair, he never hurt anyone. In fact, he'd helped people. Now, because of that, he would have to leave. It was not fair, but there was no other way.

Katya calmed down. There was a small smile on her face when she said, "Husband, we have to run. When they come for you, we'll both be gone. You're right, it's not fair. Maybe things will be better, more fair in the West."

Niki kept his eyes on Katya's face. A tear built, rolled, Katya rubbed her cheek against his hand. Then she stood and walked with him to the window. They watched the swirling snow. It was their last night together in Moscow.

Chapter Two

LITTLE ITALY, NEW YORK
October, 1984

Frankie Musca stood still in the hallway staring at the door that led to the street. The foyer was silent. A sweet-sour smell of dampness and the nutty aroma of wooden wine-grape boxes came straight up through the floor. It was a smell of home and it pleased him. But there was another smell. A horrible, bitter odor, which leaked from under the first-floor front-apartment door. That stench nauseated him. And though Frankie would never admit it, it paralyzed him as well.

"Someday I'm gonna kill the bitch," Frankie murmured to himself. He took hold of the knob and slowly opened the street door. If La Strega was in her window, she'd howl like a wolf at the sight of him. "Zips," Italians from the other side, ran at the sight of La Strega. *They* believed the bitch had powers. *They* believed she spat black magic from her window seat. To Frankie, she was a royal pain in the ass.

Once outside, Frankie looked neither left nor right, but

skipped down the steps to the street. On the sidewalk, he glanced back over his shoulder. That was a mistake. There was only one open window, it was on the tenement's first floor, and La Strega's colorless face was in it.

"*Assassino*," she screamed.

The shriek, a sound that was not human, returned Frankie's nerve. He gave her the finger. Then he rolled it back and shot her the horns. He shook his wrist, he raised his hand above his head, twisted and twirled the horn in her direction. Then he threw a fist in the air and slapped the muscle of his arm. La Strega responded by spitting, she wiggled a lizardlike tongue between brown nubbed teeth. Finally she took her best shot— a double whammy, two hands, two sets of horns. "*Eeeeeee*," she howled.

"Piss on the hole in your black heart," Frankie yelled. Fear was gone. He told himself, the bitch really was funny. He turned on his heel, and almost sprinted toward Grand Street. He never looked back.

As was his habit, Frankie hesitated and took a deep breath before entering the Grand Street traffic. Then he moved like a robber baron, invulnerable on his own turf. The early afternoon crowd was thick, he picked up speed and began his John Travolta strut. Neighborhood people moved aside, strangers slowed when they saw him. Women, as usual, held his eyes. Men glanced in his direction, then quickly turned away. Killers, like witches, are given plenty of room in Little Italy, and there was an aura of violence that surrounded Frankie Musca like a fog bank.

Frankie was a *button*, a respected and inducted member of organized crime. He was a Cosa Nostra soldier, *a made man*. At the age of twenty-four Frankie Musca was a murderer. His reputation for violent efficiency was legend. Everyone was terrified of him, everyone, that is, except La Strega.

Frankie was not easily forgotten. Tall for a Sicilian, with green eyes, and brown hair that curled with the summer humidity, he had a face that he never need shave, and skin so fair that he hid from the sun. "Babyface," they called him, "Babyface Frankie from Elizabeth Street."

He moved like a dancer now, smiling at the people he knew, waving to merchants and do-nothing "CO_2" inspectors alike. At Mulberry Street he waved to a cop. It was necessary to appear that his connections were boundless. A friendly acknowledgment from a policeman in this neighborhood did not go unnoticed. The cop smiled, but didn't wave back.

Grand Street is Little Italy's main drag. Brightly painted salumerias, coffee houses, pastry shops, and Southern Italian restaurants, with fair menus, had long since replaced pushcarts and cheap shops. This ghetto had come full circle. Grandchildren of illiterate pioneers from places like Naples, Calabria, and Taormina were getting MBAs from Harvard and Yale, and moving uptown.

When Frankie reached the corner of Grand and Centre Streets, he spotted Tony Red. Red had already taken up residence on the far side of the street just past the cheese shop.

Friends since sandbox days, the pair were a team, partners, a dynamic duo of destruction. Red, like Frankie, was a made man. He too had the medallion.

"For the luvva fuck, you wanna tell me what happened to you last night?" Red yelled as Frankie walked up and gently shoved him. It was a greeting, and Red smiled.

"I got busy," Frankie said softly.

"Too busy to get laid? Nothing personal, Frankie," Red whispered, "but I think you're turning into a faggot. Ya know what I mean? I get these two bimbos all lined up. I have the car washed. I go out and buy this new Linda Ronstadt tape. I get two bottles of Asti, a little coke, I reserve a suite, a suite mind you, at the greatest super eight motel in Jersey, and what does my *gomb* do?"

"I got busy, hey . . . I had a sit-down with my uncle. You

wanna hear about it? Or you wanna continue this pussy rap here, like I give a shit. You probably did them both."

Red had a pussy collar that made Frankie crazy. Tongues, lips, assholes, tits, and "the bush." The beautiful bushes of the world were the only things that Red thought and talked about. Frankie took it all, because when they walked side by side, shoulder to shoulder, Frankie felt a rush of kinship that sprang from alleyways and street corners, and hushed men's clubs. They were a continuation of the brotherhood carried by parents, grandparents, and great-grandparents from the mountains, valleys, and towns of a land that time forgot. They were, as Frankie often put it, "Turks of the same blood." The rest of the world were scumbags, to use, then flush away.

"You feel good," Frankie said smiling. "You ready to do some work?"

"Naturally, I'm always ready," Red grinned.

"Fine, cause we gotta go over to the club, see the gimp." As he spoke, Frankie counted, first on his thumb, then his index finger. "Then we grab the kid Philly. He's gotta get us some wheels."

Red took his sunglasses off, and held them with his left hand. With his right, he rubbed circles on his face. When Red was excited he rubbed circles on his face.

"Then," Frankie continued, "tonight we run over to Brooklyn and clip that Jew prick that embarrassed my uncle. Ya hear me? We gonna finally clip this Russian motherfucker," Frankie said simply. An enormous smile filled the face of Tony Red.

Red threw an arm around Frankie and hugged him. The two handsome young men cut princely figures as they swaggered toward the Brothers Social Club. Two blocks away, La Strega sat still in her window. She smiled and licked perspiration from her upper lip.

By the time Frankie and Red walked through the clubhouse

door, three kids had already arrived. Tanned, dressed in silk shirts and linen slacks; gold bracelets hung from their wrists, and religious medals swung when they bent their heads. The three had double-parked their cars in the street. All shiny, all new, all with the windows rolled down. Red ribbon, to fend off evil spirits, was tied in a bow around the rearview mirrors of cars with New Jersey, Pennsylvania, and Ohio plates. Hanging from the ribbon was a tiny red plastic goat's horn. It kept demons out of back seats. None of this group had been *made*. They were called kids.

The kid Philly turned a wooden chair so that he could rest his arms across the chair's back, then sat. The fact that he sat uncomfortably bothered him less than the urgent need he had to display his tattoo. On the muscle of his right arm, a skin artist had depicted an infant in diapers crouched in a fighter's stance. The baby wore boxing gloves and an evil grin. The script under the drawing said Kid Slug. Girls loved it. Men who didn't know who or what he was started fights over it. Philly nodded his head as Frankie and Red walked past him and took seats at a table in the rear of the club.

Philly, like Frankie, was tall and thin. He had a warm, deceptive smile. And, like Frankie, madness had found a home in his brain. He had a smooth, well-cared-for face, and expensively capped teeth. Philly could hit a stickball the length of a city block. And when they let him, he played with the Chinese boys from over on Mott Street. Whenever a Chinese man or woman walked past the club, Philly would bend at the waist, and say *"ah soh, ah soh."* The kids would laugh, and the Chinese people would stare at him as if he were touched. Although Philly was never sure what was south of New York— it was either New Jersey or Pennsylvania—he could count hundred-dollar bills. Once, using a hammer, Philly drove a screwdriver through a man's chest, impaling the guy to the clubhouse floor. People remembered him running through the streets of Little Italy looking for a tire iron to pry the kicking,

24

wailing, dying man loose. Philly was mean, but he smiled when Chinese people walked past the club, and said "*ah soh, ah soh*," his capped teeth glimmering, and the other kids, they laughed.

Frankie had a warm spot in his heart for Philly. Someday, he thought, he'd sic him on the witch. Philly didn't believe in that Sicilian witchy bullshit, but he wore a golden goat's horn the size of his pinkie. He wore it around his neck and rubbed it whenever he got nervous.

"Philly," Red called out, "c'mere. Take ya chair and ya tattoo and c'mere." Frankie smiled and pulled on the tip of his nose. Red liked playing with the kids, and Frankie liked to watch. Philly smiled, then glanced at Joey Legs and Richie Rags. Both the other kids leaned forward as if on cue. With their eyes they asked to be invited to the table. They weren't, and disappointment covered both their faces. Frankie knew how they felt. He understood. He'd been a kid once. But that was long ago. Before he'd been *made*, before he'd killed.

"Joey, find the gimp for us will you," Frankie said, "g'ahead, take Richie here and go and find the gimp. Tell him we need to see him."

There was nothing vague about what was going on: two made men at the club early in the day, a sit-down with the gimp, Philly chosen to join the table. Big things, big times, a big day for Philly. One did not have to know the particulars to know that the shit was on. Certainly not Joey and Richie, they could read all the signs, they saw the smiles, the crew was going to war. So with as serious an expression as they both could muster, Joey and Richie got up from their table to find Benny, the crew's armorer.

The conversation began. Special words delivered by two made men to one who wanted to belong.

"Ya know, Niki the Jew that owns the Russian club over in Brighton Beach," Frankie began.

Philly nodded his head.

"We're gonna tear out his vocal cords and strangle him with them," Red said calmly. Philly leaned back in his chair and shrugged his shoulders. Frankie smiled, he enjoyed the power he and Red had over the kids. Then Red laughed, softly at first, but when Philly said "Is that some kind a message we wanna send out, or what?" Red howled, he slapped Philly's back.

"Yeah, it's a message all right. We gotta explain to this Russian prick that we're pissed. Ya figure he'll understand?"

"Fuck, yeah," Philly said, "them Jews ain't dumb."

A sly smile from Frankie's face faded. A picture of La Strega, sitting in her open window, flashed in his mind. He leaned back in his chair and ran a hand across the tiny golden horn he wore. Something was not right. He caught a whiff of the stench that came from under La Strega's door. He lit a cigarette, drew the smoke deeply into his lungs. The feeling passed. "Tonight, Philly," he said, "tonight you make your bones."

Chapter Three

Clouds, lit by running lights, ran across the wings of the jetliner as if pushed by a giant hand. Rain streaked the window in separate lines, one followed by another, then another. Suddenly the airplane dropped. Niki heard a loud bang that seemed to come from directly beneath his seat. Katya exhaled loudly and squeezed his hand. Nikolai Zoracoff looked out of the window and saw lights, like strings of diamonds, but without shape or form. Another shudder, the huge engines whistled as they sucked air with gargantuan gulps. The liner seemed to dip to the right, then it slowly rolled left. Now the strings of diamonds were gone, the windows cold and black. And then, as if they were launched from the center of the earth, buildings appeared in the clouds; sparkling castles, with steeples of light, and highways with red, and gold, and yellow shimmer. Niki marveled at the never-ending rivers of sparkle, moving as was his life, away from the center of light, like jeweled spokes rolling into utter darkness.

"Please kindly extinguish all smoking materials. Replace your trays, and move your seats to the upright position. We will be landing at JFK International Airport shortly."

Katya smiled at Niki and Niki smiled back. The electrified excitement of New York City below now replaced the ache and pain of nostalgia for Moscow.

Each of the long days in Vienna had been riddled with an anxiety Niki could not understand. And being unable to understand his own fears, he could not explain them to Katya. Katya, it seemed to Niki, had been reborn with a cream torte and coffee cup attached to the ends of her hands. In Vienna, Niki hardly left the hotel. He wouldn't have left the room had not Katya forced him to.

It had to do with the language. What had to do with the language, he wasn't sure, but it made him anxious, caused him to turn away from people when they spoke. Embarrassing himself time and again, he stayed close to the hotel, going out only when Katya insisted.

"Why?" he asked himself, "why?"

There was no answer. He simply didn't like the people. He hoped things would be better in Rome, and they were.

Rome was better. In the past, when Niki had tried to imagine what the West would be like, it was Rome. The city was breathtakingly beautiful. Still, the people exuded a slyness that put Niki off. Not Katya, she shopped more in Rome than she did in Vienna. She bought a plate with a painting of the Colosseum, and a watch for Niki that didn't work. They walked through the streets for hours. They were refugees. They had nothing but time, and they hadn't made love since Moscow.

When the jetliner rolled to a stop, the passengers cheered. Katya let out a squeal like a child come face to face with a mountain of presents. Niki checked his wallet. He had exactly one hundred American dollars.

Petra, Yuri, and Vasily were waiting with flowers and a rented limousine. Niki and Katya would roll into American life in style.

Niki hit buttons and the car's window slid down. He pushed up on a tiny lever and the seat moved forward, then gently fell back. He flicked a switch and rock music filled the car with Dolby. Niki wrapped an arm around Katya. They looked at each other and laughed. A loud pop and Vasily held a bottle of champagne in the air. Petra produced glasses, and Yuri made a toast.

"America, the men of Moscow are here."

Katya added, "And the women."

That night, Yuri insisted that, though exhausted from the trip, they drive to Manhattan. They must see the lights of Broadway.

As they drove past the playhouses of the theater district, Katya's eyes stretched as she quietly watched the dazzle. Then they drove to Times Square, and down Forty-second Street. Niki and Katya both let loose a low moan as they looked into the powdered faces of the yellow-eyed night people. Pimps, prostitutes, clowns of all sorts filled their window.

New York's dark side. In his worst nightmares, Niki wouldn't have believed it could be this bad. He thought about the parks of Moscow and the gray and beige and brown orderliness of the Union. He wondered out loud how he would do among these people.

Yuri said, "You will be a prince, as you were in Moscow. And here it will be easier."

Yuri was the one to find the apartment. It was in an old building, six stories and brick. In the four rooms there was only one window. It was in the bedroom and it overlooked Ocean Parkway. The rooms were dark and the hallways darker still. The elevator, their closest neighbor, moved slowly and creaked.

Cold to his soul, Niki stood near the window. It was almost daybreak. Katya was breathing softly in the bed across the room. The elevator slammed, then squealed, then whined. It sounded as if it were rolling on iron wheels, through the walls and into the apartment.

Niki shivered. He lit a cigarette, drew the smoke deep into his lungs. His body felt hollow. He leaned his forehead against the cold glass windowpane and looked out into the dark street.

Across the avenue were other apartment buildings. Light flickered in some of the windows. Candles, he thought. Candles in the electrified Western Wonderland. He lay his cheek flat against the windowpane and tried to see down the avenue toward Manhattan. The rooftops of the tall buildings were dark against the morning sky.

A curious impulse came into his mind. He took the map that Vasily had given him and, with his finger, he found New York City.

The city was in the southern part of a large state also called New York. There were mountains to the north, beyond the mountains Canada, beyond Canada the polar ice, beyond the ice, home.

There was no way he could beat this city, no way he could beat his fears and this city too.

It was Niki's second night in America; the second night without sleep. His mind raced with the problem, while his hands rubbed his head. He needed rest, but he couldn't find sleep. Niki felt as though he were going insane. This inexplicable fear of people, places, and things foreign.

What was he afraid of? The Americans he'd met were friendly enough. Some too friendly, with their hugging and pressing, as if Russians hugged and kissed perfect strangers. The Americans were no less alien, no less strange, than the Romans or Viennese he'd met before them.

And then, as if he were dreaming, he heard Katya's voice call out.

"Come away from that window. You'll catch cold, come here to bed."

Niki turned and saw that Katya was smiling. She smiled a lot lately.

"Come here," she whispered, "come, come."

She looked beautiful curled in the bedding. Like a fawn in snow, he thought.

As he came near her, Katya let her nightgown slip, and she rolled to the edge of the bed. Stretching, she reached a hand toward him. When she touched him he became weak.

Her eyes were clear, in the half-light, her face had a beautiful oriental look. When Niki got into the bed she slid her hand into his pajamas, and ran her lips across his cheek.

"Lay near me, hold me, rest, Niki," she whispered.

He shut his eyes and put his cheek against Katya's breast. Then he wept, softly, as he did when he was a boy in the orphanage. Quietly, so no one could hear.

"I'm going insane, Katya, I can feel it. I can taste it. It's sour and fills my throat."

The tears ran from his eyes, over his cheeks onto Katya's breast.

She rubbed his face against her skin. In slow circles she moved his head, directing his mouth toward her breast. His face slid over her wet skin.

"You will sleep, my Niki. You will rest. Everything will be fine."

"What have I done to our lives?" he said softly.

"We're together, Niki. That's all that matters."

Then she ran her hands over his hips and slid his pajama bottom to his knees.

"I took you to a city of lunatics," he said.

31

But Katya no longer heard him. It had been weeks since Moscow, weeks since they'd touched like this. And, with her moans and shudders, she told him that she needed him. She took his hand and moved it according to her will.

The motion of Katya's body to the music of Niki's imagination was the most sensual experience he'd had in months. Her hips, arms, and shoulders moved to the sound of the fiddle and balalaika. Morning sun slowly filled the room and Niki watched as Katya danced. Her eyes were closed, her mouth was open, her hands in fists alongside her cheeks. Then her arms spread, her palms moved toward him, then away, her wrists on smooth swivels like a gypsy.

He closed his eyes, and for the first time in weeks, a smile crossed the face of Nikolai Zoracoff, as the music of home filled his head.

Chapter Four

May, 1981

Far past where the boardwalk ended, a great tower threw long shadows over the smoky tenements of Coney Island.

It was the parachute jump and lines of elderly Jews walked toward it as if someone stood on its very top blowing a great horn, calling the children of Israel home.

There were hundreds, some in pairs, many in groups of five and six. They spoke Russian with heavy Odessa accents and Yiddish, a language that made Niki's skin crawl. It was the Brighton Beach parade, they were all out.

"Do you speak Yiddish?" Niki asked, then he turned up his collar and looked toward the ocean. Along the shoreline middle-aged men quick-stepped as if they were in a race.

"I've learned some since I've been here," Yuri said, then he sniffed the air. "Spring is here," he added.

Two black boys on fine bicycles maneuvered their way between the strollers. The one in the lead blew a whistle causing a grandmother to stumble and dive out of his way.

Yuri held his hands on the railing, he moved in time to music that came from the largest radio Niki had ever seen. The black boy without the whistle carried it on his shoulder and drove his bike with one hand.

"No wonder they win gold medals," Niki said.

"They're all criminals," Yuri said.

Niki never looked at him.

"All of them?"

"Yes. The American blacks are not like the ones we knew at home. The ones we met in Moscow were Africans, they had some . . . some . . ."

"Culture," Niki said.

"That's right, these American blacks are savages."

"Why do you always wear that cowboy hat?" Niki asked after awhile.

"I like it," Yuri said quickly.

"And the boots? And the shirt? You look like a cowboy, a cowboy from Tashkent."

Yuri shrugged. He could make his face look pained without any effort. Like his brother, Mikail Yagoda, the jeweler, Yuri was nasty; like the entire Yagoda family, a bit crazy.

In Moscow Niki gave the brothers plenty of room. Now, here in America, Yuri had become a needed friend, good company. It was depressing.

Bigger than his brother, but just as dark and evil looking, Yuri would commit any crime. He had no heart, no soul, no conscience.

Yuri took Niki's elbow and led him toward the café. The sign above the café entrance said Gastronom Moscow. A man with a black leather jacket and small gray cap sat on a chair near the entrance.

"These murals I see everywhere, doesn't anyone ever clean them up?" Niki asked.

"I don't think so," Yuri said. Then he told Niki what cunt

meant. It was written in black script inside a large, green heart on the front of a closed pizza stand that was next door to the café.

Niki laughed.

Petra was waiting for them at a table in the rear of the café. He sat sipping tea and brandy watching a fat boy play Pac Man on a big, ugly, yellow machine in the corner.

They joined Petra at the table, and after a few minutes, a woman from Georgia, wearing a large golden Star of David, came over to serve them. Niki had vodka, and Yuri had a beer which was American, and to Niki tasted like water.

"Okay, Niki, today we introduce you to my American friend. The man who will make us rich," Petra said.

Niki nodded.

"When he comes you will be surprised to see how young he is," Yuri said, "but don't let his age fool you. He's an important man."

Petra laughed. "You should have seen his face when I told him that he was going to meet the Prince of Pushkin Square."

"Who is broke and needs his help," Niki said.

"I met him once and I don't like him," Yuri said.

Ah, Niki thought, the real Yuri.

"He is like all Italians, slippery like a fish."

Petra began to sing "O' Sole Mio." Yuri joined in. Then the three of them tipped drinks and sang loudly.

"But he is an American Italian," Niki said, "not like those thieves we met in Rome."

"They're all the same," Yuri said, "like eels."

"You'll see," Petra said, "he is very nice. Yuri likes no one."

"I like you."

"I'll drink to that," Niki said, "I like you too, Petra." Then he drank his vodka, the way he always drank his vodka, in a flash.

After two months in America, Niki had decided that the only way to get rich was to own a large business. And the business he'd decided on was a restaurant-nightclub. There were several in Brighton Beach, his would be the biggest, most lavish of all. Niki had already chosen the name, Moscow Nights.

Petra had met the Italian-American at a health club in Sheepshead Bay. The American, whose name was Sonny Ippolito, marveled when Petra lifted four hundred and forty pounds from a bench position. At home, in the Union, Petra had been a weight lifter.

Sonny told Petra that his accent made him laugh. One night he drove Petra home in a marvelous golden car with soft leather seats. It was one of the big American cars. Petra didn't remember the name. Unlike the European models, the American cars all looked the same to him.

When Petra said he would like to earn some money so he too could have such a car, Sonny laughed, then gave him a half-ounce of cocaine. He told Petra to reduce the half-ounce to grams, and then sell the grams for whatever he could. In two weeks he should return five hundred dollars to him. He could keep whatever profit he made.

Petra and Yuri sold the half-ounce of cocaine at the Russian club called the Wonder. They sold it all in two hours. The next day they called Sonny and ordered a full ounce. They sold that in two days, and so it went. They were earning a thousand dollars for every ounce they sold. They could get rich, but it would take time. Niki convinced them that they needed a lot of money to open Moscow Nights, and they convinced Niki that he should meet Sonny.

Sonny arrived with a man who looked like he had a shrunken head. He introduced him as Junior.

After shaking hands with Niki and his companions, Junior told Sonny that he'd wait in the car, and left. Niki felt that Junior had studied all their faces very closely. He didn't smile when he looked into Junior's eyes, and he held his hand an additional beat; Junior nodded.

Sonny wore boots that were polished to a high gleam, he wore designer jeans, and a blue blazer over a tan cashmere turtleneck sweater. A yellow silk scarf, with small red birds, hung loosely over his shoulders. He had an athlete's build, and his fingernails were polished. Around his wrist was a large gold bracelet, Niki couldn't begin to guess its value.

Sonny shook his finger at Niki like a policeman. "You are the prince that Pete told me about."

"Who is Pete? Oh, you mean Petra." Niki laughed.

The American looked at him sadly. "You don't make fun of the way I talk, and I won't correct you guys. Right, Pete? Ain't that what we agreed?"

Petra smiled and nodded.

"Of course," Niki said.

Yuri grunted.

"How long you been here, Nick?"

"Two months." Niki couldn't help but smile. This Sonny talked as if he were a young boy.

"You a Jew, like Pete?"

"Just like Pete," Niki answered. Unable to suppress a laugh, he slapped Sonny's back. "I like you, Son, we will be friends." He laughed some more, then called the Georgian woman and asked her for a glass. He poured Sonny a serious hit of vodka.

"My name's Sonny, you can call me Sonny, but not Son. My name's Sonny."

"I know," Niki said, "and my name is Niki. You can call me Niki."

Sonny smiled, put his thumb in the air, and said, "Check."

After two drinks Sonny took his jacket off and began walking around the café. He looked at the food in the glass cases and the photos of the Union that were hung on the walls for decoration. He picked up a record album by the beautiful Maya Rozova.

"Now, that's a foxy lady. I'd make her keep her hat on, ya

know what I mean? Just the hat and that string of pearls. This woman has a beautiful mouth."

"And she can sing," Petra said.

After awhile Sonny returned to the table, he *was* a handsome young man. To Niki he looked like a film star.

"Okay," Sonny said, "I don't want to keep Junior out in the car all day. If I don't get him something to eat he'll get meaner than he already is."

"There is plenty to eat here," Yuri said.

"I don't think so," Sonny answered, looking around the café as if he didn't quite understand something.

"I think Niki and I should have a little chat. And, if you two don't mind, when I chat, I chat alone. One on one, if you know what I mean."

Yuri said, "What?"

Petra said, "Why not?"

Niki said, "I understand," and motioned with his head for the other two to leave.

Niki felt as though he was in a familiar place. He could relax with Sonny. His confidence returned. He was looking at a younger reflection of himself, he thought.

Niki and Sonny looked at each other from across the table for a long time.

Sonny puckered his lips slightly, then smiled. It was an intimate gesture that made Niki a little uncomfortable. It seemed to him that this young man had power and confidence beyond his age. That Junior fellow, with the little head and enormous body, was much older than Sonny. But there was no doubt who was the *boss*.

"Can I ask how old you are?" Niki said.

"It never hurts to ask. This is America, you can ask anything."

"Well, then?"

Sonny nodded his head slowly, he smiled, and said, "You and your friends are lucky that you've met me."

38

Niki looked into Sonny's warm brown eyes. "You're young, Sonny," Niki said.

Sonny sighed and said, "Uh-huh, and there's not a thing I can't do in this city. You name it, I can do it. You want it, I can get it. And I'm gonna tell ya something else." He smiled when he said, "You can run from me, but you can't hide. You and your friends are lucky. You have made an important connection." Sonny winked.

Niki thought that he'd just been threatened, yes, threatened for sure, but nicely.

"I don't like dealing with drugs," Niki said, "I'm sure there are other things we can do."

"Somebody has to deal in drugs, and drugs are more valuable than gold. Besides, I deliver what people want, I don't force anyone to do things they don't want to do. I serve the people, Niki. I give them things they can't get anywhere else."

Niki swallowed.

"Listen, Niki, what you have to do is decide what it is you want to do, then call me. I like your friend Petra, I trust him. The little business we've done together he handled like a pro. He tells me you were a real big deal on the other side. I can help you be a big deal here."

"I want to own the biggest and best Russian nightclub and restaurant in this city. And I don't want to wait forever to get the money to do it."

Sonny frowned. "Do you know how much a business like that would cost?"

"About two hundred thousand dollars," Niki said.

Sonny's smile was full of amusement. "Is that all?"

Niki had no idea how much it would cost to get a restaurant-nightclub going. But two hundred thousand sounded good.

"You fuckin' Russians are pissers. Whadaya think we got money in U-Haul trailers around here or what?"

Niki understood little of what Sonny said, he spoke so quickly, but he was smiling in a comradely fashion. This meeting was going well. He had a new friend, someone with connections. And to a Russian, that was better than money in the bank.

"I understand that you have plenty, plenty of money. And that you need places to invest it. Is that true?" Niki asked.

"How many people do you have?" Sonny asked.

"What do you mean, people?"

"You know, guys in your crew here. How many are there?"

"Friends from home, is that what you mean?"

"Yeah, people. You know, your people."

"Not too many."

Sonny smiled. "You're a foxy fucker, Nick, but I'm gonna tell ya what I'm gonna do."

"Please, Sonny, my name is Niki, Nikolai, not Nick. And why do you curse at me? Fucker, fucker, what is this fucker?"

The fear of not understanding these New York moves was coming back to him.

"Hey, I like you, Niki, don't worry about it. We'll do some things together. But these kinda things take some time. You're not my fucking brother, ya know what I mean. But, I'll tell ya something, you're a lot smarter than he is."

"Who?" Niki felt his head pounding.

"My fucking brother, that's who."

People were coming and going in the café.

Niki drank more vodka, waiting for the kick that never came. Sonny had left his glass standing still. He seemed always to be smiling.

After a while he gave Niki a piece of paper with two phone numbers on it. He told Niki that when he wanted to reach him Niki should go to a public phone. Then dial the first number on the paper. A woman would answer. He should use the name Carl, and give her the phone number from the public phone. Sonny asked him to look at the paper, and tell him what he noticed about the two numbers.

Niki looked. It was a simple code. Each of the second set of numbers, when added to the first, made ten.

"See, I said you were smart. It took my brother three hours to figure that out."

Niki laughed. "What does your brother do?" he asked.

"Whadaya think, he works for me. If you want to leave the number 655–2110, what number would you leave with the woman?"

"455–8990, I think zeros must stay the same, right?"

"You are a slick guy, Niki. Remember after you leave the number you must wait awhile."

Niki liked this game, he liked to play any game that was easy.

"How long would I have to wait for you to call me back?"

Sonny shrugged. "A while, but not as long as you may think."

"Why all this, this? . . ."

"Because the walls have ears, Niki, the fucking cops, the police, are everywhere."

"Just like home." Niki laughed.

"Call me when you figure out what it is you want to do. If I come up with something, I'll reach you through Petra. I don't like this Yuri character. What is it with this guy?"

"He's from Tashkent, they are a little . . . you know . . ."

"Oh, I know," said Sonny, "he's like a zip from Sicily."

"Excuse me," Niki said.

"Never mind. I understand. Yuri will be okay."

Then Sonny laughed. It was a great laugh, full of open, almost childlike glee.

"I don't know why exactly, but I like you fucking Russians."

"*Fucking*," Niki thought, "always this word fucking."

"I like you fucking Americans, too," he said.

One month later Niki stood at the entrance to the Brooklyn Botanical Gardens and watched as Sonny Ippolito stepped from a parked car. Niki waved, and Sonny smiled, then nodded his head.

As had become their habit, the serious business talk was left until they had walked through the gardens to the place where the roses were planted in concentric circles, yellows in the center of bloodred American Beauties.

The gardens were crowded with people who gathered along the walks and eyed Niki and Sonny as they passed.

Finally when Sonny felt secure that they couldn't be overheard, he spoke. "It's all been arranged. If you check your bank account," he told Niki, "you'll be pleasantly surprised."

After an awkward moment, Niki asked, "How much?"

Speaking slowly, quietly, making sure that Niki understood every word, Sonny told him that two hundred and fifty thousand dollars had been deposited in his bank account.

"Fine," Niki said, and his own coolness startled him.

"Fine my ass," Sonny said, "Don't forget, you pay back ten percent a week, every week, when the restaurant opens."

Niki shrugged, turned away, and said, "I understand, Sonny, I'm very good at numbers."

"This is no joke, my Russian friend, this is serious business."

"The thing is," Niki said, "where do we have lunch today? We are up to number ten. You promised me twenty-five restaurants this month."

Sonny stood and looked at him in silence for a moment, then he smiled. "It's not me you owe the money to, Niki. It's Matty Musca. He'll send his nephew Frankie to collect."

Niki only looked at him.

"Are you getting all this, comrade, or what?" Sonny asked.

"When I draw the money from the bank in large amounts, will I have any problem?"

"You'll never have a problem with that bank. Just make sure you keep your money there."

"That's it, then," Niki said, smiling.

"Right," Sonny answered. Then he tapped Niki's shoulder with a clenched fist. "C'mon," he said, "let's go eat."

As Niki watched Sonny walk ahead of him, he thought of what Yuri had said the night he arrived in America. "You'll be a prince here as you were in Moscow, and here it will be easier."

Niki walked up to Sonny and put his arm across his shoulder and gave him a hug.

"Check," Sonny said, then he put his thumb in the air, and Niki laughed.

Chapter Five

October, 1984

Matty Musca, Frankie's uncle, was not a big man, but he was large-boned and powerful. He looked far younger than his fifty-five years. And why shouldn't he? Matty Musca took good care of himself. He belonged to an expensive health club, he watched his diet, and he visited the barber weekly for a shave, manicure, and trim. Matty Musca's face and hands were smooth. He had perfect posture; no pinched nerve bent him, and no old injury forced a limp. Like most connected criminals of his generation, Matty hadn't done a hard day's work in thirty years.

On this clear and warm day, as he walked out of the high-rise apartment building on Queens Boulevard, Matty had color in his cheeks and his chest was filled. He'd just left his mistress, a plump, bouncy woman, two years older than his oldest daughter. Matty strutted along the boulevard like Mussolini.

New York City police intelligence and FBI Mafia charts described Mathew Musca as a captain of the Don Paul Malatesta crime family. Descendants of the Genovese clan, the Malatestas were active, powerful, and rich. Such a description was about as close to accurate as law enforcement gets in these areas. It was true, Matty was an underboss, a "capo regime" of one of the seven crews of the Malatesta family. But, what was not mentioned in any intelligence folder was Matty's fundamental importance to his clan. Matty was more than a crew chief. His people, thirty men and boys, were known as the paratroopers. They were the enforcers, the warriors. Matty was the power, he was the family sword.

When Matty arrived at the spot where he'd left his car and driver, age returned to his face, his stomach did a spin, then flipped into a knot. Carlo and the Buick were gone. For a minute, Matty's world became a series of closed doors. He turned, he looked, he took a step in one direction, stopped, then moved a step or two in another direction, then stopped again. "No," he said out loud, "this is where I left him." He walked to the corner and looked down the street. The worst kind of dread had eased into him. He was unarmed, naked on the corner of a Queens street. Nothing, no one, could have forced Carlo to leave. For a second he thought about running back to Lynn's apartment. He took a deep breath. He glanced at his watch. It was one o'clock. Matty's instinct to sense danger removed the good feeling he'd been carrying. His chest and jaw tightened. He became keenly aware of every movement, every sound around him. The world began to move in slow motion, and Matty's eyes darted and danced like those of a leopard.

Matty sensed the car's presence before he saw it. He turned quickly. It was The Old Man's car. The silver Mercedes had crept along the curb and was now beside him. The driver's electric window slid down, and John Reno, Paul Malatesta's driver, smiled and said, "Hey, Matty, whadaya say."

"Hey," Matty answered, hoping he looked and sounded more pleasantly surprised than shocked. He'd counted on The

Old Man being in Europe. But there he sat, arms folded, head cocked, an ugly smile on his face. The only man in the world that could move Carlo. John Reno shook his head in what appeared to be good-natured disapproval. For a second, there was anxious anticipation in the air on the street corner. Anything could happen. Then Matty heard Paul Malatesta's voice rise from the back seat.

"Get in the car, Matty," The Old Man said, his voice soft, unthreatening.

"Where's Carlo?" Matty asked, not too calmly, as he joined The Old Man on the soft leather seat of the Mercedes. Paul Malatesta reached out and touched John Reno's shoulder.

"Let's go," he said. Then he turned to Matty. "I told Carlo to leave. I told him you'd see him later at the club. Is that okay?"

"Sure, sure, fine." Matty planted his elbow on the armrest and pinched his bottom lip. He wondered how much The Old Man knew. He knew something all right, Matty could hardly miss that.

Matty had decided to kill Niki Zoracoff the minute he'd found out that The Old Man was leaving for Europe. It was a gamble, a crap shoot. But the odds were heavily in his favor. Once in Europe, Paul Malatesta had more important things to worry about than the unauthorized hit of a Russian Jew in Brighton Beach. So Matty had thrown the dice in the person of his nephew Frankie. Now here he sat. It seemed to Matty he'd crapped out.

Matty started to say something. Paul Malatesta put his finger to his lips and a kind of tightening came around his eyes. Matty leaned back in the seat and sighed deeply.

As the Mercedes eased from the curb, Matty felt dizzy. Dizzy from the draining roll on satin sheets with Lynn's young legs and belly. Dizzy from the stupid fear of losing Carlo. Dizzy from the shame and embarrassment of having to explain. Matty didn't do well with explanations.

Matty closed his eyes when John Reno slammed down on the brakes. He was thrown forward, and bounced off the rolled leather of the front seat.

"You should wear your seatbelt," The Old Man said softly. Carlo had cut off the Mercedes.

"Now, that's a pair for ya," Matty thought. Worse yet, Carlo was yelling. People in the street were stopping. One or two passed by, then came back to stare. Matty was puzzled at first, then pleased.

"Excuse me, excuse me, sir," Carlo yelled. He had been with the Marines in Vietnam. Carlo called everyone sir. Paul Malatesta exhaled a great sigh, he ran his hands through his hair.

"Well?" he said to Matty. A nerve in his cheek jumped once, then again. Matty shrugged his shoulders.

"I don't know what's goin' on," he said.

"What the fuck is it?" John Reno shouted. Carlo looked toward the Mercedes' back seat. He answered John Reno, but he was looking at Matty.

"I need to talk to my boss for a second." Matty glanced at The Old Man. Paul Malatesta was shaking his head like a man with a problem he could not quite pin down.

"Go ahead, Matty, go and tell Don Carlo that he has nothing to worry about," he said sarcastically. "Go tell Carlo I need to talk to you. C'mon, hurry up."

There was nothing sinister in The Old Man's manner. Nevertheless Matty was glad to be out of the car, glad to be standing near Carlo.

Lying across Carlo's lap was a twenty-gauge automatic sawed-off shotgun, his favorite weapon in Nam. He stroked it as if he were petting a cat.

Carlo understood the gamble. He believed his boss to be in trouble.

He talked quietly, glancing past Matty at John Reno. Reno was a shooter, Carlo knew it and so did Matty.

"Boss, where they taking you?"

Matty shrugged.

"I'm not leaving," Carlo whispered. If the shit's on it may as well happen right here.

"Don't talk like a crazy," Matty snapped.

"Step aside, boss, and I'll turn that fuckin' Nazi car over with baby here."

"Easy," Matty said, "easy," and he gently passed his hand across Carlo's cheek.

"You're the only family I got, boss. They fuck with you, there'll be blood on the moon," Carlo said in Italian. At that moment, Matty knew he'd made a fatal mistake. The family was ready to bite at itself. Matty Musca knew enough about this life to believe that maybe he deserved to die.

"Carlo, go back to the club. I'll call if I need you to come get me. And Carlo," he said slowly, "you did the right thing coming back. Just don't lose your head."

The corners of Carlo's mouth quivered. He shot a threatening look at John Reno. "You really want me to leave, boss?" Matty nodded, and slapped the car's roof as Carlo slowly drove off.

Back in the Mercedes Matty started to say something again, and again The Old Man put his finger to his lips. Matty turned and looked out the window. Soon they were on the Whitestone Bridge. Sailboats by the hundreds were riding a good chop on Long Island Sound.

Matty turned from the window and found himself looking straight into Paul Malatesta's eyes. The Old Man must have suspected that he wanted to say something, because he began pointing around the interior of the car. He put his finger to his lips again. Fear, like pin pricks on Matty's chest and stomach, rolled on and on.

To call Paul Malatesta The Old Man was an acknowledgment of respect and a term of endearment. It was also totally inaccurate. Younger than Matty by several years, he was twenty years younger than the next youngest New York don.

One hundred soldiers, seven capos, and scores of kids referred to him as The Old Man. But, in person, within earshot, it better be Don Paul. Matty alone, only in private, called him Paul.

Sicilian born, with family ties to the "Honorable Society," Paul Malatesta was an advocate and practitioner of the *via vecchia*. He listened to counselors, even occasionally took their advice. But his word was law, his decisions final. Paul Malatesta functioned in the new world, but his strength lay in the *via vecchia*, the old way. Favoring an elegant style of dress, Paul Malatesta's manners were impeccable. Even so, his physical presence did not command immediate respect. He was small, measuring under five feet six inches. And he was thin, barely one-hundred-and-fifty pounds. But he could lead, and he could seduce. This sly little Mafia chieftain had few surviving enemies. He smiled, he stroked, his compliments were pure poetry. Under it all a temper that could cower a werewolf melded with a lust for power and wealth, producing a prototypical mafioso.

The thought of being the target of his don's rage put crabs in Matty's throat and tied knots in his bowels. It was the Jew's fault. If not for that slick Russian, he wouldn't be in this trick bag. He hated the bastard.

At about 2:00 P.M. Matty Musca stepped out of the door of the Mercedes and stood blinking. There was a stiff breeze, and the sun's reflection off Long Island Sound made him feel uncomfortable.

They were in the parking lot of Gino's City Island Restaurant. Though a nonmember, Gino had long been a friend to the family. Matty tensed, he felt surrounded when Paul Malatesta took hold of his elbow and led him down a narrow, garbage strewn path to the beach. The weirdest kind of silence came, and now lay between them. Even the breeze became still. About one hundred yards offshore a cabin cruiser held tight to its mooring. Paul Malatesta glanced at the boat, then froze. His lips clung together and his head shook from side to side.

"They're everywhere," he whispered. "You know, Matty, they have these gadgets that can pick up the slightest sound." He put his arm over Matty's shoulder and he talked so slowly that his lips barely moved. "They invade conversations. I know they're watching me," he said coolly. "They bugged my bedroom, the degenerate sonsabitches."

Matty wished he could go away, become invisible. An unfamiliar feeling had eased into him and now took command. Matty Musca was terrified. He suddenly believed he would die, here, along this filthy shore. He glanced at the cattails gathered in bunches, their stems wet with rot. They danced in the breeze like ghosts.

Paul Malatesta looked up and down the beach, then he moved to the very edge of the water. His eyes locked onto the boat. Fawn-colored, two-hundred-dollar loafers got wet and darkened above paper-thin soles. He didn't seem to mind. And this little act, if it were an act, did little to ease the circus taking place in Matty's stomach. He found himself unable to move forward, unable to move, period. And so he stood uncomfortably in swan grass and beach sand. He didn't know what was going down. And that was the worst of it. But whatever it was, he'd face it with dry feet.

For a long time Paul Malatesta stood looking out at the boat. Matty watched, wishing he'd say something. But Don Paul was off somewhere, lost in a hunted man's paranoia. Matty would have to wait for judgment.

Finally he turned and held up a little white hand. "It's all right," he said, his voice low. "There's nobody in that boat." They walked along a shore that held more empty fried-chicken boxes than sea shells. When they turned a point, and were out of sight of the cabin cruiser, Paul Malatesta turned to speak. He continued to speak as softly as Matty had ever heard him.

"So," Paul Malatesta said, his voice almost a falsetto, a smile of benign pleasure on his face.

Matty noticed that his eyes were fluttering, he tried to control them, but couldn't.

"What's wrong," Matty answered, the nervous vibration in his voice uncontrollable, and even as he said this he wondered who betrayed him.

Paul Malatesta tensed visibly. "Don't play with me," he snapped in Sicilian. Matty belched. He felt a pinch in his stomach, and a tiny bubble of air escaped from him. He prayed he hadn't dirtied himself. He tried an apology. Paul Malatesta cut him off with a flick of his little white hand. Matty heard something in the weeds behind him. He spun around. A three-legged cat was playing in the weeds with a dying crab.

"Well, goddamn it, are you going to tell me what the hell is going on?" Paul Malatesta said. Then he crossed his arms and stood waiting for a reply. Whatever good humor there was, drained from him. He shouted, "You ready to explain, or what?"

But explanations did not come easy to Matty, and he lost it. Matty began beating on his chest with the tips of his fingers. "It's me, it's me, it's what I am." Like a final emotion, a cry exploded from him. Matty screamed so loud that gulls, and a small black bird, squawked, then banged into each other in a frantic attempt to get into the air.

"That Jew cocksucker laughed at me, he laughed at me," Matty wailed. "He said he talked to you, and you gave him right." Matty had a hand the size of a baseball glove. He clenched and shook it. Paul Malatesta took a step backward. "When I told him he owed *me* the money, he laughed." Matty lowered his voice and took hold of Paul Malatesta's shoulders. "Paul, he laughed at me. We've been together from the beginning, Paul, you know me. I wouldn't go against you . . . but this man laughed at me."

Matty began to slide, he felt dizzy. He shook his head, it didn't help. He was retching. He was out of control. Just like all the cowards he'd ever known, he too began to cry. It was a simple truth, and now he fully understood it. Everybody cries before they die. And Matty Musca fully expected to hear the explosion from a pistol bouncing in the hand of John Reno. Death was breathing in his ear. Tears fell from his eyes. They left small round dots like bullet holes on his blue silk shirt. He stood still. He was through. He bowed his head and closed his eyes. The rest he thought would be easy. A bullet in the brain would be a relief. He was pleased, he'd go down like a man. He ran a hand through thinning hair and for a fleeting moment he thought of Lynn. He wondered how long she'd be alone. Now Matty Musca felt every moment of his fifty-five years.

Paul Malatesta went berserk. He slapped Matty once. Matty didn't cover his face. He slapped him again, then again. He grabbed hold of Matty with little hands, and hit him a fourth time. Finally Paul Malatesta turned it off. He pushed Matty's shoulders and walked off a step or two.

"You stupid man," he said softly, "our world is dying because of ridiculous, insane moves like the one you were going to make."

The last man to ever hit Matty had been his father. He stepped back, away from Paul Malatesta. Something snapped under the weight of his foot. The noise startled him. You're not going to die here, he told himself, this is not going to be the last minute of your life. The beach was deserted, even the three-legged cat was gone. Matty was bewildered. John Reno had not exploded a nine-millimeter into the back of his head. He was still alive.

He rubbed his cheek and couldn't stop his hand from shaking. Paul Malatesta reached out and took him by the shoulder.

"Do you think that I would really hurt you, Matty?" he asked.

The muscles in Matty's neck tightened. He twisted his face and wiped sweat from his forehead. Then he turned away.

"I'm no coward," he whispered.

"That's true, and you're also no fool. You did something stupid, but you're no fool."

"That *maza Cristo* embarrassed me in front of my nephew."

Matty's reply was so much like a child's that even to himself he sounded ridiculous.

"Don't you understand that I have reasons, and those reasons are good? We need this Russian," Paul Malatesta shouted, "we need him badly."

"Fuck him," Matty said simply.

"Fine, you can fuck him with my blessings, after he does for us what we need to get done."

Paul Malatesta stared at Matty for a long minute, then a smile came to his face. Matty started to say he was sorry. Paul Malatesta held up his hand to keep Matty from embarrassing himself any further.

"Look," Paul said, "just get a hold of Frankie and call him off. We haven't been able to reach him."

Matty understood. He was still alive only because Don Paul Malatesta needed him to stop Frankie. How important was this Russian-immigrant Jew anyway? he asked himself. What did they need him for?

"You find Frankie. You stop him. I'm leaving it in your hands. I'm counting on you."

It didn't come as a surprise that Paul Malatesta had been unable to locate his nephew. Matty knew that he wouldn't be able to find him either. But he nodded his head, and sort of grinned. For Matty the crucial thing was that he was not going to die, not here, not now, on this foul beach. But Matty also knew that there could be no forgiveness for what he had done. Paul Malatesta would come for him in his own time. Matty was no man's fool. He smiled a smile a thousand years old. He didn't think Paul Malatesta could read his face. His smile broadened as he nodded his head like a dime-store parakeet.

"Good, good," Paul Malatesta said.

He pushed his hand through Matty's arm. And then, as if Matty were a woman, he led him along the beach, back to the car.

From the Mercedes back seat, as it silently rolled toward Manhattan, Matty looked out at the city. It was the middle of the day. No matter. Big Apple traffic was murder.

Clouds had moved in and chased the sun. The sky had turned to dull silver. In the streets people grabbed tightly to light fall clothing. For the first time in months an old wind had come to visit, and stayed. Good weather for war.

Matty stepped out of the car at Forty-ninth Street near UN Plaza. It had been years since Paul Malatesta could be found near Little Italy.

"I'll explain it all to you as soon as I get back," Paul Malatesta said gently. "I'm counting on you."

The Mercedes disappeared into the traffic.

Matty jumped into a taxi and told the driver to take him to Mulberry Street, home.

"Where?" the driver asked, smiling with thick lips.

Matty looked at his license. What else, the guy was a Russian.

"Take the FDR Drive downtown to Grand Street, then go up to Mulberry."

Through the rearview mirror Matty saw the reflection of the man's smile. "I no here long time," he said. One gold and three aluminum teeth grinned.

"Too long as far as I'm concerned," Matty answered.

The driver seemed nervous. He made a sharp left, crossing three lanes of traffic. A bus slammed its brakes, and the blasts from ten horns scared a flock of pedestrians silly.

"You all crazy," the driver screamed. "The light's red."

"For you too," Matty yelled.

"No for me, for them."

"Just get me home in one piece," Matty said smoothly.

The Russian laughed and nodded his head.

Matty could not reach his nephew, he knew that. Once ordered out, Frankie got in the wind. He was an irretrievable rocket, locked on and closing. Matty figured that the Jew was already dead. He'd trained the kid well. Once you're given the nod, disappear, surface for the hit, then vanish again. He didn't expect to see Frankie for a week.

Matty shrugged. The fact that he'd escaped once consoled him. The terror that rose in his chest on that beach would not come again. He'd been dealt an impossible hand, but he'd play it. He'd prepare himself, replace fear with anger. Once the Jew was dead, Don Paul would probably come after him. Okay, Matty thought, c'mon, c'mon. This is not Palermo, this is New York, respect and honor go only so far. Survival is what it's all about. Above all else Matty Musca was a survivor. There are five New York families, and three of the other four had been recruiting him for years. True, he'd made a mistake, a slight lapse. He became angry at his own stupidity. He resolved to make Don Malatesta pay for those slaps. But first he'd let Frankie deal with the Jew. He'd told Frankie to tear twenty-dollar-bills and sprinkle them over Niki's body. The image pleased him. He closed his eyes and rested. The jostling of the cab was like a baby swing. What a joy to be alive. He thought of Lynn, of her magical velvet mouth.

The sudden stop of the cab broke his train of thought. They were at the corner of Grand and Mulberry Streets. Matty was home.

Carlo ran from the club trailed by a half-dozen kids. His people came to him, with looks of gratitude on their faces, as if he'd returned from the dead. Matty put his hands on his hips and jutted his chin. He stood on the busy corner firmly like a man of honor. Carlo hugged him, the kids surrounded him. The group then marched off to the club. Mussolini at the head of his legion. Losers on a grand scale. Not a grain of common sense could be found among the whole tribe. But for the moment, the sweet, fragrant smell of victory draped over Matty's shoulders like a hero's floral wreath. It did not seem to matter that, earlier that same day, one of his clan obviously had tipped his plans to Paul Malatesta. It didn't seem to matter, or Matty had forgotten his shock at seeing John Reno and the don on a street corner in Queens. Matty, it would seem, had a death wish that would not be denied. But then again, he had survived the morning. That was enough for him.

Paul Malatesta's black eyes were a window to his anger, and John Reno saw rage there. The Old Man had told him to pull to the curb near a public phone. It hadn't been five minutes since they'd left Matty.

"If I know my friends, I can clearly identify my enemies," Paul Malatesta thought. Matty Musca was no longer a faithful subject. He knew that Matty did not want to, and so he wouldn't, stop his nephew Frankie. The man was stupid, and now he was wild and running. He'd put everything in jeopardy over an insult. With millions of dollars at stake, Paul Malatesta could not afford to take a chance. So he telephoned Niki Zoracoff.

It took a little time, with codes and callbacks to public phones, but it was done as quickly and as safely as Paul Malatesta knew how.

Paul Malatesta told Niki to leave town for a few days. There was a problem with Matty. He didn't like the Russian's answer.

Niki Zoracoff said, "Don't worry, I can take care of myself." Then he laughed, and it was the laugh that bothered Paul

Malatesta. The Russian laughed and said, "Cowboys, stupid cowboys."

The October night had grown cold. Wind gusts flew in bursts between and around the railroad trestles on Brighton Avenue. On the street, in front of the Russian club, a crowd of people stood around illuminated in the pale light of a street lamp. Voices, colored with vodka, sent sounds into the cold night air. It was 3:00 A.M., and there were Russians everywhere.

"Will ya look at those weird sonsabitches," Frankie said.

Tony Red didn't answer. He had vanished, his mind blitzed and ablaze from the afternoon go-around with some magnificent rock coke. Philly grunted, nodded his head, then bared his capped teeth.

"Fuck them," he said.

They were seated diagonally across from the club in a stolen Malibu. Concealed by a string of other parked cars, they had an unobstructed view of the club's front and side doors.

Slouched in the back seat, Red looked wild-eyed and crazy. The kid, Philly, tense and alert, ground his teeth. He, too, had let mother coke take him up and away. Frankie tugged at the tip of his nose and hummed bits and pieces of a rock song he remembered from long ago. Their guns lay on the floor between their feet.

"Will ya look at 'em," Frankie said again. The Russians in front of the club were moving off now into double- and triple-parked cars. Each one dressed as if for a ball. Men in suits. Women in gowns. Teenagers, wearing leather pants, boots, and jackets, yelled and waved to one another, then ran to the cars. And there were children. Eight, nine, and ten year olds. Some carried flowers.

"Fuck 'em where they breath," Philly said simply.

Among the group of Russians were a half-dozen or so men

that Frankie would describe simply as "neighborhood guys." They were shorter than the others, dark-skinned, black-haired, with thick, heavy mustaches. Frankie had been at the club before, he'd seen them before. They spoke Russian, but they were different. They had the strut and move of street people. He didn't like seeing so many of them around.

Philly bent his head and took a blow of the last of the coke.

Frankie had learned to be careful. It was good to go high into a hit. Dope helped when the madness came. There was always crying . . . always begging. It was tough to watch the transformation of man to child. It screws up the head. A little coke clears the mind, eases the conscience. If you were a bit crazy, you could learn to enjoy it. The killing, that is. It was the killing that satisfied Frankie. That was the level Frankie worked on. That was the madness where he lived.

"Soon," Frankie said, "soon, Philly, we'll see what you got."

In a half-hour the street was empty. The nightclub's lights dimmed, then went out. A tiny sliver of light escaped from under the side door. It was time. Frankie felt languid, sleek as a cat. He jacked a round into the chamber of his nine-millimeter Browning and shrugged his shoulders like a matador.

"Okay, Philly," he said, "pull into the alley near the side door."

Frankie looked up, then down, the street. It was 4:00 A.M., the sidewalk was empty.

"We go in together?" Red asked.

Frankie shook his head. The coke residue that had performed magic in Red's brain was still there.

"I told you, I go in alone. You count to five, then come in. C'mon, come down, straighten up."

Frankie was irritated with Red. He'd told him to go easy with the coke. He didn't bother to reinstruct Philly. The kid was a natural. He'd wait in the alley. Frankie spoke directly to Red.

"After I go in, you count one, two, three, four, five, then come. You got it?"

Red smiled, took the gun from the floor, stuck it in his belt, then said, "Ya know, Frankie, I could go as high as ten if ya want."

They were about midway across the avenue, just past the el pillar, when Frankie saw them. Standing in the doorway of a shop near the club were two men dressed in short, zipped leather jackets, jeans, and boots. One wore a cowboy hat with a feather. He was drinking something from a styrofoam cup. Frankie told Philly not to go into the alley, but to drive off.

"Go up a few blocks," he said. "Turn around near the movie theater."

Slowly, without a hint of panic, Philly U-turned and drove three blocks, stopping just short of the Oceana Theater.

Frankie told Philly to drive back to the club. The two men he had seen earlier were gone. Philly pulled into the alley.

"Now," Frankie said, "we do him now."

Frankie moved from the car, up the steps to the club's side-door entrance. The door was open. It had been in the past, he wasn't surprised. But once inside he went numb.

"A dream," Frankie thought, "this is a fuckin' dream."

The club was in total darkness except for one, single spotlight. It shone onto the bandstand. On the edge of the cone of light, seated behind a piano, was Niki. Dressed in a black suit, with a white turtleneck sweater, he looked to Frankie like a priest. He spoke into a microphone.

"So my executioner has arrived."

Frankie, his gun already out, fired.

The spotlight went out. He heard popping sounds from behind him. Three, a pause, then *pop, pop, pop,* three more. They rang a quiet tattoo in the alley. He dove headlong into the darkness. Looking in the direction of the bandstand, he crawled like a madman, toppling tables and chairs as he went. Red and Philly were dead, he knew it. They didn't have silencers, and the only sound he'd heard were those sickening pops. Now he was on one knee behind a table. Suddenly the entire club came ablaze in a flash of light.

"Jesus Christ," he thought, "I'm a dead man. They were waiting."

Frankie rubbed his horn and held his breath. He wasn't afraid. Madness had come to Frankie, the hero's madness, an insanity that makes for legends. He threw a chair one way and dove in the opposite direction. He came to rest behind a rolling bar loaded with bottles of Gordon's vodka, Hennessey cognac, and Sambucca. He sat still and waited. Not a sound.

After what seemed an eternity, a heavily accented voice came over the microphone. It was Niki. Frankie closed his eyes and tried to concentrate on the direction of the sound. He'd get one, maybe two, shots off.

"Fucking cowboy. Fucking stupid cowboy," Niki was shouting.

Frankie giggled, got up, and fired two shots. *Pow, pow,* at nothing. He dove back down behind the bar and giggled some more.

Then there was movement, sound all around him. He had no idea how many people were in the club. But at least three were within twenty feet. He crouched low behind the bar. He couldn't figure out why they were waiting. No one had fired at him.

"I let you live, cowboy. You stand up, give it up."

It was the Russian again. His voice came from everywhere.

Frankie pushed, and the bar rolled. He began to inch toward the door.

A pop, followed by an explosion of wood and slivers of

formica, just above his head. He stopped pushing and crouched lower.

"Give me your gun, cowboy, and go home."

"Fuck you," Frankie answered.

It was an insane act of defiance, because his shout was followed by three pops, and three nickle-sized holes jolted the bar.

No way was he going to give himself up. No way, not him, not Frankie Musca. *Pop, pop, pop.* He couldn't get any lower. His head was in his crotch, his knees rubbed against his chin. The shooter was an expert. The holes were closing like a noose ringing his head. And he was getting flashes, horrible images. A picture of the Ippolito brothers hanging onto each other as he blew them away. The evil, foul-smelling garbage heap where he buried the bodies. The stench stayed with him for weeks. His ears picked up a sound close to his right, but he was afraid to move. Frankie believed that if he breathed, the next bullet would take his head off. And he wasn't ready. No, Frankie Musca was not ready to die. So he threw his gun out and stood up. Hell, he was only twenty-four years old, he'd just begun to live. There was no sound at all in the club. His eyes were out of focus. He was sweating and looking around. He stepped out from behind the bar and shouted, "Well?"

Then he caught a whiff of La Strega, and covered his face with his hands.

"I want to ride to hell in a white El Dorado, with a luscious blonde sitting on my face. A convertible with rolled, red leather seats. I wanna hear the Bee Gees singing 'Stayin' Alive' in Dolby sound." That's what he'd said when Red asked him how he wanted to die.

Frankie Musca began to cry. He was only twenty-four years old. One could hardly expect more. The popping sound caused his body to stiffen in a sudden spasm. He dug his fingers into his face. There was no one to call out for. Frankie had always been alone. So he screamed to no one and everyone. Two bullets from an Uzi set on semiautomatic shattered Frankie's chest and caused his heart to explode. He went down flat on his back, his hands still covering his face. The stinking image of a smiling Strega his only company on a well-deserved journey to hell.

Chapter Six

Detective First Grade Alexander Simon spotted Kid Vinny ("Ba-Ba") Esposito at the far end of the bar and nodded. Vinny looked up and saw him, then turned away. Alex was late, and Vinny was pouting.

It was a bitterly cold New York day. There was a taste of snow in the air, and the city was gearing up for the holidays. Alex had expected that the hotel would be crowded, but not like this. The place was a zoo.

The Algonquin Hotel is an elegant relic of New York's Edwardian past, a traditional place with Greek waiters trying to look English scurrying about, carrying gin tonics and Jim Beam on the rocks to a lot of sunken cheeks in three-piece suits. A perfect place to meet an informant. Alex and Vinny had been meeting there for years.

People moving through the lobby to the sitting room found the couches full and the chairs taken. With no place to go, they moved to the tiny Blue Bar. Twenty people and it's full. Alex was forced to inch his way past the half-lit patrons to get to Vinny.

"You're a fuckin' half-hour late," Vinny said loudly.

Half a dozen people seated at the bar tipped their heads, as if pinched in the back.

"I'm not a half-hour late, I'm only fifteen minutes late, and would you try and keep it down to a roar, you're not on Court Street."

The idea was to have as little conversation as possible, draw as little attention to yourself as possible. But Vinny Ba-Ba didn't worry about such things. He was a man of the street, and in the street to be self-conscious was a sign of weakness. Vinny had discovered long ago that if you were loud, people paid attention. He also knew that if he looked directly into people's eyes it made them uncomfortable.

"Is that guy gonna come or what?" Vinny asked with a very serious look.

"Uh-huh," Alex whispered. And he gently slipped a room key into Vinny's coat pocket.

Vinny was puckering his lips, frowning and shaking his head as if he were beyond tired.

"Look," he said, "you know I don't like to talk to anyone but you. Why you gotta insist on bringing this turd around?"

Alex exhaled. Bar patrons began moving in their seats in the way people do when they'd rather be anywhere else but have no place to go. Heads dropped between shoulders and bodies moved away from the space Vinny occupied. Vinny Ba-Ba was just under six feet tall and weighed 297 pounds. And he always looked mean. For as long as Alex knew him, Kid Vinny Ba-Ba Esposito looked as though he was on the verge of taking someone's head off.

Then Alex heard a familiar voice, looked over his shoulder, and saw Chief Inspector Ross. The chief was standing in the doorway and pointing with his chin toward the elevators.

"Is that the turd?" Vinny asked.

"Lovely language," a voice said. And someone else sighed.

"Jesus Christ," Alex hissed, "the man's a chief inspector in the police department, show a little respect."

"Fuck his mother where she breathes," Vinny Ba-Ba said clearly, distinctly.

A guy in a six-hundred-dollar, light gray Brooks Brothers pin-stripe dropped a martini glass. At the same time, Alex lay a five-dollar bill on the bar, turned, and walked out.

Vinny Ba-Ba Esposito's hair was light brown, almost blond, and he had curls, too many curls. They looked man-made. His nose was flat. His lips were full, round, and thick. He had gray eyes that sometimes looked blue. Round indentations behind his hands, scars the size of dimes, were a clue to the raging junk habit he had in earlier years. He had no neck.

Ba-Ba was the rarest of all informants. He did it because he loved his control, Alexander Simon. He wasn't homosexual, though there were times Alex wondered. His affection for Alex was unnerving. Alex constantly wondered what Vinny Ba-Ba was thinking.

Vinny was incredibly strong. In his dope-shooting street days, he was known as a gorilla. Robbing other addicts of their cure.

Once Vinny carried a black hooker nine blocks to an emergency room. She'd overdosed. Ba-Ba saw her drop. He carried her as if she were a baby.

Three weeks later, when the hooker was back in the street turning tricks for two and ten (two dollars for the room, ten dollars for her), Vinny robbed her of an entire night's profits, and called her bitch more than once.

A table and two chairs were the only furniture that Vinny'd left in his widowed mother's apartment. He'd sold everything else for the white lady.

One weekend, after running in the street, Ba-Ba came home to find his mother dead of a stroke on the kitchen floor. He lay beside her for two days. It took five cops to move him.

Alex met him during his rustling days.

The wholesale meat markets on Atlantic and Flatbush avenues in Brooklyn hung sides of beef at railroad and truck sidings, huge things, weighing a couple-of-hundred pounds. Ba-Ba would walk up, lift one off the hook, and waddle off with it. He'd sell the beef to local butchers for thirty dollars— his morning cure.

One morning, two patrol cops, while having a breakfast of coffee and sweet rolls, saw what they were later to describe as a blond, curly-haired monster shuffling down Atlantic Avenue carrying half a cow. When they drove alongside him, Ba-Ba threw the side of beef through the windshield of the police cruiser, and took off into the morning traffic.

Then the door of an old Chevy opened up, and the driver yelled, "Quick, jump in!" He did.

The Chevy took off, and Ba-Ba said, "Man, I really don't know how to thank you. No shit, you saved my life."

Then he slid down in the seat, his hands covering his face. The driver was holding a .38-caliber police special pointed at Vinny's blond curls.

"You have a choice? We could go to the 76th or the 78th precinct. Which would you prefer?"

It was Vinny Ba-Ba's introduction to Detective Alexander Simon of the Intelligence Division. What they did that day was a measure of how their relationship would develop. Detective Alexander Simon didn't arrest Vinny. Instead they made a date to meet later that night. An arrest would have been a rare thing for Alex. As an intelligence detective, he simply accumulated information and passed it on to other units of the department. To make himself known was stupid. On impulse, he'd opened his car door to let Ba-Ba in. Alexander Simon had acted without thinking, something he almost never did.

Certain policemen get off locking people up. Alexander Simon's pleasures came from the drawing together of information. He had a good feeling about this giant of a madman in curls. Because he did, because he trusted his instincts, because he showed Vinny Ba-Ba compassion, he had an informant for life . . . which suited Alex fine. Ba-Ba turned out to be something rare.

The crowd was thick in the Algonquin lobby. The glorious antique of a hotel, with its little round tables and chintz couches, had rarely seen the likes of Vinny Ba-Ba Esposito. Everyone made room for him.

When he got on the elevator it was just he and Alex and the inspector. Vinny looked at the inspector, the inspector looked at Alex, and Alex looked at his shoes.

"I gave you the room key," Alex said. "You should have waited awhile. What's the point of trying to hide in this hotel if you ride on the elevator with us?"

Vinny didn't answer. He looked past Alex to the chief.

"Whadaya got in the bag?" Vinny asked.

"Just some pictures," the inspector said. "I'll show them to you when we get to the room."

The room was small, cold, and dark, with a brass bed, a chest of drawers, and one chair. It would do for the meeting.

"I couldn't get laid in here," Vinny said.

Alex nodded his head, then shook it when he sat on the bed.

"Right, Vinny, you couldn't get laid in here."

The inspector leaned against the wall near the dresser, and Vinny dropped his three-hundred-pound mass on the only chair in the room.

"Okay, when do the broads show up," he said.

"I want you to take a look at these photos," Chief Ross said, then handed Vinny the folder.

"Frankie Musca," Vinny cried. "Holy shit, and Red. I don't know this other guy."

"They were found in a Dempsey Dumpster near the boardwalk in Coney Island," Alex said.

Smiling, panting a bit, Vinny studied the photographs of

violent death. He turned the pictures this way and that, held them upside down, laid them on the bed, side by side. Then he looked in the folder for more. Finding none, he seemed disappointed.

"Gee, don't they look cute," he said, smiling.

Though a nonmember, Vinny was close to the Columbo family, and the Columbos, for years, had locked horns with the Malatestas. Short, violent wars would erupt for a few weeks. There'd be bodies all over town. Then things would quiet down. These three bodies, Alex figured, were the opening round of yet another battle.

"Am I to assume from your response that you're no fan of these guys?" Chief Ross asked.

"Right. This is one wake I'll skip."

"What do you think's happening?" Alex asked.

"Fuck do I know? These guys go ta war for exercise. You're lookin' at two of the worse shooters around. These guys, and this guy Frankie's uncle, Matty, knock people off like they wuz changin' underwear."

Vinny was laughing. "Ain't they cute," he kept saying. His eyes settled on Frankie Musca's picture.

"Ya see this guy here," he said, "this kid took out a seventy-five-year-old nobody. Then whacked his two grandchildren who went around to their club to ask why. Sonny and Mikey Ippolito, two kids—he popped them like nothing. And this other guy, this guy Red here, he's Frankie's crime partner. A couple of real winners these two. But, let me tell ya something. As bad as these guys are, or were," he said, "the kid Frankie's uncle makes them look like boy scouts. He's a real mad hatter."

"You mean Matty Musca?" Alex asked.

Vinny nodded, then said, "There's gonna be a whole lot of real busy florists in Brooklyn over the next few weeks. If I wuz you guys, I'd go on vacation, come back in a month and pick up the pieces. Ya know what I mean, fuck 'em all, do yourselves a favor and take a rest."

"Do you think you could find out what's going on?" Alex asked.

"Who, me?" Vinny said. "Sure."

"We'd really appreciate it," Inspector Ross said. Then he began to put the pictures back in his folder.

The chief explained that Alex was going to work on the case. He'd need help. They'd like to stop a war before it began.

"Can we do anything for you?" The chief asked.

"Yeah, my gun permit, get me a gun permit."

"You're crazy," Alex said.

"Then how about a driver's license? I don't need no gun permit anyway."

"Sure," the inspector said. Alex was looking at the pictures, he did not look up. Vinny was constantly asking him for a driver's license. And there was no way Alex could get him one. It was embarrassing; he thought the inspector was putting Vinny on.

"No shit, you can get me a driver's license?"

"I said I would."

"I ain't never had a driver's license. Hey, Alex, the boss here sez he's gonna get me a driver's license. With my picture on it and all that shit? Then maybe I can get my own cab. You can make some serious money with your own cab, right, Alex?"

"Right," the inspector said, "with your picture on it and all that shit."

Afterward, when Vinny Ba-Ba left, Alex asked Inspector Ross if he really intended to get him a driver's license. The inspector told him to be serious, why would he want to get this jerk a driver's license?

Forty-five minutes later, Alexander Simon parked his car across from the Eastern District of New York's courthouse. The Federal Building is home to the Organized Crime Strike Force, handling hundreds of cases involving loan sharking, extortion, pornography, narcotics, stock fraud, murder for hire, and organized-crime interests in the garment center, construction industry, private carting, real estate, and meat packing.

Alex had enormous respect for the strike force, but he didn't want to work there. There were simply too many agencies, twenty-two at last count. They even had a guy from the Royal Canadian Mounted Police—too many bosses.

Alex liked to work alone. But it was Friday evening, the building would be quiet, the button-downs took early blows on Friday.

Alexander Simon was thirty-seven years old. He'd been a policeman for fifteen of those years, and he'd never spent a day in uniform. Sometimes that bothered him. He never got to play with the toys, the whistle, the stick, the car with the light that goes round and round. Taken right from his academy recruit class and placed in intelligence, Alex had a very unusual police career. Well-educated (he had a master's degree in American Literature) and well-traveled (he'd spent his junior college year in England), Alex was a rare find for the department.

For fifteen years he'd specialized in accumulating information on organized crime. Now, he was the in-house expert.

Reporting to no one but Chief Ross, Alex worked his own hours, installed his own wiretaps and bugs, and never had to make an arrest. He did undercover work, identified targets, then passed the information to enforcement groups. He'd never testified in open court, only in grand juries. Alex hoped that, before he retired, he'd just once get to use those two magical words: "You're busted!" The thought sent a thrill through him as he stepped off the fourth-floor elevator and saw Tom Delaney, his FBI counterpart, waiting.

Delaney was bulging out of his three-piece suit, and his leg, crossed at the knee, slipped to the floor when he handed Alex the folder he carried.

When Alex gave a signal, Delaney was always ready to help. All smiles, with backslapping and handshaking, fingers running through his short-cropped hair, Delaney seemed to Alex like someone who didn't know how to be mean.

Little League was more important to Tom Delaney than how members of the five families spent their weekends. But not to Alex. Even so, Alex liked him.

"Nothing, we have nothing," Delaney said. "We don't see any of the families getting down for war. This was some sort of freak shooting. None of the families are going to take on the Malatestas, not with the army of madmen they have."

Mafia soldiers, like Indian politicians, never die alone. Alex didn't understand it, but he felt it, something was really strange. And the more he wondered, the more nervous he got. Could something be going down he knew nothing about? He doubted that. He had access to every wiretap that in any way touched on organized crime. And even with Delaney giving him strike-force intelligence, he had a good handle on nothing.

"Do you know who took out the Ippolito brothers?" Alex asked.

Delaney rubbed his neck.

"No," he said, "we don't know for certain. But I'd guess Matty Musca."

"Hum, that's interesting."

"What's interesting?"

"That you don't know."

"Do you?"

"I'll tell you in a day or two."

The Ippolito double murder had been an open homicide for awhile. Vinny Ba-Ba had let drop that Frankie Musca and his buddy Red had been the shooters. Like Delaney, Alex had figured it was Matty. The Ippolitos were from Brooklyn. This shooting could be a payback.

"Are we going to have a war?"

Alex shrugged.

"I hope so," Delaney said. "We could use one. Clear the decks, so to speak. Thin out my files."

"Can I keep this?" Alex asked.

"Sure, they're photocopies of reports, nothing sensitive. You only get what everybody knows."

"Now that you raised the issue, I've been giving you a lot better stuff than you've been giving me lately."

"That's right," Delaney said, "so bring your business someplace else."

"Maybe I will."

In the past when Delaney joked with him, Alex hadn't taken it seriously. Friendly kidding between competitors was how he thought of it. It had always worked; this time it didn't.

"There's nothing going on here you wouldn't tell me, is there, Tom?"

Delaney looked troubled, thoughtful, undecided, but then he smiled. It was a small smile, weak, forced.

"Would I do that to you?"

"Don't play with me, Tom," Alex said sharply.

Delaney blinked.

"What time is it, eight, eight thirty? I gave the eagle two hours overtime waiting for you. That's two hours of my life the government got gratis. I'm not you, Alex. If it was up to me these guinea hoods could kill themselves in wholesale lots, and I'd give the country a day off. I want to get home and watch TV with my kids.

"Yours are out in Long Island, somewhere, with their stepfather. And you, you'll go home tonight to that pit you call an apartment. And two dozen of these characters in that folder I just gave you will be watching the midnight show in Atlantic City. It's all fog, mist, and bullshit, Alex. Nobody really gives a shit."

"I do."

"Right, that's why you and I are standing here, and your boys are watching 'Fantasy Island' with the Toyota dealer."

"Honda," Alex corrected.

"Same thing."

"Some intelligence officer you are. What's going on, Tom? Why are you laying this crap on me?"

Delaney looked up at him.

"See, Alex, that's where you and I part company. What you're doing is crap; what I'm talking about is real."

"You mean 'Fantasy Island' and Little League, and P.T.A. and crabgrass? That's real, Tom? Well, if that's real, I'll take the mist and the fog. At least I can feel mist, it makes me know I'm alive."

Delaney waved and walked through the double doors into the world of button-down collars and wing-tipped shoes. Alex felt uneasy. Something was moving around him and he couldn't tell what it was. He looked at his watch. It was eight thirty. He thought for a moment about what his boys might be doing tonight. He'd see them tomorrow, Saturday. But Saturday morning would be a great time to get on Matty Musca. He shook all this off. He had work to do. What in the hell got into Delaney anyway? He pushed the button for the elevator and laughed. It was time to return to the pit.

"What do we have here?" Vinny Ba-Ba asked Willie ("Peejays") Deluca on the morning after his meeting with Alex Simon and the inspector. Peejays was sitting on a stool in front of his Uncle Nino's pizzeria, on Court Street in South Brooklyn, eating clams from a bucket and reading the morning paper, which was full of the same violent pictures Ba-Ba had seen the night before.

"Something, ain't it?" Peejays said, sucking down a clam.

"So you finally took a piece back," Ba-Ba said with a low whistle. He ran his finger through the story, looking for the name of the third guy with Frankie Musca and Red.

"Ya see what I wuz tellin' you that time? Everybody likes

you, Ba-Ba, but you still got dope in your brain. That shit never goes away. It scars them—them tissues and things in the brain and all."

"Fuck you, Peejays. Whada you, a fuckin' genius sitting here eating clams when it's thirty below? If your Uncle Nino didn't take these guys out, he shudda."

No words were spoken while Peejays fought with a monster of a cherrystone that had ice all over it.

"The Ippolito thing was straightened out a long time ago. We had nothin' to do with this. My uncle said it wuz Russians," Peejays finally said, and he said this without his usual drama.

Vinny nodded. "Russians, no shit?"

"It's the truth. These guys been dead a few days. This is old news here."

"Russians," Alex yelled into the phone, "what Russians?"

"I don't know, but I could find out, I guess, if I spend the day with Nino Balsamo's nephew."

"Well, good, Vinny, do it."

"Just like that, do it, do it. I got other things ta do, ya know. I don't get no check like you, ya know. By the way, you find out about my driver's license?"

Alex held the phone a long time, then let go a great sigh.

"Ya see, ya see," Vinny yelled, "you don't care about me. Inspector Ross, he cares, he's gonna get me a license. You probably never even bothered to ask the guy, right? And me asking you all the time. You don't even follow it up."

"I'll follow it up," Alex finally said. "I promise, Vinny, I'll look into it."

"You gonna come out today or what?" Vinny said softly.

"I don't know, I'm supposed to see my boys today, but I don't have any money."

"Hey, they're your kids, they'll understand. Your kids miss ya, Alex, go see them. And, by the way, dress warm, it's fuckin' freezing out here."

"Hey, Vinny, find out about this Russian stuff, will ya?"

"Gotcha, partner, I'm on the job."

Alexander Simon's degree in literature was not of any great help in the police department. He'd graduated from New York University with enough teaching credits so that he could find a job teaching high-school English. It was terrible, he hated it. Within a year, he'd decided that he'd rather arrest the students than teach them. Teaching had kept him out of Vietnam. Someone his age had gone, someone had taken his place. He often thought about that guy, wondering who he was and whether he'd made it back in one piece.

Alex remembered the day Marsha didn't look at him.

It was a Sunday morning. He'd gone out for two bagels, two jelly doughnuts, two crumb buns, the *New York Times*, and the *Daily News*. Sunday morning.

When he returned home, the coffee hadn't been made, the boys weren't up, and Marsha sat in that red robe her parents had given her for her birthday. She sat in the kitchen, a place she never liked to be. After Alex put the bag of buns and bagels on the table, and after he set the coffeepot, Marsha said, "I want a divorce. I want a divorce and I want to marry Sy Alweiss."

"He's your cousin," Alex yelled.

"My third cousin, it's perfectly legal. And he owns a Honda dealership on Northern Boulevard."

"He doesn't own it, Marsha, he's part owner with his father and two uncles."

"Shit, I hate it when you start that crap. As if you're the only one that does anything important with your life."

He remembered that he stood up and began buttering the bagels, all the while thinking, great, get lost, who the hell wants to be married?

All during this conversation he remembered Marsha staring. She was hypnotized, it seemed, by the little metal magnets that held the boys' pediatrician appointments onto the refrigerator. He remembered asking her if she was really serious.

"Alex," she'd said, "I can't stand the thought that the intelligent, romantic literature professor I married has given up his dreams, and has become a goyim cop. I can't stand to think about it anymore."

"I wasn't a professor, Marsha. I was a high-school English teacher. I hated every minute of it. It was your dream, not mine. I tried, but those kids tore it out of me." He couldn't believe his luck; she really did want a divorce. He leaned in close to her and whispered, "Sy Alweiss, the guy that walks like a duck, and has an ass like a frog. You're going to divorce me, me you're going to divorce to marry frog-ass Alweiss. I can't believe it."

"Believe it, Alex, believe it. He'll come home at night. He'll be home on weekends and holidays. I won't have to sit around all day wondering where you get those cheap perfume smells on your shirts and sweaters and around your fly."

"You've been smelling my fly, Marsha? That's sick, that's really sick. And what about my boys? What about Josh and David? You think Frog Ass will be able to bring them up?"

"You'll be able to visit, don't worry. We're not going far, just to Roslyn Heights."

"You've gone JAP on me, Marsha. I can't believe it. When I wasn't looking, you turned into a princess."

"Tell me something, Alex, why in the world did you become a cop?"

"Cops tell the funniest stories, Marsha. You just never listened."

"I know this isn't funny, Alex, but try and deal with it like the man I once knew."

Alex remembered trying very hard not to smile. Then he thought about Vinny, and Russians, and Delaney. He tried hard not to think about Josh, and David, and Frog Ass.

Chapter Seven

"Everyone knows that Michael Burns loves cops. Isn't that true, Alex? I'm Assistant District Attorney Michael Burns of the Queens D.A.'s office, I'm a cop lover and proud of it. Hell, last week I spoke at this month's PBA communion breakfast. You were there, weren't you?"

Alex shook his head.

"That's dumb, I'm sorry, Alex, of course you wouldn't be there. Your people don't take communion, do they?"

Alex shook his head a second time.

"Anyway, I gave a speech, a speech in support of the death penalty. The cops stood and cheered. I got a standing ovation. I spoke boldly, Alex, boldly. 'Fry the fuckers' is what I said. Well, I didn't say fuckers, it being a communion breakfast and all, but you understand."

Alex nodded.

"And now, just a week later, do you know what I'm forced to do?"

"What's that?"

"Me, Michael Burns, a man whose very own father retired

from the thin blue line a short five years ago. A man whose only brother is a detective assigned to the Manhattan North Homicide Squad. A man whose very blood runs blue and gold. I have to call a press conference to announce the arrest of four police officers for burglary.

"And, not just any four cops. No, Alex, these four are matched pairs. Two men, two women. Between them they have thirty citations for bravery, and seven children.

"Here, let me read the press release. I worked on it for three hours. The man downstairs loves it. You're sensitive to this sort of thing, being an intelligence officer and all."

Alex suppressed a yawn.

" 'Queens District Attorney, John Santangelo, announced today the indictment of four police officers. The officers, all assigned to the 119th Precinct, were indicted for burglary, in the second degree. If convicted of the charges alleged in the indictment, the officers could face up to thirty years imprisonment.'

"How's that?"

Alex didn't hide his yawn. Still Burns went on.

" 'On the night in question, the officers responded to a call of burglary in progress at the Grand Union market at 179th Street and Hillside Avenue. When they arrived on the scene, the officers found the burglars gone, and the door to the market open. After discovering sophisticated safe-cracking tools, and a locked safe, Officer Janet Martin suggested to the others that they complete what the burglars had begun.

" 'For four hours the women officers stood lookout while their male partners cracked the safe. A patrol sergeant spotted them placing bags of money in one of the patrol cars. Janet Martin, who testified under a grant of immunity, told members of the D.A.'s office, and the grand jury, that the officers had been lovers for over a year. They planned to use the money to begin new lives in Mexico.' "

"All four?" Alex asked.

D.A. Burns rubbed his hands and all his features came together in a red-flecked ball.

"Yup," he said, "two loving couples is what we have here."

"You should have seen Officer Martin at the grand jury, Alex," Burns whispered. "She actually pissed. You couldn't see it at first. No one noticed. You know how the grand jury room is. She was seated behind a desk. You know what I mean, there's that wood paneling in front. The jury foreman yelled *she's pissing.*' He must have seen the puddle alongside her chair. Sad, isn't it?"

Alex shut his eyes and cringed.

"Tragic," he said.

Looking at D.A. Burns made Alex drowsy.

"I'll probably never get invited to another PBA communion breakfast."

"Probably not."

Burns shrugged, then smiled. "Well, what can I do for you? Wait, let me guess. Another wiretap, I bet."

"Right."

"On who?"

"A woman, a girl, really, Lynn Backman. She's the girlfriend of Mathew, Matty, Musca."

"Does Musca live with her?"

"No."

"And the telephone, it's listed in the girl's name?"

"Yes."

"Are you sure he uses that phone for business?"

"He doesn't use his home phone. I've checked, there's not one toll call to New York City. And the guy lives in Fort Lee, New Jersey."

"Weren't you on him once before?"

"Last year, I had a wire on the Brothers Social Club. But they tore that phone off the wall."

"What is Musca into?"

80

"Name it. Drugs, hijacking, extortion, murder. Mathew Musca is a major organized crime guy, Michael."

"Yes, but he doesn't live there, Alex. And the phone is not in his name, Alex. And you are not sure what would be said on that phone. Isn't that true?"

Alex heard himself sigh, loudly. "Damn you," he thought, "you asshole."

It had been a weekend of being totally at the mercy of events. Events that ground his teeth and made his prick disappear.

First it was the boys, then it was Vinny.

Saturday morning, though he really wanted to get on Matty Musca, he'd decided that Josh and David needed to see him. Truth was, he needed to see them, but he was broke, and the boys would expect dinner and a show. Still, it was *his* weekend. So he drove out to the land of the golden community centers in his beat-up Chevy, with its broken heater.

When he got to the home of Frog Ass, Marsha yelled to him from behind a locked door. She said that the boys had gone into the city to a boat show. Marsha reminded him that he'd missed his last two weekends, and since he hadn't called, there was no way they thought he'd be coming.

So he sat in the Chevy on Frog Ass's driveway and read *Last Exit to Brooklyn*. He waited for six hours.

When the boys and Frog Ass finally arrived, he threatened Frog Ass. Frog Ass ran to the house screaming for Marsha to call the police.

He and the boys went for Chinese.

These scenes with Marsha made Josh nervous. The kid threw up all over a waitress from Manila.

When he brought the boys back, Frog Ass, Marsha, and two Nassau County policemen were waiting.

More yelling, more screaming. Josh threw up again.

When he finally got home, there was a message on his machine from Vinny. He'd been arrested with Peejays, for assault and police impersonation. It took all of Sunday to get him out of jail.

"Alex, like I was saying, let me read this memo to you. It's from the man himself."

"For christsake, Michael, don't read it, just tell me what it's about."

"Okay, simply put, this office is not going to be giving out any more wiretap orders unless we know they are going to be successful."

"How's that?" Alex asked.

"No more applications will be submitted to the court unless we are sure they will net results."

"You're kidding. You have to be. How the hell am I supposed to know that a wire is going to be successful till I put it in?"

"That's your problem."

"Last year, this office submitted fifty wiretap applications. They were all approved."

"You had more than your share, ol' buddy. Of the fifty taps, thirty-five turned out to be losers, nonproductive. Fifteen led to arrests, and of that fifteen, ten were suppressed at hearings, before trial. Only five resulted in convictions. We're not giving out any more tap orders unless we know they are going to be productive.

"Got that, Alex? None of these ghost wires like the one you want to drop on citizen Musca."

"You're not going to give me a wiretap order?"

"Not unless you first make sure that Musca is talking business on that phone. Don't take it personally, it's office policy."

"You want to tell me how I'm supposed to know if the guy's talking business, before I get on his goddamn phone?"

"You figure it out, you're a bright guy."

When Alex pulled himself from the chair, D.A. Burns winked. It was a sly, evil kind of wink.

Alex thought that this was a totally useless human being. He smiled, nodded, then left the room.

Detective Alexander Simon spent five seconds examining the moral and legal implications of what he was about to do, then he looked into his toolbox. He checked the handset and the tape recorders. He made doubly sure he had an extension cord and enough telephone wire. He'd return the keys for the front and basement doors to the super, just as soon as he was sure the dupes he'd made worked.

Alex smiled when he walked across the Boulevard and saw his reflection from the glass of the building's front door. It was 3:00 A.M.

Dressed in a Consolidated Edison uniform, he was alone in the street, then alone in the building foyer. He would most certainly be alone in the basement. The keys worked fine. He walked directly to the door that led to the basement. He opened it and went down a flight of stairs. First there was a large room filled with bicycles and discarded refrigerators. Then a hallway that ran from the basement room to the laundry room, and then to the furnace room. The telephone box was on the laundry room wall.

It was a large, gray metal box and, like all telephone company boxes, left unlocked.

Alex lifted off the front shield; the pairs were clearly marked. He looked for apartment 7B, found it, and marked it with a Band-Aid.

Inside the box itself, telephone wires are stripped of their insulation. Once they left the box to enter the main cable, the color of the insulated wires was clearly visible. Phone company installers always use an off-white, almost beige-colored, line. The brighter white strand, coming out of the box, immediately caught Alex's experienced eye. He followed it back down into the box to the place where it'd been stripped. Then he traced the stripped line directly to the back of a pair of set screws. The apartment number beneath the screws was marked 7B. Alex yelled "shit," frightening himself. His voice exploded and echoed in the empty basement.

He retraced the line.

It joined the cable, then separated and went off on its own. Making a ninety-degree turn, it ran along the top of the wall till it traveled the full length of the room. Stapled to the furnace room ceiling, it had been strung in a straight line to the window. There it exited the building alongside the window frame.

In the rear yard, Alex used his flashlight to follow the line up the side of the building. It went straight up to the roof.

On the elevator he wondered who the hell could have this tap. He'd already eliminated the FBI. They leased lines directly from the telephone company. The FBI ran wiretaps right from their desks. No, it wasn't the bureau. To use wire that was different from telephone company issue was an amateur move. When it came to wiretapping, the FBI was anything but amateur.

On the roof, whoever did the work had joined the wire to television antenna cable, then ran it to the adjoining building. It stretched over the parapet to the opposite side of the building, down two stories, and into an apartment.

Alex stood on the roof; he looked at his watch. He had three hours to kill before he could speak to the super.

It was 4:00 A.M., he was alone on a rooftop in Queens, and he had to pee. "The whole world's a toilet," he thought, and he pissed on the white telephone line. Who was the sonofabitch that was playing fuckaround with his case, he wondered.

In his car, he opened his toolbox, his magical bag of tricks and toys. "Alexander Simon, you are the master of fuckaround," he thought. Wrapping himself in a blanket and setting his alarm for seven, he went to sleep. Five minutes into a fitful rest, he realized he had an erection.

"Yes, I'm the super of that building, too," said Jimmy Melina, the man from Argentina, who understood all too well the dangers of foreign terrorists.

Two days earlier, Alex had flashed his shield and ID card at Jimmy. He told him he was involved in a supersecret investigation involving a diversified group of communists, religious fanatics, and pedophilic baby fuckers who were using the building for clandestine meetings. He said he couldn't tell Jimmy who the people were yet, but he'd let him know the day before any arrests were made. Jimmy'd winked, and said he knew exactly who the people were. He'd never trusted those Cuban Pentecostal *putas* on the sixth floor. Always wearing white, and crossing themselves whenever they saw him.

Alex had shrugged and smiled, and gave Jimmy a bottle of good dark rum. Jimmy gave him the keys to the building.

"You have new tenants on the fourth floor of the other building," Alex said softly, drawing Jimmy into his patriotic conspiracy.

"Um-hum," Jimmy said, not at all surprised that Alex should have such current and accurate information. After all, he was a secret agent. "A young American couple. They paid three months rent in advance."

"Not American," Alex said, "Bulgarian, the same people that tried to kill the pope. They have the world's best language schools. They can fool anyone."

"The pope," Jimmy said.

Alex nodded.

"They seemed so all-American."

"And that, my friend, is their genius."

Jimmy slid his passkey into the lock, turned it, and nothing happened.

"Bucking sneaky Bulgarians," Jimmy said, "they changed the bucking lock."

For fifteen minutes Alex played with his pick set . . . and zip. He couldn't work these things. He'd studied for a month with a locksmith in Brooklyn. And there were some locks that he could pick. But not with a dead bolt. And that's exactly what this one had. He smiled at Jimmy and Jimmy smiled back as if he were watching brain surgery. Alex held the bar probe and ran the pick one more time. Suddenly he felt it go. Jimmy applauded when he heard the click. Alex smiled confidently; they were in communion. He turned the knob and opened the door.

Alex walked straight through the vacant apartment to the back bedroom. Jimmy waited in the hallway. A footlocker secured with a combination lock lay against the wall. The white wire came in under the window frame, and ran straight into the locker.

Alex felt as though there were ghosts in the room, ghosts of people just like himself.

He asked Jimmy to wait in the downstairs foyer near the bells. If the Bulgarians came into the building, he should buzz him. He'd need ten minutes.

Jimmy said sure, and marched off as if on a mission.

Alex closed and locked the door, then opened his toolbox. He took out a screwdriver and removed the double wall outlet across from the footlocker. He replaced it with another double outlet. An exact duplicate of the first with one small difference. Only the bottom receptacle worked. The one on top, though it looked perfectly ordinary, was, in fact, the microphone of a transmitter. If anyone tried to plug into it, they would think it was broken and use the bottom half.

This much done, he returned his tools to his box, exited the apartment, and closed the door. The snap lock was in place but the dead bolt was not. So he took out his pick set and started playing with it again. Then he heard the apartment buzzer. He took his things and ran up the stairs.

Alex kept going until he reached the roof. In any case, the roof was to be his next stop. Alex had no great need to see who was going into the apartment; he'd know soon enough.

Once out on the roof he found the white wire among the television antenna lines. He shaved a one-inch section of insulation from the line, and attached a line bug. This particular bug was powered by a nine-volt battery. He'd have to change it every three days. The transmitter in the apartment had its own power source. If not discovered, it would last forever. He taped the line bug securely in place, knowing that if anyone checked this line they would have to be brain damaged not to find it. But, then again, why would anyone look? Both bugs in place, he went over the roof into the building where Lynn Backman, Matty's girlfriend, lived.

In the lobby he found Jimmy sitting in a chair reading *La Prensa*.

"It was one of the Bulgarians," Jimmy whispered. "The female. She didn't even say hello to me when she came in the building."

"Terrorists have no manners, especially Bulgarian terrorists," Alex said. Then he thanked Jimmy for his patriotic help, and told him he'd be checking with him again soon.

In the trunk of the Chevy, Alex had two FM radio receivers. On one, the FM band was cleared to receive signals from the room bug. The other should pick up conversation from Lynn's phone. The room bug he had no doubts would work perfectly. He did have some concern for the line bug. If the connection wasn't perfect, he'd get a broken signal. Alex turned the radio on and tuned to a spot just between 108 FM and 110 FM. If he got a signal, he'd be tapping a wiretap. He was the master of fuckaround.

"I'll have him call you," the female voice said.

"Cause I wanna leave soon," a soft, almost whiny, male voice answered.

"Call me back in ten minutes. I'll see if I can find him."

A hang up, a dial tone, then the *beat-beat, beat-beat-beat* of an outgoing finger-dialed call. The muffled buzz of a ring, one, then again, a pick up.

"Whadaya say?"

"Yeah."

"Wha'?"

"Listen, ya want me ta? Paulie just called, he wants to talk to you."

"All right, is he home?"

"Yeah."

"All right, I'll call him now."

"Okay, cause he's gonna call back here in ten minutes. If you don't call, get ahold of him. I'll tell him where you are."

"No, I'll call him right now."

"Right."

"No, I'll call him right up."

"All right, bye."

"Bye, baby."

Hang up.

"A home run." Alex laughed to himself. The bug worked as well as a direct line to a recorder. But he couldn't sit here all day. So he jacked the FM radio into an impulse-activated tape recorder, a Sony, his best piece of equipment. No sooner had he set the recorder on automatic than the spools began turning. He flipped the monitor switch, and turned up the volume.

Outgoing: *beat, beat, beat* . . .

Loud rock music in the background, a ring, then another ring, then another.

Matty's voice, loud and clear. "Oh, this shit I need."

"Matty's voice," Alex yelled; where the hell was he. Lynn called him not two minutes ago. Damn, there's a second apartment, and it must be on the same floor, probably right next door.

A pick up. "Hello, hello."

"Will you lower that fuckin' thing," Matty yelled.

The voice on the other end of the line repeated, "Hello, hello."

"Who's this?"

"Matty?"

"Yeah."

"Tell him that Anthony is gonna come over to pick that package up."

"Whatsamatta, you sound outta breath?"

"No, it's a . . . listen, tell Joey to call Anthony."

"Uh-huh."

"Ya hear?"

"When will we see ya?"

"Why?"

"No reason."

"Okay then, I'll see ya later."

After jacking the second radio into the other tape recorder, Alex put both pieces of equipment into the Chevy's trunk. The line bug should work beautifully. It was a transmitter on the roof of a building directing its signal straight down to the car. The room transmitter, with the electrical outlet as a power source, could throw a strong signal. The tape recorder was voice activated. It would receive conversation from the room. Trouble was, the signal had to bang its way through the walls. Alex wouldn't know how that was working until someone joined the woman in the apartment.

A familiar thrill, an excitement that he could describe to no one, came over him. His breathing was rapid as he walked along Queens Boulevard to the subway. He'd go into the office and pick up another car.

On the subway, he was crowded by two kids who used motherfucker screams and scowled at the passengers. When they caught his eye, he stared at them flatly. One started to say something, and move toward him. Alex had both his hands in his jacket pockets.

The punks studied him carefully. When it seemed they were on the point of decision, Alex pulled the handle of his PPK automatic from his jacket pocket so they could see it.

The train stopped at Queens Plaza, the doors slid open, and the kids quickly got off.

Alex thought about Marsha. He thought about teaching high school. He laughed. Soon it became uncontrollable. People in the car began to move away from him. He stroked the PPK in his pocket. Alexander Simon felt like superman.

Chapter Eight

Vinny tried three clubs and two bars looking for Peejays, but Peejays was nowhere to be seen. On Court Street, he saw Toto Deluca, Peejays' brother, and called to him.

"Toto, hey, Toto, you see your mutt brother?"

Toto pointed, like shooting a pistol, in the direction of the Merry Boys Social Club.

Vinny opened the door to the club and stood. He stood like he didn't care who was in the club, or what was happening. He stood like he was bad and seriously pissed; which he wasn't. But he did look terrible. Vinny Ba-Ba Esposito could always look fierce.

"Here he is, Peejays," Long John Crespo called out.

Peejays ran into the bathroom and slammed the door.

Vinny took a chair and sat. He sat right in front of the bathroom.

Long John asked if he wanted a coffee.

Vinny sat, and sat there, looking at the bathroom. Finally he said, "I can't take this suspense, Peejays. Come out now and catch your slaps; get it over with."

"Damn you, Vinny, I didn't do anything," he said in that familiar whining Peejays tone.

"I layed up the whole weekend with yams and *oyes* dribbling and throwing up all over me. You get bail and don't jerk me out. You're a one-way prick, Peejays."

Peejays said "Shit," and the sound of his voice made Vinny giggle; he couldn't help it.

"My uncle got me out, Vinny. I tol' him about you, I did! C'mon, let me outta here."

"Peejays, how many times do I hafta tell ya? Ya can't let fear stop ya from doing what you gotta do. And, Peejays, you gotta come out sooner or later. Get hold of yerself, man, and c'mon out."

"You gonna hit me?" Peejays asked softly.

"Just once, maybe twice. Whadaya think, Long John? Does this one-way prick need to get two slaps or what?"

Long John shrugged and said, "I dunno, I gotta get bread, or my mother is gonna beat hell outta me." Long John walked to the door, then called back, "See ya later, Peejays."

After a while Peejays came out of the bathroom, and Vinny pinned him neatly against the wall.

"I do you a favor. I get involved in something that's none of my business, and wind up busted. Then you leave me to sit in the can. Peejays, I oughtta break your fucking face is what I oughtta do. But I'm gonna give you one slap, and call it even."

"C'mon," Peejays pleaded. Vinny slapped him so hard that four old-timers, who spend their time waiting to die, playing seven and a half, under a painting of Naples speckled with fly shit, looked up.

One looked sympathetic and said, "Hey."

"Go plays cards, do what you gotta do. I gotta talk to Peejays here."

"Hey," the old guy yelled. Vinny looked and swallowed hard. It was Old Man Balsamo, Peejays' uncle, a made man.

"Dumbo," he said, "take your games outside. You see we're playing here." Then he said, "I took my nephew out. You wanna tell me how you, mister bust out, made bail?"

"My aunt hadda come get me," Vinny said.

Vinny was in awe of made guys, even if they were seventy, arthritic, and ugly as death.

Old Man Balsamo smiled at him. Then turned back to his game.

"After I got home," Peejays whispered, "I took the bank-book and went back, but you were gone."

Vinny moved less confidently now, and that delighted Pee-jays. He smiled in the direction of his uncle, and said loudly so all could hear, "You know you earned a little respect with that help you gave me."

"From who?" Vinny asked.

"People know what you did."

"Thanks."

"You better believe it. People are watching you, Vinny. They'd like to give you another shot. You'd like to stay at the club, wouldn't ya? You'd like to belong here?"

He'd once dreamed of being a made guy. No more, not him. These guys used you, then threw you to the dogs. A button, big deal, ain't nobody gonna push his button. No. Not him, not Vinny Ba-Ba Esposito.

He'd take care of himself. Do a little dipping and dabbing. And, when he got jammed up, he'd call Alex. Someday he'd make a big score. Then he'd buy his own cab. Be a business-man. Have a checkbook with his name on it. Right now he wanted to find out about the Russians for Alex, but he wasn't sure what questions to ask.

Vinny liked it when Alex smiled, and patted his back, and called him partner.

"I see Frankie Musca got himself wasted," Vinny said to Old Man Balsamo.

"His father shoulda jerked him off in Jamaica Bay. The kid

was a mad dog," Balsamo said, flicking the top of his card with the tip of his thumb.

"A mad dog," Peejays said, nodding his head and rubbing his cheek.

"Well, he fucked with the wrong guys this time," Vinny smiled.

Old Man Balsamo shrugged.

"But his uncle is gonna come a-calling," Vinny hastened to add.

"Yeah, his uncle is a . . . ." Peejays started to say.

"Who gives a shit for these Jews in Coney Island or these Lower East Side crazies? And why is a dumbo like you interested anyway?" Old Man Balsamo seemed genuinely annoyed. Vinny got nervous.

"No reason. I know the kid Frankie from around, he's a shit."

"Uh-huh, a shit, you mean he *was* a shit."

"Yeah," Vinny laughed, "a shit that ended in a garbage can."

Vinny stared at Balsamo. He tried a smile, but it wouldn't come. Balsamo looked at him a long time, then shook his head slowly.

"I gotta go," Vinny said. He tapped Peejays' shoulder. "The next time you want somebody leaned on, make sure he's not gonna call the cops. Now I gotta worry if the guy's gonna come to court to press charges."

"He's not," Old Man Balsamo said, and Vinny believed him.

On the street, Vinny felt the eyes of Balsamo on him. "That's an evil old fucker," he thought.

In the club, Balsamo took hold of Peejays' shirt, and twisted. "I smell rat all over that fat sonofabitch junkie *gavone*," he hissed. "You stay away from him. You got other people here you can use. I don't wanna see him around here anymore. He asks too many questions that ain't none of his business. Or don't you listen?"

"Too many questions," Peejays said, "the sonofabitch asks too many questions."

Vinny bought a slice of pizza, then zoomed down the avenue toward the pay phone on Union Street. Russian Jews in Coney Island, that's who did Frankie Musca. He giggled when he thought of the pictures Chief Ross and Alex showed him. Three guys in one garbage can.

Vinny smiled politely at a little old lady dressed in black and pulling a shopping cart loaded with washed and folded laundry.

"You a nice boy, Vinny," she said.

He didn't remember who she was. Probably somebody he met in his dope-shooting days. Probably somebody's grandmother. Yeah, Sally Boy Clemente's grandmother, that's who she was. Vinny remembered the day he and Sally Boy robbed her TV. He wondered what happened to ol' Sally Boy. He hadn't seen him in years. Man, Sally Boy really hated his grandmother.

Russians from Coney Island took out Frankie Musca. Get them Russians was what he was gonna say to Alex. He'd make him laugh. Vinny liked Alex a lot. He liked to talk to him every day. Alex made him feel safe.

Vinny's hand was shaking as he put the coin in the telephone.

"Hey, dumbo," he heard, "c'mere, I wanna ask you something."

Balsamo leaned against the building smoking one of those guinea stinkers. It looked like a short, black, twisted snake coming out of his mouth. Balsamo's cheeks were sick pink, and his teeth were long and streaked brown.

Pretending he felt honored, Vinny hung up the phone and joined Balsamo on the corner.

"What can I do for ya?" he asked.

"How would you like to make a few easy bucks?"

Vinny shrugged.

"You wanna earn or what?" Balsamo asked again.

"I guess so," Vinny said, trying to sound enthusiastic, and thinking "this guy smells like a headache."

"You gotta car?"

"No."

"Never mind, Junior can drive ya."

"What is it ya want me ta do?"

"Never mind, Junior will tell ya on the way there."

"Where?"

"Never mind."

Vinny felt like he was getting leaned on. Screwed is what it felt like. Screwed softly, but screwed nevertheless.

Should he ride with this, or make up some lame excuse? Be smart, he thought, you can outfox this old brown-toothed greaser.

Balsamo held up his hand. "Five," he said, "think that'll make you happy? Five hundred, I wanna make you happy, Vinny. I want you to show me you're no dumbo."

Vinny laughed. "I'm no dumbo," he said.

"Junior will pick you up right here in a couple of minutes."

Balsamo turned and limped off. He had a mean limp. People said it was an old wound; a bullet from a cop thirty, forty years ago. Peejays said he did it for effect. Vinny believed Peejays.

Vinny began to stink. Whenever he got nervous, anxious, or afraid, Vinny sweated like a race horse, and smelled worse. It made him self-conscious, so he wiped his nose on his sleeve and sniffed. Later, next time, he wouldn't be afraid to tell the old greaser Balsamo to piss off. Just like that, piss off, you old geezer. I got things to do, people to see, money to make. Piss off, old man, you're slowing down my fucking day. Vinny hitched up his pants and waited for Junior.

When Junior showed, he got into the car. He pretended it was funny that they weren't telling him what he had to do to earn the five hundred.

"Who do I hafta kill?" he joked.

"Kill, whadaya talking, kill? We don't kill nobody. Naw, you just gotta pick up a trailer down the Hook and bring it to Staten Island. You can drive a truck, right? I seen you drive a truck once, didn't I?"

"Wha' kinda truck?" Vinny asked, knowing that he'd just slid into a trick bag. Now the trick was to pop out in one piece. These guys thought they were so slick. They had a hot truck, that was it. The truck was probably glowing so bright you'd need sun glasses to get within a block of the damn thing. Sure, that was it, cops were probably sitting all over the fucker.

And these slick guys, not wanting to send one of their own, are gonna use me, he thought, dumbo. I fuck 'em where they breathe.

Vinny pretended he felt better, he pretended he knew what to do.

On the far side of Red Hook, on a dead-end street near the water, Vinny saw the eighteen-wheeler.

Junior handed him one key, and said he should drive out of the Hook via Hamilton Avenue. At the Hamilton Avenue entrance to the expressway, Toto and Balsamo would be waiting. He'd follow them to Staten Island. Toto would give him the money at the end of the trip.

Vinny was impressed. Junior was running a good game on him. He listened closely, it didn't get better. He was in trouble.

He needed to get to a phone, needed to call Alex. Junior would be watching.

"Hey, Junior," he said, "when Balsamo talked to me I was just about to call my girl. I'm supposed to meet her in an hour, ya know. She's gonna be waiting on a corner, waiting for me to show."

"Give me her number, I'll call her for ya."

Vinny laughed and slapped Junior's back. "You slick son-ofabitch, you'd be peeking in my girl's laundry bag before I got to Staten Island. Naw, Junior, I can't give you her number. She's married. We go through these changes and all. I ring her phone, she rings me back, then I meet her. If she thought I told somebody who she was, she'd be all pissed off."

"Then she's gonna be pissed off waiting. Because the way I see it, and I'm trying to see it every possible way, the bitch is gonna be pissed, cuz you ain't calling nobody."

"I'm gonna call her, Junior. You wanna tell Balsamo, you go ahead."

"Vinny, you contracted to drive the truck. You drive the truck. If you stop for any reason you kill your contract, and I'm gonna kill you."

A hot stink rolled from Junior's mouth. Accented with garlic, his words cut like razors.

Vinny laughed a little, very quietly, then he got out of the car and walked the block to the tractor-trailer.

He thought he'd make a dry run. See if he could draw a tip. There was not a house, not a building, on the street. The truck was parked along the curb next to the playground that hadn't been used in years. The swings were gone, and the wood from the benches had been torn off. The park house was covered with graffiti. There was a jagged hole from a roof fire.

In this part of Brooklyn, they burn the park houses down.

Somebody could easily lay up in there and wait, Vinny thought. The place could be full of cops; cops waiting for a dumbo to come by and pick up a glowing tractor-trailer full of Vinny didn't know what.

He checked the tractor's door; it was locked. Then he turned and walked through a hole in the playground's fence. He went directly to the little brick house with the hole in the roof.

When he went through the door, the stink hit. It hit like a

stone wall. Kid Vinny Esposito had run in the street for years, he'd seen some bad shit, but for pure stink, this place took the cup, going away.

People had been using the place for a toilet for a year, maybe more. And the light that dripped in through the roof made the interior of the house look weird, haunted by junkie ghosts. "Geez," Vinny thought, "I could never shoot junk again. When I shot junk, this stink never bothered me. What a sick fucker I was. Thank God for Alex, Alex washed that stink off me."

He imagined it clearly, hiding in a basement, or a roof landing, or an abandoned building; they all stank, just like this place. He'd tie up and rub a fat vein. He'd play with a cooker and a spike. Images danced in his head, and the smell disappeared. Even now Vinny started to get dizzy, he felt a horribly familiar presence. The sleeping beast that was his habit rolled in his stomach, it reached a claw to his chest, and squeezed his heart.

He moaned. Vinny Ba-Ba wanted to get high. He heard the song and felt the sweet breath of the white lady. Vinny ran from the park house, he ran on fat legs and leather-soled shoes; he ran, slipping and sliding, to the door of the tractor-trailer and opened it with the key. He got in and started the engine. Fuck whoever was watching, he hadda get outta here.

Vinny bounced along in the tractor-trailer. He played with the air horn and scared hell out of a car full of PRs in a big old Chrysler that had a picture of two palm trees on its rear window. Under the palm-tree picture, written in green script, were the words Puerto Rico, Island of Enchantment. Vinny ran the eighteen-wheeler right up to their rear bumper and yanked the air horn. The PRs inside jumped around like mice in a shoe box. Vinny laughed. He picked up the CB microphone and yelled, "Breaker 10–4, I love this shit." The beast in his stomach, disappointed, went back to sleep.

On the Staten Island side of the Verrazano Narrows Bridge, Toto and Balsamo had pulled to the shoulder of the highway.

They waited till he paid the toll, then motioned for him to follow. In his rearview, he saw Junior riding with a guy he'd never seen before. Vinny reached a hand under his arm; he was dripping.

He struggled to keep an eye on Toto, and his mind clear. The stink of the park house haunted his nostrils; he had a bitter taste, like heroin, dripping in the back of his throat. But he knew the beast slept and that made him proud.

They rode the expressway as far as the Victory Boulevard exit. Vinny followed Toto down the ramp, across the boulevard, then up a narrow paved road in to an enormous junkyard that was surrounded by an eight-foot fence with curled razor wire on top. The gate to the yard was open. Vinny followed Toto inside; he took a deep breath when the gate closed behind the trailer. Easing the giant truck near a machine that looked like it could crush a tank, he shut the engine and waited.

Balsamo and Toto stood near the office talking with a short, fat man. A guy who Vinny *had* seen before—he'd seen him at the Merry Boys. His name was Fat Anthony and he drove a white Mercedes convertible with Florida plates. Vinny remembered the car, it was special.

He sat in the tractor until Junior tapped on the window and motioned with his head for him to get out and follow.

Inside the office, Vinny dropped onto a brown leatherette couch. Toto and Fat Anthony stood near him; Balsamo and Junior were out of sight, but he could hear them; they were laughing.

He was here; there was nothing to do, but he wished Alex was nearby. Alex had a funny way of laughing when things got sticky. It was like he was having fun.

Toto took a roll of bills from his pocket, looked at it, then put it back.

"I got something better than money for you, Ba-Ba," he

said. Then he reached into his other pocket and took out a spoon bag of skag.

"How'd ya like this. There ain't nothing better in the street. This here will turn you loose, bring you up and away, right, Anthony?"

"Best babanya in the world; straight from Sicily; it'll take ya home."

Vinny's hand was shaking; he could smell the shit in the park house. Then he heard Alex laugh, and said, "What for? I don't do that shit anymore."

"Once a junkie . . ."

Vinny shook his head and sniffed. He couldn't believe it; his nose was running.

"Hey," he said, "I drove your truck, I got it here. Balsamo said I'd get five hundred."

"Mister Balsamo to you," Toto said.

"You gonna beat me for the five? Is that it? You guys are from the neighborhood; what the hell is going on?"

Toto laughed and Fat Anthony yawned.

Vinny turned his best smile on them; then he thought fuck this, and got up.

"What the fuck is going on here?" he screamed, and when he screamed lights went off in his head. You could only push Vinny Ba-Ba so far and then the connections lapsed and the gorilla took command.

He picked Toto up with one hand, lifted him off the floor. Toto dropped the bag of junk and grabbed Vinny's shoulders and yelled, "Whoa, Vinny, whoa! What are you doing?"

"I'm gonna throw you through the fucking roof, is what I'm gonna do."

From the corner of his eye he saw Fat Anthony reach for his pocket.

"You fat fuck, you make a move, I'll break this prick in half and beat you to death with the fucking pieces. What game you guys running over here? You think I'm a punk or something? You think you're fucking with Peejays or something? I'll kill you scumbags."

The door to the office slammed open. Balsamo and Junior, with the guy Vinny didn't know, came into the room.

"Whoa," Balsamo yelled. "Whadaya doing? You gone crazy or what?"

"Put me down," Toto pleaded.

"You Americans crazy, like red indians, all crazy," the stranger with Balsamo said.

Vinny threw Toto onto the plastic couch and looked at this weird-sounding little character who was now standing in the office, wearing a large cowboy hat with a little red feather.

Vinny shrugged. "For old-times sake," he said, "you guys wanna tell me what's going down here?"

"You ask too many questions, dumbo," Balsamo said.

"Yeah, dumbo, too many fucking questions," Toto said.

"I ask too many questions? About what?"

"How did you know those guys ended up in a garbage can? This morning, at the club, you said Frankie Musca ended up in a garbage can. How do you know that?"

"Oh, man," Vinny said sadly, "It was in the paper. I read it in the paper."

"Show me," Balsamo said, and he handed Vinny a copy of the *Daily News*. Balsamo suddenly seemed to be amused, and the strange little fucker with the cowboy hat was now sitting on the couch, cleaning his nails with a switchblade.

He found the line in the article he wanted, then handed the paper back to Balsamo.

"It says they were found in a Dempsey Dumpster, that's a big garbage can," Vinny said. Then he walked over to Toto.

"You put junk in my face again, I'm going to blind you," he said with a smile that convinced everyone there that he meant it.

"Good for you, Toto," Balsamo said.

Fat Anthony asked if anyone wanted a veal-and-pepper hero, or a VCR; he had plenty of both. The weird man in the cowboy hat closed his knife, introduced himself as Yuri, then laughed. Vinny thought he laughed with an accent like all zips.

It had been one helluva day, and when it ended Vinny knelt in his bedroom and prayed to Saint Jude, his patron, who, along with Alex, beat down the long nails of the white lady and helped him put the beast to sleep.

It was only to Jude that Vinny spoke honestly. Yes, there was Alex, but Alex, though Vinny loved him, was a cop.

"What the hell did I do to deserve the shit you put me through today?" he asked the plaster figure. "I oughtta put out your candle, is what I oughtta do."

Vinny turned the statue toward the wall and said, "Okay, smart ass, check out the roaches, I don't wanna see your face for a week."

The day hadn't been all bad.

He did make five hundred dollars, right at the end, right at the time he thought they would kill him, then squash him *splat* in that machine. That machine that boxed cars to the size of a small portable TV.

Where did the bones go, he wondered? Probably just got squished up, all gooey and sticky, then mixed with the plastic, and metal, and rubber of the splatted car. It made him woozy to think about it.

If he were in an elevator that fell, he thought, he'd jump in the air just before it hit. He'd get banged around a bit, but he'd survive. Whenever he rode an elevator, he thought about that. Just count one, two, three, jump—zippedy do—he'd be okay. But nobody had to tell him that he'd be squashed flat in one of those car fuckeruppers. No way. He'd get squished sure as hell; unless, maybe, he had a steel bar, or something to wedge in there. But where was he going to find a steel bar? And they'd probably shoot and stab him, and otherwise totally fuck him around first. Buncha degenerates. He'd rather deal with junkies any day. Junkies, he thought, had hearts, feelings.

Funny to catch a break like that, meeting the Russian zip and all.

Weird-looking fucker with the cowboy hat. Yuri, Yuri, weird fucker spending time picking his fingernails with a shank. And, when he laughed, those aluminum teeth . . . weird.

Alex laughed, man did he laugh, when he told him. He heard Alex clap his hands. He did, he clapped and said, "Ba-Ba, you are the best, goddamn it. You're the greatest."

Of course, Alex got his reasons to be happy, but Vinny hoped Alex didn't think of him as a stool pigeon.

He's nobody's rat; couldn't live with that jacket. He helped Alex because Alex treated him with respect, and called him partner. But, most important, Alex helped him tame the beast; Alex and methadone.

Methadone, phew, what a mother jones that was to kick. But he'd done it, and he'd done it righteous, too. He'd turkeyed that mother habit, almost died doing it.

Vinny quietly prayed to Saint Jude.

A tear rolled along his big round cheek. "Please, Jude," he said, "please give Toto, Junior, Fat Anthony, and Old Man Balsamo cancer of the asshole. Do that for me and we'll be friends again."

He didn't put horns on Peejays. Peejays wasn't bad, just dumb as a stick.

Chapter Nine

It was late, and everyone had left the nightclub, except an old man who sat in the corner drinking cognac. He sat there even as the lights went out and he was left in the glow of just one. He sat in shadow, sipping cognac, and looking at Niki.

Petra and Yuri and two waiters, one from Odessa and one from Riga, kept watch on him.

"He's been here all night," Petra said.

"Do we know him?" Niki asked.

"I don't," said Yuri.

And Petra said, "Me neither."

They all sat together at a table close to the bandstand near the side door that exited to the alleyway. It was through that door Frankie Musca came in the night they killed him and his two cowboy friends.

Niki had four people from Uzbekistan on the street and in the alley. He was ready; he wasn't going to run from his club. It'd taken too much to get it.

Nikolai Zoracoff had been in America eighteen months, and

he now headed a small Russian army; an army that stepped back from nobody.

It had to be so in America. In America, Niki found that to step back is to be stepped on. Everybody's crazy.

"What is he drinking?" Niki asked the waiter from Riga.

"Cognac."

Niki went to the bar and took a bottle of Hennessey, put it on a silver tray, and walked to the old man's table.

"Can I join you?" he asked.

"I've been waiting for you."

"For me?"

"Yes."

He was seventy-five, maybe eighty, tall and lean with smooth olive skin. His hands were large, his fingers long and thin. Around his wrist was a gold bracelet; a bracelet Niki had seen before—it was Sonny's. Sonny, the movie star; Sonny, the first American criminal he'd met. Sonny, the only American he cared for. Sonny, the one Frankie Musca had killed, along with Mikey, his stupid brother.

"That's a nice bracelet," Niki said.

"It was my grandnephew's. They killed him and his brother; buried them in garbage."

"I know," Niki said.

"And my brother, you know, they killed my brother, too."

"I know."

"I'm the last of the Ippolitos. Maybe they'll kill me, too, and that'll be it."

"We don't have to talk about this, you know. I mean you don't have to tell me these things. It really is none of my business." He liked this man who sat tall and straight, and had the callouses of a laborer on his hands.

"My name is Joseph, Joseph Ippolito. I had a vegetable store in South Brooklyn for thirty years. Made a lot of money; I worked hard. Look at my hands."

"I noticed," Niki said. Then he asked, "Would you like to go for a walk?"

"Where to?"

"To the boardwalk?"

"The boardwalk? What for?"

"It is late, I'm tired from the smoke and the heat in here. Let's walk near the beach, it's only a short distance."

"I want to talk to you," Joseph Ippolito said.

His speech was ominous, and there was pressure in his manner. But he was an old man. Niki liked and respected old men, especially men who, unlike himself, had worked with their hands all their lives.

"Can't we talk while we're walking?" Niki asked.

"Sure, but I can't walk far," Ippolito said, "I'm no kid like you, you know."

"It's a half-block to the boardwalk. We can sit, it's a nice night. We can sit, and you can tell me what it is you want to tell me. The people here would like to go home." Niki smiled, and Joseph Ippolito, Sonny's great-uncle, smiled back.

"Don't go alone," Ippolito whispered.

"Are you here to hurt me?"

"No, to warn you. To thank you and to warn you."

It was a cool night on the Brighton Beach boardwalk. Fishing boats were a long way from shore, but by the full moon and the boat lights, you could see the studied way they trolled. Niki loved to watch ships at sea.

He came to this place often, to sit, and think, and plan. Sometimes he came with Katya, sometimes with Yuri, Petra, or Vasily. But mostly he came alone.

Since the shooting, he was never totally alone. Yuri and Yuri's people were always nearby.

Joseph Ippolito motioned with his finger, then tapped the side of his head. "It is a wonderful place, America is. If you are smart you can live well. But you have to work hard, nobody gives you nothing for nothing here."

"It is a violent place, your America. I have never dreamed there could be such violence."

Ippolito stared down at his hands; there was a lost look on his face, and it made Niki sad.

"I have worked all my life. I never hurt anyone. I am not a violent man and I don't do violent things. I only work hard. My family is another story. All of them, every last one, either died in prison or on the street. But the truth is, none of them wanted to work. Work was for stupid people. So now the stupid one of the family is the only one in the family that is alive."

Niki shrugged. "Sonny was not violent."

Ippolito looked at him but did not answer.

"Sonny showed me New York. He loved this city, and he arranged for me to buy my restaurant. Sonny lent me money, and hardly knew me.

"I paid much back, nearly every penny, and the interest was high." Niki laughed. "I guess high interest was how he earned his money. It was better than his other business. We were partners in a restaurant, a restaurant where Sonny never ate the food. Sonny always talked about life, and love and travel and food. He loved music, you know," Niki said, "Sonny didn't like our food, but he loved our music."

Ippolito remained silent.

"Anyway, we became close friends. He was the only American friend I had. I hope you don't think I had anything to do with . . ."

"Oh, no, no. I know how he died, and I know why he died. And his brother Mikey died only because he was with him. I know everything."

"You sold vegetables?" Niki asked.

"Yes."

"You know," Niki said, "you can come from anywhere on this earth, and in a year you can consider yourself a New Yorker. Sonny taught me that."

"Sonny was very smart. You know, his teachers said he had a gift. His brother Mikey was a lump. He was older than Sonny, but a lump. Their parents died when they were babies. Sonny, I think was no more than a year old, his brother was . . . I don't know . . . older. I think by five, six years. My nephew raised them both."

"How old are you?" Niki asked.

Ippolito put his hand on Niki's shoulder and squeezed. "I'm eighty years old," he said.

"No."

"You're fuckin' *A*, and I'm still alive, and like the ladies," Ippolito winked.

Niki watched him for a few seconds, then he shook his head and said, "I'm glad to know you."

"They will come for you, you know. No matter what they promise, no matter what they say, they'll join together in the end, and come for you. You're not one of them. They turn on each other, they lie and cheat each other, so you, you will be easy."

"They need me," Niki said.

"And, when they don't need you anymore, they'll come."

"I'll be here, I'm not running. I think this Paul Malatesta is the biggest of the big. He told me the crazy ones are coming."

"Only because he needs you."

"Why are you telling me all this?"

"Because Sonny liked you, he liked you a lot. And they killed him. And my brother, and my other grandnephew. You avenged my family. Sonny would have wanted me to warn you. Why don't you take your money and go home?"

"I have no place to go. I can't go home. I stay here; I'm making this my new home. But soon, maybe very soon, I'll leave New York and go somewhere else."

"They'll find you."

"Then I have no choice, do I?"

"No, not unless you go to the police."

"I have no choice then."

Ippolito stood up, he stretched and turned to Niki and smiled. There was a warmth there Niki had not seen in a while. It made him feel good.

"You disapprove of me?" Niki asked.

"I disapprove of all of you who think the world is yours for the taking. I disapproved of everyone in my own family. But I loved them all, nonetheless."

Lighting one of those strange, ugly Italian cigars, Ippolito began to walk off.

"I have to go, I am tired," he said.

Niki gave him a big smile. It was very late; four o'clock in the morning; nothing moved in the street; the moon was full and it was bright.

Niki looked up and down the deserted boardwalk. He knew Yuri and Petra were watching.

"Come with me," he told Ippolito. "It's not a good idea to walk around here when it's so late and you're all alone."

"I'll call a cab," Ippolito said.

"Not at this hour, you won't. No, I'll have someone drive you home. Make sure you arrive safely."

They walked from the boardwalk along a side street. Part way up the block, car lights flashed, once, then again.

"I hope that's your friends," Ippolito said.

"It is."

Ippolito looked at him for a moment, smiled, then nodded. "Okay," he said, "I'd appreciate a ride home."

Niki opened the door to Yuri's car. It was another new one, a Mercedes. In the panel light it seemed that Yuri was smiling, but you could never be sure with him.

"Take him wherever he needs to go. I'll wait for you back at the restaurant."

"All right," Yuri said.

Petra and Vasily seemed to appear from nowhere, and Ippolito smiled approvingly.

"You'll be careful, won't you?" Ippolito said.

"Always," Niki said, "I'm always careful!"

Niki stood near the corner of Brighton Avenue and Seventeenth Street, looking up at a howling train covered with murals—graffiti, the Americans called it.

A blue and white police car sped by, its lights flashing. Niki could get just a glimpse of two black men inside. They were young and both were smoking. Petra, who stood nearby, smiled and said, "Well, what do you think? Will you change your mind?"

Niki hummed the first few bars of "The Flowers of Kalina," and shook his head. "No, " he said, "I haven't changed my mind. I'm going to get this man Matty before he can come for me."

"And Paul Malatesta, the big boss?" Petra asked.

"He is a mystery; he helped us. Without his warning, we would have been finished. But I don't trust him. Among that group Sonny was the only one I trusted."

"There are too many of them," Petra said.

"This is one of those times when you have to be optimistic. Maybe things aren't as bad as they seem. These people are jealous of each other."

"Is there anyone among them we can trust?" Petra asked.

"Not if we want to survive."

"And this man, Sonny's relative? What did he have to say?"

"He said we're a long way from home."

Petra laughed, and his laugh turned into a worried frown. "Did he really say that?" he asked.

Niki smiled and took Petra's arm. They walked along Brighton Avenue, past the shops with Russian lettering, past the pizza parlor and the furniture store. They turned into the street where Moscow Nights stood on the corner, all glittery and looking new.

Niki concentrated on the order of things; his first months in America. How crazy it all seemed, and how, for a while, after Sonny, it all sort of fell into place. Then he thought of Frankie Musca and his friends; the night he witnessed the American dream in action.

Nikolai Zoracoff was guided by the philosophy that important friends could turn one's life around. That's how it had been with Viktor in Moscow. He thought it would be that way again with Sonny, then Matty Musca, and then Paul Malatesta. Over money—granted, a lot of money—his friends had turned into dangerous enemies. The trick was to maintain a sense of humor; that was it, that was the trick.

Chapter Ten

Alex parked his car one street from the courthouse in a frighteningly large pothole. It was a parking lot, Bronx style.

He drove down and in, parked and locked, then walked up and out. He counted back from ten as he went. At zero he turned around. The car was still there; he stood on the rise and watched it a while. Chances were he might not see it again.

It had been a while since Alex had been in the Bronx; he didn't miss it, but when he reached 161st Street and the Concourse, he saw change.

The Concourse Plaza Hotel, diagonally across the avenue from the courthouse, had been renovated. Remodeled, it almost looked new.

Not long ago, it was a pad for winos and junkies, a crib for burnouts and blowaways, that kept three precinct sector cars hopping twenty-four hours a day. Returned to its glory days, it now reached back to a time when the Concourse was truly grand. But that was long ago, when Alex was a boy and the Dodgers were still in Brooklyn, and the Giants played in

Harlem, and junk was something thrown in a garbage can. Then he saw a column of smoke from *between* chimneys.

More landlord renovation.

Alex did very little work in the Bronx, and that suited him fine; the place was a war zone.

He had an appointment to meet Tom Delaney and some other feds at a D.A.'s office on the sixth floor of the criminal courts building. He was already fifteen minutes late. He began to jog to the side entrance; Delaney hated to wait. Four junkies spread themselves across the entrance steps. Holding tight to their noses for balance, eyes shut, they sailed around the moon at ninety-degree angles from the pavement. But they straightened up as Alex passed, then slowly began to collapse in sections, knees, waist, elbows held tight to their sides. Then, as if on cue, they shot straight up again. Hey-hey, whadaya say; it was the Bronx two-step, the heroin hop.

Law and Order Enforced with Justice and by Strength Lie at the Foundations of Civilization. Law Must Be Based upon Justice Else it Cannot Stand and It Must Be Enforced with Resolute Firmness, was chiseled in the granite above the oversized revolving door.

Mad Mike, Zulu Clara, and Savage Skulls-L.A.M.F., was spray-painted in white and pink and blue on the same stone.

On the main floor, Alex fought his way through cops and lawyers and bondsmen, victims and predators and packs of people who could undergo multiple bypass surgery without anesthesia. The great white horse was still free and running loose in the Bronx.

On the elevator, he ran into two old-timers, courtroom regulars, trial buffs who could give Justice Burger an hour's lecture on the ramifications of the Miranda decision. They were locked in a heated argument.

"Whadaya mean? I was here last week."

"I didn't see ya."

"I saw you eating liver across the street. Me, I never eat liver out."

"I like it with mushrooms; I call 'em little umbrellas."

"I'd rather eat liver home. I like the way my wife makes it."

One of the old-timers asked Alex if he was a lawyer.

Alex shook his head, then he glanced at his watch. When he looked up, the old gent was smiling.

"Crook?"

"No, I'm not a crook, and I'm not a lawyer. You wanna keep going?"

"You're a cop," he said, as if a two-year-old could tell. Alex nodded.

"I'm a widower. Been a widower for thirty years. It's not so bad. Except . . . I gotta eat liver out." Then he cleared his throat, scratched his cheek, and removed from his head the ugliest, most beat-up, gray fedora Alex had ever seen. He was wearing a blue Yamulka. It was handmade, Alex could tell. His hair was white and full; coarse as wire.

"Are you Jewish?" the other one asked.

Alex nodded again.

"With that face you think maybe he's from Sweden?" the widower said.

Alex smiled, then asked, "What's good in the courthouse?"

"The double murder on the ninth floor, in part 1-A1. The detective is a terrific witness."

The married man disagreed. "He looks at his notes too much."

"Yeah, but when he testifies he smiles at the jury. They love him and that's more important."

"Whadaya know?"

"Whadaya mean, whada I know? This is my six-hundredth trial."

"What is your name?" the married man asked Alex.

"Alex Simon."

"A nice Jewish name. You a patrolman? A sergeant? A what?"

"A detective, a first grade detective."

"Well, Detective First Grade Simon, let me tell you something. This schmuck eats liver out, and he's telling me it's more important to smile at the jury than to know the facts of a case. Give us your professional opinion, if you please?"

Alex shrugged. "Well," he said . . .

"This man, Detective Alex Simon, first grade, you can take my word for it, is a schmuck. He's my friend for thirty years maybe. Still, he's a schmuck. Just like the detective who shakes his head to every other question and says, 'I can't recall—' a schmuck."

The married man dropped his head into his hand and said, "Sol, you talk, you talk, you talk. Why I listen, I'll never understand. Maybe you're right. Maybe I am schmuck."

"Can I ask you two something?" Alex said.

"Ask."

"What do you know about Russia. I mean, Russian Jews?"

"Ask him," Sol said, "he was born there."

Alex asked the married man, "Do you know anything about Russian Jews, you know, the ones who have come over recently?"

The elevator traveled to the ninth floor. The doors opened, and the married man took Alex by the elbow. He walked him to a place where no one could hear. Then he spoke as if someone were listening in the next booth.

"Detective, let me tell you something. Russians hate Jews. Russians have always hated Jews. *Even Russian Jews hate Jews.* I met some of these émigrés. My daughter, the social worker, brought a couple of these—these Russians to my house. They live in this place, Odessa Beach."

"Where?" Alex asked.

"You know, in Brooklyn, in Brighton Beach. I call it Odessa Beach because that's where they all come from. Odessa.

"They're crooks, they're shit, they're no good. Jimmy Carter, he didn't do us any favors."

That was it; Alex couldn't help but laugh.

"That can't be true of all of them," he said.

"Go ahead, laugh. You asked, I told you. Sakharov doesn't live on Brighton Avenue."

"C'mon," Alex said, "they're immigrants. They have to start somewhere."

The married man folded his arms and leaned back on his heals.

"Did you ever meet any of these characters?"

"I don't think so," Alex said.

"Well, maybe you will, and when you do, take a good look at them. How many Jews do you know have tattoos?"

"You're condemning them for having tattoos?"

"Jews don't have tattoos, Detective Simon. And let me tell you, there are no tattoo parlors in the Soviet Union. Do you know where you get tattooed in Russia? In jail is where you get tattooed."

"My friend, you can go to jail in the Soviet Union for combing your hair."

"Well, you asked, I answered. Believe what you want."

Jews, Alex thought, could be some of the worst anti-Semites. Close to eighty thousand Russian émigrés are not criminals. The married man, who ate liver home, had met two, and judged the whole group bad news. Tattoos, he thought. If anyone should understand tattoos, Jews should.

The guy Vinny described with the cowboy hat and red feather—now that guy sounded interesting. Alex decided that his next stop would be Odessa Beach. The thought pleased him; looking for a Russian cowboy with a red feather, that was all right, that would be fun.

117

Alex found the elevators jammed and the hallways crowded. Delaney was waiting, but he was preoccupied with stories of Russians and Jews that were doing business with Nino Balsamo and Fat Anthony. Vinny was a gem, a regular gem.

Looking at women moving through the hallways, he recalled that it had been awhile since he'd played. A month actually, since he'd last raised a skirt. He decided that was long enough. It was time again for Goodey, Gloria Goodman, the old standby, the greatest mouth of any white woman in the Western World. When he arrived at the office, and told the secretary he was there to meet with some feds, she didn't look up from her crossword, just pointed with her thumb.

"They're inside," she said.

Alex considered how the secretary would be in bed. It had been too long. She was probably sitting at this desk when he was chasing Gloria around grade school. But then again, there had been times, and there had been pleasant surprises. He asked the secretary her name. She didn't look up and just flicked her thumb.

"Well, it's the PD's in-house genius," Delaney crooned.

Delaney and two other FBI agents stood with such deference that Alex might have been the attorney general.

"Meet Jim Corso and Frank Rivera."

"A pleasure," Alex exclaimed. "Are you two responsible for dragging me up here to Combat City?"

Rivera smiled and shook his hand. Corso sat back in a chair and played with a folder.

Alex walked to the center of the room and said, "Well?"

"We have something we think you should see," Delaney said.

Delaney's two friends sat together on a couch. They were field agents, Alex could tell. They looked like hit men when compared to Delaney in his button-down, and wing tips.

They appeared nervous and glanced at the folder. They wouldn't look at him.

The Latin guy handed Alex an eight-by-ten black and white photo. Alex, already alarmed, took the photo and examined it closely.

"So," Delaney said.

Alex sat on a chair and handed the photo back to Delaney. Delaney looked sympathetic; he looked like a schoolteacher who'd caught his favorite student cheating. He looked like he was still a friend. But low whistles were going off in Alex's head. Show time, he thought.

"So, yourself," Alex said, smiling.

"Do you know what we have here?" Delaney asked.

Alex suddenly felt afraid. It was clear Vinny was in serious trouble. He was not ready to say anything.

The Latin agent smiled. "You got quite a rep," he said. "You're the man with all the information. Mister Intelligence himself."

"What a combo," Alex thought. "Delancy's brains and these two guys' street smarts. The bureau has come quite a way."

"I think your guy has a real problem."

"My guy?" Alex said.

"Look, I talked to Inspector Ross. This gorilla is your main C.I., or stool, as you call him."

"I don't call him anything of the kind," Alex said. "Ross should have told you that. The guy's no stool pigeon, just someone I know."

"Hey, I sympathize with wanting to protect a good C.I."

"Not everyone does," Alex said.

"You kept him a dark secret because he's close to the Columbos. Real close, according to that picture."

"And no one knows," Alex said. "Nobody, that's why he's still alive."

Delaney shook his head thoughtfully. He looked at Alex and smiled.

"We know, and I'm sorry to tell you, but now he's mine."

"No he's not," Alex said.

"We got him."

Alex shrugged. "You got a picture of a guy stepping out of a truck in a junkyard."

"A hijacked truck. A hijacked truck whose driver was killed in New Jersey."

"He's a killer, your friend is a killer," the Latin agent said.

"What?"

"I said he's a fucking wop killer."

"He's not."

"When can we talk to him?" Delaney said.

Alex thought about it.

"If it was up to me you'd never talk to him."

"But it's not up to you. And the truth is, we can help him, keep him out of the can, relocate him, straighten out his life."

"You can get him killed, is what you can do."

Delaney laughed. "How long ago did you learn not to fall in love with an informant, Alex?"

The agent whose name was John Corso said, "You know what I think? I think we're supposed to be on the same side."

Alex didn't answer.

"Your guy Esposito is in the middle of the hopper. A hijacking-murder; no joke, Alex."

"That's bullshit," Alex said. "Vinny wouldn't kill anybody."

"Were you there?" Delaney said disgustedly. "He's a wop hood, that's all he is, Alex. And according to his sheet, a junkie too."

"I got him off junk. He doesn't use junk anymore."

"Once a junkie—"

"Well, you're wrong, Tom. So where do we go from here?"

Delaney leaned forward confidently.

"You bring him to a meet with us. We want Nino Balsamo. He can make him."

"You got Balsamo, don't ya? Isn't that him in the picture?"

"We want him tight, on tape, talking about this hijack and loan sharking."

"You want Vinny to wear a wire? You must be kidding."

The Latin agent stood up.

"Listen, your guy's dead. We have him cold. He wears a wire for us or he's busted. You know we can help him. Stop playing his lawyer, you're doing a shitty job of it."

"I see," Alex said. "He wears a wire, then, of course, he has to testify and in six months we find him in a car trunk."

He wanted to tell them that Vinny was a decent man, not brilliant, not even honest in the pure sense. But a good human being. The only thing the guy wants is to get a driver's license so he can get a cab, for christsake.

Delaney sat down and looked at Alex impatiently.

"Alex, cut the bullshit. We don't need you to pick him up. I'm giving you a little professional consideration, so to speak."

"He won't work for you unless I tell him to," Alex said sharply.

"Don't you think we know that?"

Time, Alex thought, he needed time to think about this. If he were to tell Vinny to jump in with Delaney's people, he'd do it. He'd do anything he'd ask him to. They'd have him wear a wire for sure. If he survives that, then they'll have him testify at a grand jury, and then at trials.

There is the witness protection program. But Vinny couldn't make that work. Once they took him out of South Brooklyn, he'd go mad. He'd probably come back. And then he'd be chop meat.

He tried to explain to Delaney that Vinny was a simple neighborhood guy. No big deal.

"He can put a lot of people away, Alex," Delaney said.

"They'd blow him away sooner or later," Alex hastened to add.

"One less wop bad guy," Delaney said, and the two agents laughed. Even the one named Corso laughed.

121

"Seriously, Alex, who are we talking about here?" Delaney said.

"I think," Alex said, "that I'd better talk to him."

They all looked thoughtful, then Delaney smiled.

"Right, Alex, talk to him. Explain to him that he has a patriotic responsibility."

"Tell him his uncle needs him," the agent whose name was Corso said. Delaney was staring at Alex.

"Sure," Alex said, "I'll tell him he's going to be a certified hero. Vinny will like that."

It was this vestigial prejudice against trusting the FBI that made Alex stop in the outer office and speak to the secretary.

She was still bent over her puzzle, and not at all bad looking. But, he couldn't see below the waist, which he thought might be a bit large. She had a round open face like a woman that made TV milk commercials. Wholesome, sort of, with black, short hair streaked with gray. But it was the giant breasts that made Alex twitch.

She looked up at him and there was a hint of a smile. No, he wouldn't mind camping for an afternoon with this lady.

"Terrific guys, these FBI agents, aren't they?" he said mildly.

"Well, they certainly are better mannered than you cops," she said.

Whoops, he thought, try a smile.

"They so rarely come up to the Bronx, you only get to meet the nice ones."

"They're here all the time."

"Really?" He was trying desperately to overhear the conversation that was now taking place behind the closed office door.

"I've been here before, I haven't seen you," he said.

"Oh," she said, "I've been here two years. Hardly miss a day."

He was running out of words, and he couldn't hear diddley from the office.

"I want to warn you, I'm a desperate man. My wife left me, I've been alone for months. Don't know how to approach women anymore. You know, when you're out of the flow of things. I don't know how to flirt."

She pointed to the ring on her finger.

"I'm happily married. I have four children. What are you up to, detective?"

"I'm going to proposition you, is all."

She looked happy.

"Well, thank you, but no thanks."

She didn't seem angry, but then again, she wasn't tearing at his clothes. There's nothing like a compliment to build a failing conversation.

"You can't blame me for trying. You're a very pretty lady."

"You cops should learn from the FBI. They're so polite and professional."

"You mean they don't flirt? Maybe they're gay."

She got up from her desk shaking her head. She walked to a filing cabinet. Great legs, tight ass—four kids or not, this lady was looking better all the time. Or was it this month living like a monk. He suddenly had an image of Gloria Goodman's mouth. Thoughts of Gloria were always oral. She was a dentist, after all.

"What is it you want, detective?"

"Well, that's sort of straightforward, isn't it?"

"C'mon," she said, "I have work to do."

"I'd like to know what these feds are doing here in the Bronx."

"You just had a meeting with them, why didn't you ask?"

"You know how the feds are. They treat us city employees like we're lesser human beings." Municipal pride, that might help.

Now she looked startled.

"They're perfect gentlemen. They occasionally come here and take Anatole Pavlovich to lunch."

"Who?"

"Anatole Pavlovich. He's a Russian immigrant. His office is next door. He does social research for us."

"No kidding."

"And, do you know that Spanish FBI agent, Mister Rivera, he speaks beautiful Russian. I heard him speaking to Doctor Pavlovich. I was really shocked."

"No shit."

"You see! I never once heard an FBI agent curse. Certainly not in front of a woman. You cops have a lot to learn from the FBI."

Chapter Eleven

The telephone rang. Niki glanced at his watch. It was 8:00 A.M. He'd been asleep three hours.

"Yes," he said wearily.

"Consider the time here. Remember how I love my afternoon nap. And appreciate what it is I do for you."

"Vika?"

"Who else?"

"Well, how is life among the ruins and the eels?" he asked loudly.

"For me, wonderful, here is where *you* should be living. The people are beautiful, the women, elegant, and the men adore me."

"Naturally," Niki laughed.

"And you? The most handsome and sexiest Muscovite ever!"

Niki glanced at Katya, who continued to sleep, her head resting comfortably in the crook of her arm.

"I'm all right."

"Just all right? You're such a typical Russian, Niki. The better things get, the more depressed you become."

Vika was a close friend. She was an Armenian who had worked her way to Moscow with her heels in the air. Along the way she'd broken more than a few hearts and, some said, a man's back or two. To be in bed with Vika, Niki remembered, was to be in bed with a leopard. Slow and long licks, followed by scratches and clawing, and finally purrs that turned to growls of passion. A wondrous lady, too big a handful for Niki.

Vika went where she wanted, when she wanted, and did whatever fancy danced into her beautiful head. Such things were not easy in Moscow, but Vika knew how.

She now lived in Rome. Other than Jews, Armenians were the only Soviet citizens allowed to emigrate.

"And your lovers, Vika, how are your lovers?"

"I have a twenty-year-old who crawls from my bed in the morning, saying, 'Gràtzia, gràtzia.' Then he runs home to his mother."

The hearty Vika laugh boomed from across the ocean.

"And the other?" Niki asked. "Is he well?"

He'd hesitated to ask, but this is what it was all about. This was why Paul Malatesta, for the moment, treated him as an equal.

There was silence on the other end of the line.

"How important is this to you, Niki?"

"It couldn't be more important."

Vika began to laugh, it was a quiet, sad laugh.

"My prince, what trouble have you got yourself into?"

His trouble, Niki thought, was that he was alone. There was no one here that could match his intellect. No one here whose advice he trusted. Viktor was in Moscow, and Sonny was dead. For all of his ability to judge character, these American gangsters might as well be from Mars, they defied understanding.

"I need your help, Vika." Niki knew there was despair in his voice, and he was embarrassed.

126

"The man is from a town in Sicily called Villalba. My John Carlo and other government officials discuss things with him. But he has said nothing that they don't already know."

"So he has not yet informed?"

"No, I'm sure he hasn't."

"Does John Carlo think he will?"

"Yes. But in his own time."

"This information, Vika, can make you very rich."

Again, a long silence on the line, then Vika said, "This is your business, Niki. I don't like it. But I look on the bright side. If I can help my Niki, who helped me more times than I can remember, there is no question, I do it. We Armenians never forget our friends, or forgive our enemies."

"You sound like the Mafia."

They both laughed. . . .

"I miss you, Vika," Niki said softly, hoping she'd understand. He thought he sounded like a child.

"You are careful?" she asked.

"I am."

"Why not leave that place and come to Rome?" Vika said sharply.

Niki didn't answer.

"How is our beautiful Katya?"

Before he hung up the telephone, before he said good-by, Niki told Vika that Katya was sleeping.

Vika was always at the center of things. She made people laugh. She had a way of taking your hand and holding it, smiling and saying yes. Niki's friends in Moscow were in awe of her.

She'd left the Union shortly after he and Katya left. Niki hoped that she'd follow them to America. Vika would have been truly good company, a real friend from home.

127

But she had fallen in love with Italy. So Vika had stayed in Rome.

After his arrival in the States, Niki made several attempts to locate her, without success. It was Vika who found him.

One Saturday morning the phone rang, and there was that laugh. When he asked if she was fundamentally happy, Vika said she wasn't, but it was likely that she soon would be. You see, there was a man, a wonderful rich Italian bureaucrat. His name was John Carlo and he had a very large family and a very tired wife. Niki told her something of his adventures with American Italians, something of the restaurant. A restaurant he'd named Moscow Nights. There was talk about late nights with old friends, of music, and vodka, of a time when they were both, each in their own way, stars.

The transatlantic calls continued. They were a Saturday-morning ritual. It was during one of these calls that Vika told him of John Carlo's meeting with the Sicilian Mafioso chief, the one whose family had been shotgunned on the steps of his hometown church, the one who knew all there was to know of Mafia business, both in Sicily and in America. She gave him priceless information. And Niki knew how to use it.

At the time, he was deeply in debt to Matty Musca. Sonny Ippolito had introduced them. Musca, it turned out, had the brain of a donkey, impossible to deal with. Niki begged Sonny to bring him to the real boss, the real chief. Obviously, it couldn't be Musca. Sonny had laughed, and said, "Fucking Russian, you are crazy." But when Niki hinted, just hinted, at what he knew, Sonny stopped laughing, and said, "That's not funny, Niki."

They met at the Plaza Hotel, he and Paul Malatesta. Niki went alone, by taxi. Sonny had never brought him to such a grand place. Nothing he'd seen compared to the grandeur of the Plaza.

They had lunch. During coffee he'd wondered what the

point of it all was. Not one word of business had passed between them.

It was when they were getting their coats that Malatesta said, "You have thirty seconds. What do you want to say to me?"

He told him, "I owe Matty Musca two hundred and fifty thousand dollars. Every week I pay an interest of ten percent. I want the interest to stop, and I want time to pay the entire amount. In return, I will tell you the name of a man who is prepared to destroy you, and everyone like you, both here and in Italy. I know someone who at this very moment is talking to this man. I know who you are, and what you are, and I know you are too intelligent to think I would dream up such a story. You must have ways to check such things."

Paul Malatesta gave no sign. He did not smile, did not nod his head, made no gesture at all. He put on his topcoat and left.

The following day Niki received a telephone call from Sonny. It would be their last conversation. The handsome young man Niki had met on the boardwalk, with his beautiful gold bracelet and look and strut of a movie star, the one that said there was nothing he couldn't do in this city, would pay for reaching above Matty Musca in order to help Niki.

In cold, dead serious tones, he told Niki that he could consider his outstanding bill paid.

"Paid in full?"

"Paid in full."

And when the name and the location of the informant is passed to Mister Malatesta four times the amount of the bill would be deposited in Niki's name in any bank in the world. Niki was staggered. Overnight he could be a millionaire. Niki felt as though he had been born into a new age.

A week later Matty Musca showed up at the restaurant. In Niki's office, Musca ranted. He screamed like a crazy man, and his nephew Frankie stood in the doorway. If they expected panic from him, there was none. He simply told them to talk to Mr. Malatesta. When the older Musca said, "It's my money, I could squash you for the price of a drink," Niki laughed and said, "Don't be foolish. Speak to your boss."

Within days, Sonny, his dullard brother, and their uncle paid the price for setting the stage of Matty Musca's embarrassment. Frankie Musca and his crime partner Red buried them all in a Queens garbage dump.

A month later they came for Niki, Matty's nephew and his two friends. They were killers, crazy men. Then again, Yuri and his people were little better. It was all madness.

They came wanting to kill us, Yuri had said, you're lucky to be alive. He said that after he executed Frankie Musca, it could be described no other way. Frankie Musca had killed Sonny. That much Niki knew. He had no tears for this crazy cowboy Frankie Musca.

Now he had to decide whether to sell a man's life for a million dollars. A man whom he did not know, a man who had lost his entire family to other madmen in another country populated by lunatics.

Niki longed for some peace of mind, longed for Vika's laugh, for Viktor's wisdom, longed for the dullness that was Moscow.

Chapter Twelve

Jimmy, the super, at half-past seven in the morning, said, "Yesterday the bucking Bulgarians were all over. They were everywhere. They ran out of that apartment like the building was on fire."

Alex handed him a bottle of Bacardi Dark, the kind he liked.

"What are you talking about?" he asked.

Jimmy took the bottle and again started talking loud and fast.

"Yesterday morning, I was moppin' de hallway in front of de apartment and they come out de door good and pissed and dey 'most knocked me down, *coño*; and she was dere, *una rubia*, and de oder one was yellin' and, and dere were oder ones, de place was full of dem, in dis building, in de basement, on de roof, dey look panic. *Un viejo gordo* come and say to me go back to work, *cabron*! And he was de man, de head man and look buckin' wild and, and . . . bucking Bulgarians, *coño*."

"Right," Alex said. Then he ran out of the building to the Chevy he'd parked in the street. He opened the trunk and checked the tape recorders. They were in place.

The car had stood at a parking meter for two days, and there were two summonses. The city doesn't tow cars in Queens. Considering the car's location was perfect to receive transmitted signals, Alex thought he should have great recordings.

The tape counters had run several hundred clicks. He felt anxious, but he also felt good. It was a familiar sensation. He had conversation.

Alex started the car and drove off. Twice he made wrong turns. The Macy's garage was what he was looking for. He finally had to stop and think about where he was, exactly. He then drove directly to the garage, and though there were spaces on the lower decks, he went to the roof. He felt at home on a roof.

After removing the machines from the trunk, it occurred to him that maybe the batteries had grown weak. He checked both machines, they were fine. He rewound the tapes, took a deep breath, then pushed the play button on the machine that recorded conversations from the apartment.

He heard the first voice, then the second, then the third. He threw his arms in the air, shook his head, and screamed, "Delaney, you sly . . . I'd never guessed it. . . . But, ol' buddy, you forgot the most important thing. . . . I'm the master of fuckaround, *heh-heh-heh.*" He rewound the tape, and played it again.

There were four of them, all talking at once, like policemen do when they first enter a wiretap plant. There was excitement, the sound of expectancy in their voices.

Alex immediately identified Delaney's growl, and the two agents he'd met at the Bronx D.A.'s office. The fourth was a woman.

Delaney began with a question that made Alex smile.

"Did somebody bring coffee? I'm starved."

"We can make our own," the woman said.

"Frank, get the machine out, will you? Let's see who's been calling ol' Matty. And, please, I really do need a coffee."

"If someone will get breakfast things, I'll make coffee," the woman said. "We need milk and sugar. There's a bagel place across the street."

"Your foot's not nailed to the floor," said the agent whose name was Rivera.

Rivera was a tough one, a hard one. Though they met only one time, Alex didn't like him. Rivera had that air of FBI superiority about him.

"I drink my coffee black," said Delaney. "Make some, Janice, you can plug the pot in here, stand it on the footlocker."

"Do we have any cups?" Rivera asked.

"Mister Delaney, I brought the coffee, the coffee pot, and some cups. But, I tell you this, I'm not playing housemother."

"That's it," Alex said. "Stand up to the chauvinist creeps." There were times Alex talked to his tape recorders.

The footlocker was opened, then closed. They began talking about coffee again. Delaney said to knock it off, he wanted to hear who had called Matty. Silence. Alex could barely make out Matty's voice, faint in the background.

Water running.

Alex realized that the woman would try to plug the coffee pot into his transmitter.

"Well," the woman called out, "who is going for milk and things?"

There was no reply.

Suddenly a terrific amount of static.

"What the hell?" the woman said. "I can't get the plug in."

Delaney said, "Why not?"

The static was gone, and the woman said, "It's okay, that should do it."

"Why couldn't you use the top one?" Delaney asked, and Alex could hear the anxiety in his voice.

"It's broken, stuffed up or something."

The excitement Alex felt was physical. He moved the tips of his fingers across his lips and waited.

Delaney knew his business, the room went silent.

Then Alex heard labored breathing, Delaney studying the outlet.

"Sonofabitch," Delaney whispered, and Alex smiled.

"I know it's you. You've done it this time."

"What is it?" the woman called out.

"You want to be enemies, you jerk." Delaney whispered into the receptacle. "Is that what you want?"

"No," Alex thought, "actually I want a cigarette." He hadn't smoked in a year, but it was times like these that brought back the itch.

"I got it, you bastard," Delaney hissed, then he yelled, and Alex moved back in the car seat, back away from the machine.

"Look in the street, see if you can find Simon," Delaney yelled. "He can't be far. Alex," he hissed, "if your print is on this cheap piece of crap, I'll have your head. . . . This is a federal crime, you moron."

Then Delaney yelled, "Janice, get me a knife!"

"We don't have one."

"Find something, anything. . . ."

The door to the apartment opened, then slammed shut, then opened again. Alex heard Jimmy, the super, yell, "Hey, man."

Then the transmitter went dead. Delaney tore it loose. One hundred and fifty dollars down the tubes.

Alex bought his own bugs from a Korean in the Village. He'd had this one for years. Now, like Vinny, it was Delaney's. But fingerprints, that was a Delaney pipe dream. There were no fingerprints. Alex was daring, but he was not stupid.

Alex shook his head. Delaney had gone batshit, but there was respect in his voice. And Alex liked that. He now turned on the other machine, the one that recorded the telephone conversations from Matty Musca's girlfriend's apartment.

Outgoing: *ring-ring* . . .

"Hello."

"Where you been?" Matty's voice.

"Oh, I been uptown."

"I figured, I thought maybe you were still going from the other day."

"No, no, I came back." Laughter, there was deference in Matty's tone. This was not one of his soldiers, this was a peer.

Alex was becoming impatient with Matty's monotone, and his girlfriend, Lynn, was worse. Her voice grated, she yelled in the background.

"Say hello for me. C'mon, Matty, say hello."

Alex couldn't concentrate. The Delaney discovery had taken place the day before. What was Delaney up to today? He wouldn't make an official complaint. He hadn't caught Alex on the wire. There were no fingerprints. Delaney had nothing more than suspicions. He knew all right, but, in fact, he couldn't prove a thing. Their next meeting should be bizarre.

"Do you hear this bitch?" Matty's voice on the telephone. Then Lynn on the extension.

"I am no bitch."

"You sure are," the other voice said.

"You're a bitch yourself." Lynn was high.

"What are you doing?" the voice asked Lynn.

"Nothing. Eating a potato chip. Why not?"

"Why not is right."

"Tell her why not," Matty said.

"You're gonna get fat," the voice answered.

"Fuck you, I don't wanna talk to you anymore, good-by."

The great Mafia at play, Alex thought, good God.

Lynn got off the phone, and Matty got serious.

"So what's doing?" he asked.

"We're ready, you just say when."

"I'll be there in fifteen, twenty minutes. I gotta make a call first. But you're ready, right?"

"Oh, yeah, we're ready."

"Okay, I'll be there in a little while. Take care."

"Good enough."

135

Alex was used to listening to telephone conversations. It didn't strike him as strange that these people talked so freely on telephones they thought were safe. Amazing what people say on the telephone.

He'd decided to listen to one or two more calls, then listen to the rest at home. He was tired, and he was worried about Vinny. Poor Vinny. Delaney would come down on him. He'd take out on Vinny what he couldn't on Alex. In his position, Alex would do the same. It was all a game.

Outgoing: *ring-ring* . . . Matty was breathing heavily, like he'd just run a mile . . . *ring*.

"Good morning, the FBI."

"Agent Delaney, please."

"Ohmigod," Alex said out loud, "I don't believe it. Delaney and Musca. Musca's turned, he's working for Delaney. Then why the wire? Delaney doesn't trust him, simple as that."

"Mister Delaney is in the field. Can I take a message?"

"Sure, honey, tell him Stanley called."

"Stanley," Alex said to the machine, "Stanley, you see what middle age does to a man."

He drove from the garage feeling an excitement rising in his stomach. Then that familiar, complicated emotion, the joy of the game and the dread of losing. To Delaney and Alex, it was a sport, even to himself he'd never been able to explain this rush. He looked at the machines lying now on the back seat. Vinny Ba-Ba was a decent human being, and Delaney, though he didn't mean to, would kill him. He stopped at a light, hardly breathing. "I'm sorry, Vinny," he moaned. Then he shrugged as car horns blared. "People are no damn good," Alex Simon said to the machines on his back seat.

*   *   *

Vinny Esposito, at seven o'clock that night, said, "Are you guys really from the FBI? Now don't bullshit me, are you two really feds?"

Agent Rivera and Agent Corso stood in Vinny's kitchen and studied him.

"You saw our credentials. Now get dressed, you're coming with us," the one who said his name was Rivera said.

Vinny tried hard, without success, to smile.

"Oh, yeah! You got a warrant?"

"We don't need a warrant. You're coming with us willingly for investigation."

"You wanna bet?"

"Look, *paisan*, we can take you out of here in chains, or you can walk out like a man. I'm Italian, like you. I don't want to embarrass you in front of your *gombas* around here," the one who said his name was Corso said.

"Fuck you, and your Sons of Italy routine. That shit went out when I wuz a kid. I trust you wop cops less than anyone else."

Rivera walked to the telephone, picked up the receiver, and pointed it toward him.

"Call your friend Simon, and ask him what you should do. Go ahead, call your Jewish lawyer."

Well, what the hell was this supposed to mean? How did these two know about Alex and him? Vinny was confused, he half got up, then he sat back down.

"What am I supposed to have done?"

"No one said you did anything. We need to talk to you, have a little chat. Go ahead, call Simon."

"I will," Vinny said, and when he got up from the stool he felt his knees tremble a little.

He'd never felt worse. Alex said he should go with them. Just to talk, and to listen to what they had to say. This was crap, he couldn't just walk out of his apartment with these two agents. Well, maybe they didn't look like agents, but they were agents. It just didn't look good. And, Alex's voice sounded sad, really sad. Vinny was worried. Then again he hadn't done anything the feds should be hot about. So why should Alex be so upset? It was a bitch; he couldn't figure this out. But whatever it was, it wasn't going to make him happy, of that he was sure.

Vinny smiled and cocked his head. "Okay," he said, "take me to your leader." He thought that was funny, but the agents didn't laugh.

Afterward Vinny lay in his bed going over and over in his mind the proposition the feds made him.

They wanted him to borrow money, five thousand dollars, from Balsamo. They wanted him to make Balsamo explain to him how the vig worked. Ten points a week, he knew that. Why would Balsamo have to explain it to him? He'd wear this gismo around his chest and under his arm. The place where he sweated so much. He'd jam Balsamo's ass good and proper. That would be fun, that would be a laugh. The feds would pay him, he'd be on salary, he'd be an agent. And they would forget that he drove a hijacked truck. He wouldn't be an informant, he'd be an agent; there was a difference.

They had some office, with flags and pictures of presidents. At least, he thought they were presidents—could have just been big bosses of the bureau. The bureau . . . he'd be an agent, get paid, and they said his driver's license was a snap. They'd do it with a phone call. Alex never did, said he couldn't. As he lay thinking, he began to feel proud. He'd be working for the United States of America, secret agent Vinny Ba-Ba Esposito. Maybe someday they'd make a movie about him; maybe the president would give him an award. He felt bad his mother was dead, she'd be proud. He wondered why Alex sounded so sad when he told him he was going to go ahead and do his part. That's what the agents said, "Do your part for America." Alex should be proud, but he wasn't, he was sad. Maybe Alex was jealous. He understood that, silly Alex thought that he'd leave him forever to work for the government. He'd never do that, he loved Alex. Vinny lay for a long time looking up at the ceiling, thinking.

Chapter Thirteen

Niki saw him sitting on a bench, the one nearest the ramp that went down onto the beach. In his outfit you could hardly miss him. He sat as if on a pew.

He was small, you could even say tiny, and he wore the long, black coat and fur-rimmed hat of a religious Jew. His beard was red, thick and tight like a black's. Niki guessed his age to be close to his own, thirty-three or -four.

Three hooligans stood over him, taunting, abusing him.

"Silly-looking fool," Niki said to himself, "I wonder if he knows what he looks like."

The morning air was gray and cool, dark clouds dropped lead streaks into the ocean. Except for the five of them, the boardwalk was empty. Niki watched from twenty feet away, on the fringe really. The hooligans whirled and shouted and pointed at the man. Niki hoped they would stay where they were, away from him.

He'd gone to the nightclub to work on the books. He was

140

making money, a lot of money. He could expand, maybe open another restaurant. But this business with Malatesta haunted him. So he'd walked to the beach to deal with his plans, his strategies. To dream a dream and look at the sea. He wasn't up to dealing with three hooligans and a Jew.

"One million dollars," he thought, "one million dollars for a telephone call, a little telephone call. Who wouldn't do it?"

He recalled his important connections, the way he always did. How they'd helped. How clever he was to use them, all of them, yes, even Viktor. In eighteen months he hadn't heard a single word from Viktor. Maybe the old policeman's liver had exploded and he was dead.

He looked toward the Jew, the hooligans were really carrying on. Niki said nothing, and breathed slowly.

The Jew seemed calm or he pretended to be. His hands played on the top of the bench and he kept his eyes straight ahead.

The hooligans laughed their heads off.

They called him kike, "fucking weird-looking kike." They were trying to work him up, yet he sat still, and said nothing.

At last the Jew got up from the bench. He moved along the boardwalk slowly, dragging a leg, stumbled and sat down, closer to Niki now.

The hooligans followed.

Niki wanted to leave, turn his back and go. But somehow he couldn't. He looked straight into the Jew's eyes. Niki felt his mouth twitch and he smiled. After a long moment, the Jew smiled back. But Niki could see that his fingers were trembling.

The hooligans persisted. Then one took the fur-rimmed hat and laughed *he-he-he*, like a crazy man.

The Jew seemed just on the point of speaking, but he only shook his head and smiled broadly at Niki.

Niki didn't have to go far, three steps and he was between them.

"I want to tell you something," he told the hooligan holding the hat. But his English failed, and he groped for words.

The Jew spoke, quickly, loudly, in Yiddish.

The hooligans laughed harder, wilder, when Niki said, "Don't speak that language to me. I don't understand that language."

But then they saw they'd made a mistake.

Niki grabbed the biggest one by the collar and pulled. He tore the fur-rimmed hat from his hand.

"You're a stupid fuck," he said. Niki was finding there were times he liked using that word.

The hooligans stepped back. They came shoulder to shoulder and smiled like crazed Siamese triplets.

"Please," the Jew said, "please," and held up his hand. Then he asked Niki for his hat back, in lightly accented English.

"Please," the smaller one said, drawing the word heavily and slowly from his mouth.

"How would you like us to kick your ass?" asked the biggest one.

"Whyn't you mind your own business," added the one in the middle.

And the small one called out, "Yeah, go back where you belong. Go back wherever you came from." Then he cleared his throat loudly and spat on the boardwalk.

Yuri, Petra, and Vasily had been standing behind the hooligans for a while. The hooligans, lost in their game, had not noticed the three of them come up onto the boardwalk.

These days Niki was never alone.

"I think you should just go. Get out of here," Niki said quickly.

The hooligans laughed loudly, together, as one.

"Yeah. We'll go, man, soon as you come off ten dollars for us," the small one said.

The big one moved toward Niki and pointed with his finger at Niki's chest. "You gotta learn to mind your own business, tough man. This is our neighborhood. We're gonna get upside your head in about two seconds, you don't get off the ten."

"Give him the ten dollars, Niki," Yuri called out, "he'll need it for the hospital."

Yuri spoke in Russian, then he laughed. The hooligans began to back away. Petra and Vasily moved toward them. The small one turned as if to run, but Yuri stood blocking him, his cowboy hat back on his head, his switchblade tapping the side of his nose.

"Please, please," the Jew said, "they're just boys. Chase them, but let them go." He spoke in Russian, perfect well-educated Russian, the best Russian Niki had heard since leaving Moscow.

Niki motioned for Yuri to move aside, and let the boys pass.

The little hooligan said to the big one, "Those are the biggest Jews I've ever seen."

"They're not Jews," the big one said, "they're communists."

Petra laughed, and Vasily too. Yuri said, "Get out of here. Get going before we throw you in a garbage can where you belong."

The Jew stood, took Niki's hand, and said, "Thank you."

Niki smiled and nodded.

"Nikolai Zoracoff," he said. There was a long silence between them. Finally the Jew said, "My name is Jakob Grossman, thank you again. Those boys . . ." He paused, shook his head, and smiled.

His Russian was elegant, lyrical. Niki was impressed, he was also furious.

"Boys?" he shouted. Yuri, Petra, and Vasily, who had moved off a bit, stopped and turned back.

"Those were not boys," Niki said. "Those three were gangsters."

"They were boys," Jakob said, then he struggled to get up from the bench. Niki reached a hand to him and pulled him upright.

"What's the problem, are you hurt?"

"No, I'm not hurt. I have one leg, and this prosthesis bothers me. I can't seem to get used to it."

"I'm sorry," Niki said.

"Is it your fault I have diabetes?"

"I don't think so." Niki laughed.

"Then you have nothing to be sorry about."

Niki suddenly felt terribly sad. He had no doubt that this man felt as ridiculous as he looked. "God's people," he thought, "take some kind of weird pleasure in being abused. Why else would they come out into the world looking so different, so bizarre?"

Jakob Grossman stood fine now, and asked Niki for a cigarette.

"Of course," Niki said, and he gave him one of his Dunhills.

After lighting it for him, Niki asked, "How much abuse would you have taken before—"

"I would fight?"

"Protect yourself."

"I only have one leg, I'm not exactly Muhammad Ali."

Yuri stood close by, he listened carefully, then spoke loudly in his gutter Russian.

"These people don't fight. They let the world shit on them. They don't defend themselves or the people they care for. If you ask me, you'll excuse me, Rabbi, they're full of shit."

"I'm not a rabbi," Jakob said, laughing, "and you are wrong. If I'm understanding you correctly, you are wrong. But it's not important. Thank you all. I was in a mess, wasn't I? You helped me, thank you."

Niki glared at Yuri, then he turned back to Jakob.

"It's important to me. I'd like to know when you do fight. I've always understood that your people are pacifists. You don't fight, or even defend yourselves."

"They're full of shit," Yuri yelled.

"Petra, please," Niki said and motioned with his head. Petra took Yuri's arm and led him away.

"I am not full of shit," Jakob said.

Niki was shocked, he folded his arms and leaned back against the boardwalk railing.

"You smoke, you curse, you surprise me," he said.

"I make love. I gamble. I'm a sinner. I'm man, not God."

Niki questioned Jakob about many things, and he listened attentively as Jakob discussed aspects of his life. He was fascinated. It was the first time that he had spoken at any length to a religious Jew. Niki wanted Jakob to speak about fighting, because, in the places he'd been, and by the people he'd spoken to, he'd always been told that religious Jews, Orthodox Jews, wouldn't fight. Niki could not respect a people that wouldn't defend itself.

"I think it's more important that you understand when I would not fight than when I would," Jakob said, lighting one of Niki's cigarettes.

"Okay," Niki said, "when wouldn't you fight?"

"I would never fight for power, or financial gain. Though your friend doesn't think so, I would defend myself, and my family, but I would not enjoy it, or take pleasure in a victory."

"But those criminals, those gangsters that attacked you, wouldn't you take pleasure in slapping them down?"

"Nikolai," Jakob said, "I am a religious man. I believe there is a God. How could I take pleasure in slapping down, as you put it, children of God? Everyone's life is precious in the eyes of God."

"Excuse me, my friend, but you don't really believe that crap, do you?" Niki said.

Jakob Grossman had a wonderful smile. All his features seemed to light up and his eyes glittered.

"Of course I believe that, and I also believe that you do as well."

"You're wrong," Niki said, and he winked. "You see, I don't believe in a God, any God."

Jakob Grossman took a deep breath, turned his head toward

the ocean. "Really, Nikolai Zoracoff," he said, "really, that is such an easy way out. Isn't it?"

Later that day Niki sat in his office at the rear of the nightclub. He turned pages of a newspaper. It seemed he was looking at the same faces he'd looked at the day before: wild-eyed, dumb, reckless faces, victims of crime and criminals. All children of God, he thought.

Petra and Vasily came in laughing and poking fun at one another. Petra stopped at the door. "I'll get a car," he said. Niki shook his head.

"I want to drive you," Petra said quickly.

"I don't want any of you to drive me. I'll take a taxi. Call one of our friends and have him pick me up here."

"Niki," Vasily said sharply, "someone should go with you."

"I'll go alone. The message said to come alone—so I will."

Vasily looked at him with a worried frown. "Are you sure, Niki?" he asked.

Niki nodded, but he wasn't sure, he wasn't sure of anything, let alone what Paul Malatesta was planning. But that man was plotting something, of that Niki had no doubt.

He'd received a message from Paul Malatesta. They were to meet at five o'clock at the Oyster Bar of the Plaza Hotel. The message was clear, he should come alone.

"You can't trust him," Vasily said.

"I know, I know," Niki said sharply, "I can't trust anyone."

Vasily seemed hurt and he lowered his head. Petra said Niki should go on holiday.

"Holiday! Petra, we're in the middle of a war. There are people right now, this moment, planning to kill us. Holiday?"

Vasily said, "You need a rest, Niki."

"Where did Yuri go?" Niki asked.

No answer from Petra or Vasily. Niki felt a chill, something desperate had touched him. Where was Yuri? He needed to know where they all were, at every moment. . . .

There were times the others behaved like children, playing,

pretending, it was somehow a game. Yuri was the worst of all. Niki believed it was the cocaine. Yuri used too much cocaine, it froze his mind as well as his nose.

"Where is Yuri?" he asked.

Petra looked to Vasily and Vasily looked at the floor.

Something moved in Niki's stomach when Petra said, "Yuri went to see Italians in Brooklyn. People that he had done business with."

When Niki asked what kind of business, Petra told him about a truckload of television sets, stolen television sets.

Yuri had gone out on his own, not out of greed, not because he needed the money, simply because he believed he could make an alliance with Italians from Brooklyn who he thought were enemies of the Muscas.

"Why didn't he ask me? Why didn't either of *you* tell me? Petra, Vasily, you are both smarter than Yuri. You both know that this is a foolish, foolish thing to do. We don't know these people, we are strangers. We are, for God's sake, the common enemy."

"You are going to speak to this Malatesta," Vasily said softly, fear creeping into his face.

"Yes, because I know what he wants from me. I know he needs me."

Niki exhaled loudly. "Yuri doesn't think," he shouted.

"Yuri knows these Brooklyn Italians," Petra said, "he's done cocaine business with them."

"Are you going to surprise me again, Petra?" Niki asked. "Are you going to tell me that you and Yuri are still doing that business?"

"No, no, no, we are not. They brought us some ounces, but that was long ago. They hate the Muscas, they are different people. Niki, maybe you don't understand. These are different people. A separate group from the Muscas."

Niki slammed his fist on the desk. Petra, all two hundred and fifty pounds of him, jumped.

147

"How often must I tell you, Petra, we are the ones that are different. We are the only ones that are separate. If we don't secure ourselves they will crush us as if we were never here. Can you call Yuri? Do you know where to reach him?"

"No," Petra said, "you know Yuri, he goes like the wind."

"Then he's gone?" Niki said.

"He'll be fine. Yuri is a cat—a sly cat. He knows what he is doing," Vasily said.

"I hope to God that he does," Niki said. Then he thought of Jakob Grossman and lit a cigarette from the one he was already smoking.

"Goddamn that Yuri," he said.

Chapter Fourteen

Vinny was walking from his apartment on First Street to the Merry Boys Social Club on Third and Court Street, the Nagra tape recorder strapped under his arm, the microphone taped to his chest. Corso, the Italian fed, had shaved a one-inch swatch through his chest hair. The procedure had made Vinny laugh, but now he sweated, and his chest burned.

Peejays and Toto sat on stools in front of the club taking in the afternoon sun. Although he'd made up his mind that this was going to be fun, recording every word that was said to him, he suddenly found himself picking at his fingernails; he felt his sweat running like a creek through the center of his back.

They both waved, seemed happy to see him. He wanted to get Toto on this tape, but not Peejays. That would be a trick.

"Hi, Peejays," was all he said, then he turned to Toto, bent and whispered so that Toto would have to talk into his chest.

"I need to see Balsamo," he said. "I gotta business thing for 'em."

Toto got up from the stool, took him by the elbow, and said, "C'mon, let's walk."

Vinny waved to Peejays, who smiled and nodded his head as if he understood that Vinny and Toto needed to be alone. Peejays was a harmless stick.

"Balsamo and Junior are not around. They won't be back till later tonight."

"Shit," Vinny said, "I need to talk to him."

"He'll be here tonight."

"Maybe you can give me a hand with this, huh, Toto? You know, I'm sorry about that junk business the other day. I just don't want any dope around me, that's all."

Toto leaned against a parking meter and looked straight into Vinny's eyes.

"What do you want, Ba-Ba? What headache you got for us?"

"I need a loan."

"A loan?" Toto said. "For a loan you go to the bank."

"C'mon," Vinny said.

"Don't give me c'mon. Who the fuck is gonna lend you money? You crazy or what?"

Suddenly the words wouldn't come. He didn't think there was a chance that these people would turn him down. He knew how they felt about him, him being an ex-junkie and all. But he'd done the right thing the other day, did everything they wanted.

"Then get me some junk," he said. "I'll move it. I need the money real bad."

"C'mon, Vinny, whadaya trying ta do here, asking me for junk? What kind of money do you need anyway, and for what?"

"I wanna get a cab. I need five thousand."

"For a cab, Vinny, you only need a license. What are you talking about?"

"I want a gypsy cab. I gotta buy a car. I want my own business."

Vinny knew that he had to handle this just right. He had to show Toto that he had it together, and that he needed and respected him. The fact was that he wanted to strangle Toto and throw him under a bus. It wasn't going to be easy; he had his pride.

"Look, Toto," he said, bowing his head, "I'm clean, been clean for a long time. I know you think I'm a jerk-off, but I'm not. I'm here for you whenever you need me. Just ask me to do somethin', and it's done."

"Vinny, nobody knows you anymore. You ain't been around, nobody knows what you been doin', who you been doin' it with. Hey, you gotta come around, Vinny, you gotta show us. You know what I mean?"

"Shit," he thought, "I gotta kiss this moron's ass."

"You're the boss," he said, "but I'll only do things for you, Toto. I trust you. You're smarter than the others. You know how to do the right thing, Toto. You're good people."

Vinny kept his head down and talked softly with respect, throughout the conversation. Every so often he'd glance up at Toto, smile nervously, and nod his head.

"Okay," Toto said, "I'll give you a shot." Then he threw an arm around Vinny and hugged him.

"You're a dumbo, Vinny, but I like ya."

Vinny bit into his tongue, then tried a smile. It wasn't easy.

"Good, Vinny, good. I could use you, no doubt about it."

"So you'll talk to Balsamo?"

"In time. But maybe you won't even have to go to Balsamo. You do the right thing for me, and I'll see that you earn."

Vinny made himself smile.

Then Vinny heard the Peejay's whistle, quick and sharp. He turned to look up the street and saw Balsamo, Junior, and Fat Anthony go into the club. A car pulled to the curb and parked behind Fat Anthony's. Two people Vinny had not seen before got out. Suddenly, as if from a dream, the face of one seemed familiar. He'd seen it before, though maybe not in person, maybe in a photograph.

"C'mon, Vinny," Toto said. "Stay with me and keep your mouth shut."

They walked up the street and into the club.

Balsamo was sitting with Junior and Fat Anthony. The two people that had driven up to the club stood over the table, above Balsamo, looking down. Toto left Vinny by the door; he, too, joined the table and sat looking up at a man Vinny was sure he recognized, but couldn't place. He began to sweat; water ran from him and the Nagra tape recorder silently turned in his armpit.

Balsamo glanced at Vinny and said, "Hey, what is dumbo doing here?"

Toto whispered something and Balsamo shook his head violently. Vinny didn't move, he knew they would ask him to leave; still he didn't move.

Toto got up from the table and walked directly to him.

"You gotta go, Vinny," Toto said.

"Sure, boss, I'll wait on the corner. You need your car washed or anything?"

Toto grinned, he was beyond pleased. "Naw, kid, you don't wash cars. Grab hold of Peejays and make him do it, okay?"

"Sure, boss," Vinny said, "sure, boss. Heavy shit, hah?" Then Vinny pointed with his chin toward the big man standing over Balsamo.

"Ga 'head, grab Peejays and wash the car." Toto lead him out the door.

On the street Peejays said, "That's Matty Musca, Vinny, nobody else but."

Niki was stepping out of his taxi at the corner of Fifty-sixth Street and Fifth Avenue. It was the rush hour, and the glitter and glamour of the city poured into the street in designer clothes and jeweled fingers. New York's women are by far the world's most beautiful, Niki thought, but what would they do without their paints, and creams, scents, shampoos, and rinses? He wondered how these women would do among the crowds and lines of Moscow. Powdered and pampered, it all came so easy to them.

But they smiled, and were friendly, and Niki turned more than one dainty American head as he walked west on Fifty-Eighth Street to the Oyster Bar. The Prince of Pushkin Square was going to the Plaza. The thought pleased him.

Just before he reached the entrance of the bar, a hand tapped on his shoulder. He turned quickly, ready for anything.

A dapper looking man in a suit and top coat, wearing the largest sapphire pinky ring Niki had ever seen, smiled warmly and asked, "Niki Zoracoff?"

Niki nodded.

"My name is John Reno," the man continued, "I'm Mister Malatesta's driver. I'm to take you to him."

"Fine." Niki shrugged; he'd almost made it to the Plaza.

John Reno held the door and Niki got into the back seat of a Mercedes, not unlike Yuri's. It made him smile.

They rode in silence for several minutes, then John Reno asked, "You like America?"

"It's wonderful," Niki said flatly. Then he said, "I really haven't seen much."

John Reno smiled, it was a gesture without words, he nodded and smiled again. But Niki could tell that John Reno was studying him through the rearview mirror. It felt uncomfortable.

"Where are we going?" Niki asked.

"Not far."

Looking out of the car's window, he remembered that these Americans spoke in code and half-finished sentences.

"You should get to see Vegas," John Reno said, "and Atlantic City, the real America. Ya know what I mean? New

York's nothing—nothing. You gotta see Vegas, man, what a place!"

"Maybe someday I will."

John Reno moved the car in and out of traffic, neatly avoiding pedestrians. He dashed through traffic signals just as they turned red. The streets and avenues swarmed with all sorts of traffic, still it seemed the Mercedes rarely slowed, and never stopped. Niki marveled at the ease in which John Reno moved through the New York streets.

"I heard that Vermont and Maine are beautiful," Niki said.

"Where?"

"Maine and Vermont. I heard that all of New England is beautiful."

"Naw," John Reno said, "nothing but rocks and trees. Sure, if ya like snow and ice, it's beautiful. But there ain't nothin' ta do there."

They were out of the inner-city traffic now, moving onto a bridge. Traffic slowed at the toll plaza. Then suddenly, without warning or signal, John Reno spun a U-turn, he ran down cones that divided city-bound and outgoing traffic. Horns blared and Niki expected to see police cars; there were none.

John Reno cut across three lanes of traffic, then headed back toward the city, glancing in the rearview as he went. John Reno was a pro, Niki was impressed. But for the first time, he felt a flutter of fear, just a tiny bubble. It rose in his chest, then disappeared when he swallowed.

"Sorry about that," John Reno said. "Like I was saying, Vermont and Maine—there ain't much to see. And not a good Italian restaurant for miles."

They drove into a garage that was beneath a high-rise apartment building. Two black men with Caribbean accents approached. One asked for the car key and the other began to write a parking receipt.

"What are you guys, new or what?" John Reno said.

He walked past the pair and handed the car key to a grim-faced man who took it, got in the car, and adjusted the seat as if he expected to be there for awhile.

John Reno put his arm over Niki's shoulder and walked him through a door that led to the building's lobby. Niki noticed television cameras everywhere—two that scanned the garage, one in the hallway that led from the garage into the lobby, another in the lobby that faced the street entrance, and another one that scanned the elevators. Lubyanka prison, in Moscow, had less security.

They rode the elevator to the eighth floor. The building was quiet and elegant, with luxurious carpeting, polished brass, and fine waxed paneling.

They entered an apartment that was not one apartment but several. Renovated, they were joined by French doors, one opening to another, then to another.

Niki stood on a polished parquet floor. A blue-and-white oriental rug cut a neat square in the center of a large room. The room was lit by a delicate crystal chandelier. The walls were decorated with three mirrors trimmed in gold and one painting, a misty Venetian oil. Two chairs and a couch were separated by a low table that had one tiny porcelain figurine on its center.

In Moscow, Viktor Vosk had taught Niki a great deal about antiques. This was great furniture, not made for practical purposes, but it did impress.

Paul Malatesta, if this was his home, lived in a beautiful setting. He was the most powerful of the powerful, and he lived among the best of the best.

John Reno asked Niki to make himself comfortable on the couch, then he left the room.

In seconds Paul Malatesta entered, wearing black brushed-corduroy slacks, a red cashmere V-neck sweater, and loafers. Niki noticed that he wasn't wearing socks.

He looked tanned and healthy, and he smiled as if Niki were an old friend, or maybe a relative; certainly a comrade.

"Niki, how are you, my friend? You look great, but a little tired."

When Niki got up from the couch to greet him, Paul Malatesta hugged him, then patted his cheek with a small soft hand. Niki tightened.

"You work too hard, Niki. You have no color. You need a vacation," he said warmly. Then he sat in a chair that was tall and had elaborate carvings.

Niki would not have been surprised to see ladies in bunched silk and jewels enter the room and kneel at the feet of Don Paul Malatesta.

On a sideboard across the room Niki saw a French vase and a helmut bowl, but there was not an ashtray in sight.

"Do you mind if I smoke?" he asked.

"Not at all, but it will kill you. Sooner or later it will kill you. Smoking, that is." Then Paul Malatesta smiled.

"It's unavoidable," Niki said.

"Smoking?"

"No . . . death. I'm more concerned about how I live than how I die." Niki took out a cigarette and lit it.

Malatesta sat back in the chair and laughed. Then John Reno entered the room carrying a silver tray with coffee, sandwiches, and a bottle of Niki's favorite brandy. There were two cut-crystal glasses, tiny ones, for the brandy. John Reno set down the tray, then ran from the room, returning immediately with an ashtray.

No one would be killed in this room, Niki thought. Paul Malatesta would not permit the mess. Not a day passed that Niki didn't appreciate the lessons learned from Viktor. Look at the eyes, the old policeman said, madness and fear are roommates in the eyes. The trick is to be able to distinguish between them.

"You look well," Niki said.

"The Italian sun and Moorish genes will do that for you."

"Maybe that's where I should be living."

"In Italy?"

"Yes, I have some friends there."

"So I understand. But Italy is not for you, Niki. The whole country is full of communists and criminals and terrorists. Italy has gone to the dogs, red ones, if you know what I mean."

Niki did not trust his voice or his hearing. His English was good, he thought, still there were words he missed, meanings that escaped him, body language that was confusing.

When he explained all this to him, Paul Malatesta sympathized.

"Coming to a foreign country, playing a new game, by new rules, is difficult, close to impossible," he said. "But, you're doing well, be proud."

Their conversation took on a rhythm of friendship. Paul Malatesta was a seducer, a charmer. Niki wanted a vodka.

They talked for half an hour about life in the States, about the nightclub, about life in Moscow. The sandwiches were delicious and the coffee, wonderful. New, different tastes. The brandy was of the very best quality. It warmed Niki, made him relax. Alcohol, the Russian opiate . . . Niki almost dropped his guard.

"Your information was very accurate," Paul Malatesta said at last.

Niki nodded, and said, "I'm glad I could help."

"You could work for me, you know. Do you think you would like that? Jews and Italians do well together. We have a long, successful history, here in the States."

Niki had not the faintest notion of what Paul Malatesta was talking about. What history? And he didn't want to get into his Jewishness.

He could never be Paul Malatesta's friend; the man was an eel.

"Why did Frankie Musca kill my friend, Sonny Ippolito, his brother, and his uncle?" was what he wanted to ask, the warm cognac stirring memories and anger. But Niki didn't

157

trust his voice. He could tell when his English was beginning to fade. It may have been foolish, but he was not afraid of Paul Malatesta. This man did not do violence, Niki could tell. Still, he did not want to say something that would be misunderstood. He had spent enough time on the dark side to know the difference between a chess game and a knife fight. And he hadn't forgotten about the ever-present John Reno. Now that man is a killer, he thought.

"Sonny Ippolito did not deserve to die," Niki said, surprising himself.

"Don't be so certain that I had anything to do with that. Matty Musca is a madman," Paul Malatesta said, and handed Niki another drink.

"Don't you deal with people that are stupid, and act on their own?"

"Yes," Niki said, thinking of Yuri and suddenly wondering where he was, and if he was all right.

"But let's not waste time talking about fools. We have much more important things to discuss."

"Musca is planning to come for me. I know he is," Niki said.

"Trust me, he'll never have the chance." Paul Malatesta smiled, then went on. "Please tell me where you got this information about the man in Italy."

"From a friend in Rome," Niki answered.

"Your friend is absolutely correct. We know who the man is. What we need to know is where he is. For that information you will earn your million dollars."

"I'm not sure I can find that out," Niki told him.

For a moment Paul Malatesta seemed to be suffering.

"I was afraid you were going to say that."

"I'm sorry," Niki said, "I think, in time, I probably can."

As he said this, Niki wondered about Vika, and if she would be able to get such information from her Italian lover.

"Oh," Paul Malatesta said, "that's good, that's very good.

But we must know quickly, as soon as possible. You understand that?"

Niki was beginning to feel anxious again. He asked for another drink. It didn't help; he felt a shiver and rubbed his hands across his chest.

"I'll need two, maybe three, days," Niki said.

Paul Malatesta rubbed his face, thinking, thinking about survival, Niki suspected. When he looked into Niki's eyes his expression was that of a man who was suffering with far-off problems, problems that he could not solve.

"You know, two or three *hours* could be too late," he said finally.

For the first time Niki saw fear in the eyes of Paul Malatesta. The man in Rome could destroy him. Now Niki had power, he knew it, he was playing chess with three queens. Knowledge was lethal, and Niki, people said, could have been a chess master.

"I will do my best to help you," he said, "but what if"— he paused and locked on Malatesta's eyes—"when all this is done, and you are safe"—Paul Malatesta twitched when he said *safe*—"my friends and I are not left in peace? How can I be sure that you won't decide that I know too much? What will stop you from coming after me?" He said all this softly, slowly.

Paul Malatesta reached to the table, took a sip of coffee, then a sip of cognac. Then he touched Niki's shoulder and squeezed.

"You have to trust me, Niki. What else can I say?"

Paul Malatesta seemed sincere, but for Niki it was always this foreign thing, this alien thing. He saw no kindness in this man. Paul Malatesta was a villain. His eyes squinted when he spoke, pushing sincerity. Niki was an outsider, he wouldn't doubt that for an instant. Did Paul Malatesta see him as a person, as a comrade? Or as a foreigner who knows nothing of his world, his loyalties, his bonds? Could Malatesta un-

159

derstand his need to be left in peace? Could a man like this respect that? He gazed at Paul Malatesta, wanting to see the warm openness he'd found in Sonny, and Sonny's granduncle. What he saw was an eel, an eel that smiled, curled in the corner of a trap. A trap that for the moment would not kill him, but would also not release him. Using the hand of friendship, Paul Malatesta was searching for a key. Could this man understand friendship?

Yes, something had gone wrong in Paul Malatesta's life, a mistake had been made. How many people would die as a result of one mistake? When would Paul Malatesta feel safe, secure?

Paul Malatesta took a small bite from a sandwich, then set it back on the tray. As he chewed, his eyes never left Niki's. . . . Could he somehow guess Niki's thoughts?

"Trust is an interesting thing," Niki said. "I've trusted more than a few people in my life, and those that I trusted have never betrayed me. Trust is part of the Russian personality. We Russians trust everyone."

"Really?" Paul Malatesta said, surprised. "Not according to what I read. I understand that you Russians are the paranoia superstars of history. I know you're more intelligent than that. At least I hope you are, because if you're not, and I've been wrong about you. . . ."

"When you talk about fear and paranoia," Niki cut in, "you're talking about a state, a government, not a people. The Russian people are a warm, trusting people. The government is something else again."

"Oh, excuse me, I've forgotten. The Russian government is run by Frenchmen, or is it Greeks. C'mon, Niki, be serious."

But for Nikolai Zoracoff it was all serious, these foreigners, these aliens, these Americans who thought they knew all there was to know about the Union. Their smugness and stupidity amazed him.

"First of all," he said, "it's the Soviet Union, not Russia.

Only in America do people call everyone from the Soviet Union, a country with eighteen different states, Russia. Russia is one state, one of many."

"As far as I'm concerned, you're all Russians."

"Well, you're wrong."

"Have another sandwich," Paul Malatesta said, "and don't get so uptight over the small stuff."

"What do you mean, small stuff?" Niki asked.

"As far as you and I are concerned, governments are all bullshit. It's all trick or treat."

"I'm sorry, but I don't understand."

"Niki, you and I exist in one world, everyone else lives in another place. We have the courage to take the world by the balls and squeeze. We can see all the liars. Whether it's here, or in Russia, or in Japan, or Europe, or, or . . . it doesn't matter. People like us are united by a secret bond. We have courage."

"To spirit," Niki said, then he paused, lowered his eyes, then raised them slowly. Paul Malatesta wore a full grin. Niki drank his brandy.

"Seriously, Niki, how long do you think I would last in Russia?" Paul Malatesta asked.

A door to his mind opened, and Niki looked in. The man was serious, how curious these Americans.

"About thirty seconds." And then, in the way he did when the alcohol had taken its effect and eased his nerves, Niki laughed and clapped his hands. Niki spread his arms as if to fly. "To live like this in the Union you would have to be the premier, the head of state, the most important man in the country."

"What makes you think it's any different here?" Paul Malatesta said. Then he too laughed, and poured more brandy, spilling a bit on the fine polished wood of the table.

*   *   *

161

Except for Peejays, no one had come out of the club for an hour. Now they all were in the street, moving to parked cars, and whispering to each other as they went.

Toto motioned for Vinny to come with him, then he walked toward his car. He was smoking and he moved in that pigeon-toed stride of his; hands stuffed into his jacket pocket, eyes studying cracks in the pavement.

"You drive, Vinny, just go where I tell you."

Toto seemed anxious and pissed off.

Vinny had spent the hour in the street trying to figure a way to shut off the tape recorder. Corso told him he could record for ninety minutes, no more, then the tape would run out. Vinny wanted to save some tape; he didn't want to spend the hour talking to Peejays about stick-minded madness, but that is what he'd done. And now he was sure the tape was finished. Corso, the fed, had also told him, he should never, under any circumstances, shut off the recorder then restart it. Such a recording, he told him, would be useless in a court of law. And since Vinny was an agent now, he had to make doubly sure he obeyed the law. So Corso had taped the ON button down in such a way that Vinny would have to undress in order to get to it.

"Don't drive so slow," Toto said sharply, "get going."

"What a moron," Vinny thought, "he hasn't told me where to go."

"Where we going?" Vinny asked.

"Go down Court and make a right at Fourth, my sister's is the third one on the right."

Vinny parked the car at a fire hydrant off the corner of Fourth and Court. Toto looked at Vinny with a faint smile.

"I convinced Balsamo you deserved a shot," he said, "and you know what? You lucked out. We got a job, a heavyweight job. Important people will be there. I like you, Ba-Ba, you got more heart than a lot of people in this crew."

Vinny nodded and began to sweat.

"I'm gonna run into my sister's and pick up something. Then we gonna run over to that junkyard, ya know, Anthony's place. We gonna squash that little fuckin' Russian with the cowboy hat. Remember that little prick from the other day?"

Vinny nodded again.

"Well, he's counting back from ten right now, and he doesn't know it. *Heh-heh*, I love this shit."

"Balsamo said it's okay for me to come along?" Vinny asked.

"Come along? Ba-Ba, my man, you gotta be the luckiest guy in the world. You're gonna get to jerk the trigger. Can you believe that? You're gonna make your bones first night out. And me, Vinny, I couldn't be happier for ya."

Vinny cleared his throat and looked at Toto in sullen silence. Toto nodded and then patted Vinny's head as if offering a blessing.

"Ya know," Vinny said, "I always knew I'd get this kinda break."

"Well, Vinny, you show respect, and good things happen."

Toto moved closer to Vinny. If he kisses me I'm a dead man, Vinny thought, I'd have to strangle the sonofabitch.

"Welcome in brotherhood to La Cosa Nostra," Toto said reverently.

"Terrific," Vinny thought, "now get the fuck out of here, I gotta make a phone call."

"Thank you," Vinny said, "and God bless you too, Toto."

Toto left the car and pigeon-toed off toward his sister's house. When he entered the building, Vinny bolted from the car.

God is good, God is kind, and God lives in South Brooklyn, he told himself as he ran to the phone booth on the corner. He dropped in a quarter and dialed Alex's number, repeating God is good, God is kind, be home, Alex, be home. The phone rang once, then again, then the machine.

"You know who this is, wait for the sound of the beep and leave a message. I'll get back to you as quickly as I can. . . ."

"Alex, if you don't help me I'm gonna kill a Russian in Staten Island," Vinny said. Then he yelled into the phone, "Ya hear me, they want me ta clip one a dem Russians, the one with the cowboy hat. Geez, Alex, I don't know what to do."

Vinny was back in the car before Toto left the building.

"Ya ready?" he asked Vinny.

"Sure, let's get going."

The night was without moon or stars and the air that came onto Staten Island from New Jersey was heavy with stink. Though Yuri kept the windows of the Mercedes closed, a foul smell found its way into the car, then into his nose, which was sensitive and bled easily when he rubbed it.

Too much cocaine, but Yuri didn't think of that. And if he did, it didn't seem to bother him, because he'd already sucked away three lines by the time he saw the headlights of the first car turn into the street. The car parked next to him, in front of Fat Anthony's Junkyard.

A second, then a third, and finally a fourth, set of headlights followed the first. It was not clear to Yuri why there should be so many people coming to meet him, but he didn't see it as a complication, more as a sign of his own importance.

Fat Anthony and Balsamo were in the first car. Yuri didn't look to see who was in the others.

The gate to the junkyard shuddered, then slid open. Balsamo waved for Yuri to come ahead. After pulling the Mercedes into the yard, Yuri hesitated getting out. The ground was muddy and he'd spent a half-hour shining his boots.

A light went on in the small building that Fat Anthony used as an office. Balsamo came into the light and waved impatiently for Yuri to come ahead.

Yuri had made his decision the day before, and had telephoned Balsamo. The morning's incident with the Jew on the boardwalk had confirmed his worst fears. A shadow had settled between himself and Niki. Petra was replacing him in the order of things.

When Niki had turned to Petra, and told Petra to take him away, away from the Jew because he was embarrassing Niki, Yuri knew he'd been right to call Balsamo. Right to take matters into his own hands.

Petra, like Niki, didn't really know the Americans. Not like he did. He, Yuri, knew their sly ways. How to use them, one against the other.

Balsamo had let slip more than once that he thought Matty Musca was a fool. An insane fool, flying high and wild. A man he'd love to see come down. So Yuri had telephoned Balsamo to arrange this meeting. He'd tell Balsamo that he'd do it. He'd bring Musca down.

Then wouldn't Niki be happy. They'd have a party at the club. He, Yuri Yagoda, would be guest of honor. Niki would announce the opening of another restaurant, a wonderful nightclub that Yuri could operate on his own. Maybe he'd do just a little of the cocaine business on the side. Not much, not like he and Petra did with Sonny, but enough to pay the bills. And bills were high. Cocaine was expensive. Yuri found that in America he could not live without cocaine, or his cowboy hat.

Vinny walked into Fat Anthony's office, Toto right in front of him leading the way. The strange little man, the Russian with the cowboy hat, looked up as though this was a private party and Vinny was uninvited—a surprise.

The Russian was dark-skinned, and Vinny didn't quite understand that. He thought that Russians were blond with blue eyes, or bald with big bellies. This fellow was short and squat and had brown eyes that Vinny could tell were blitzed from coke, way too much coke.

The man was going to die, Vinny knew that much. But the Russian didn't, or else he was crazy, because he didn't look frightened. Just sort of dumb. Silly looking.

There were six people in the room. Balsamo sat behind Fat Anthony's desk. Fat Anthony, Junior, and Toto all sat on chairs; Vinny and the Russian were seated on the brown plastic couch.

Balsamo went into his pocket, took one of those stinking little cigars, then slid it into his mouth. He moved it around, in and out. To Vinny, that little guinea cigar looked like a monkey's prick.

He'd seen plenty of monkey pricks when he'd cut school and run to the Bronx to buy dope.

He'd get loaded and hang around the zoo all day, looking at lions and tigers, stinking penguins and monkey pricks. "Why am I thinking about this now," he thought. "Christ, I'm more afraid than that silly damn Russian with that stupid cowboy hat."

The office reeked of the Russian's death, but the silly sonofabitch didn't know what was going on, Vinny thought, or did he, because now the Russian seemed uncomfortable, nervous. He took off his cowboy hat and played with it on his lap.

"We got a lot to talk about here. So whadaya wanna say?" asked Balsamo, not looking at the Russian, but twirling his cigar and staring down at the desk as if he were studying a paper or reading a note.

"Maybe," the Russian said, "maybe you can help me find this Matty Musca, and I will do you all a favor. No charge. No fee."

Balsamo didn't answer him. He took his cigar, ran it around slowly between his fingers, and turned to Junior, who was ready with a light from a wooden match.

"Why should we help you find Matty?" Fat Anthony said, shrugging, wagging his head, not talking to the Russian but answering him and looking at Balsamo.

"Matty's our *gomb*," Balsamo said.

Vinny swallowed hard and looked at Toto, who was licking his lips and glancing around the room.

"Do you know what *gomb* means, asshole?" Junior said, and Fat Anthony laughed and Balsamo said, "Enough, enough."

The Russian played with his hat, put it on, then took it off, and, as if it were a signal, the door to the office opened and Matty Musca filled it.

"Can I come in?" he said.

Everyone in the room, like a chorus of admirers, called out his name. Everyone, that is, except Vinny and the Russian, whose name Vinny just remembered, and who was now breathing heavily on the couch.

Vinny shut his eyes, and for a second he believed he could disappear. Fly off to wherever it was he could find Alex. He thought about the feds. Maybe they were watching, lying in the cut just out of sight in their cool fed way; talking to each other by radio, in code; waiting for the right moment to come crashing through the door, big golden badges in their hands, yelling, "It's the FBI. The game's over." Vinny shut his eyes so tight that he could see it all in living color.

He heard the Russian say, "Why do you always make trouble? Nobody here wants trouble. You're a crazy man. You make so much trouble."

In a hoarse, almost choking voice, Matty screamed at the Russian, and pounded his chest in the way that he did when he was out of control.

"You little fuck, did you think these people would set me up for you, for you, you little prick?"

It seemed that everyone had a gun, everyone, that is, except Vinny and the Russian. Toto hit Vinny's shoulder and tried to hand him one. But it was too late, Vinny was already diving for the floor.

Shots—*pow, pow,* then *pow-pow-pow.*

Vinny had seen the knife come out from under the Russian's

cowboy hat. He'd seen the Russian snap it open and throw it like magic. He'd heard a shrill scream from the Russian as he'd thrown the knife. He saw it stick in the doorframe above Matty's head.

He would have liked to see more but he couldn't because he was lying on the floor, at the foot of the couch, and the Russian, whose name he remembered was Yuri, was draped over him, bleeding and mumbling and foaming white and red bubbles from his mouth.

Vinny threw the Russian off, then stumbled, as he tried to get to his feet. He slipped on the Russian's blood, then went into the air and fell backwards, down on his back. All two hundred and ninety pounds of him landed on his elbow, and he felt the firelike pain shoot from the elbow down his arm into his hand. He heard Balsamo shriek, "What the fuck is that?" He looked down and saw the tape recorder hanging out from under his shirt.

"Waste him," Junior screamed, "that's a fuckin' tape recorder. Clip the rat fuck."

"Don't shoot him," Matty Musca yelled. He was frantic, he began tugging at Yuri who had rolled from the couch and was lying across Vinny's legs.

Balsamo screamed, "Toto, ya see! Toto, ya see! I tol' you, I tol' you he asks too many questions."

Vinny had shut his eyes, and was whispering to himself. "God is good, God is good, Saint Jude make me disappear."

Vinny's eyes filled with Alex, his arm was numb, dead, gone. He couldn't move. Then he smelled Junior's breath, heavy with garlic and hot with fear and craziness.

"Now I'm gonna waste you, you big fat sonofabitch."

Junior punched Vinny in the face, pulled his hand back quickly and punched him again. Vinny grinned, and Junior punched him once more.

Fat Anthony had the tape recorder. He was examining it.

Trying to open it. "What *is* this fuckin' thing?" he moaned.

Matty Musca said, "Whadaya think it is?"

Somehow Vinny held on to the edge of the couch, and got up. Toto shot him in the shoulder.

The impact spun him, but he stayed on his feet. "You stupid son-of-a-bitch," Matty Musca screamed. He punched Toto and sent him sprawling across the room. Balsamo caught him before he fell.

Vinny sat on a chair. The whole right side of his body felt like it died. He began to rock, and as he rocked he looked around the room gauging his chances for survival.

Junior and Toto dragged the dead Russian from the office. Vinny heard the trunk of a car slam.

His eyes met Matty's, and he turned away.

He looked at Fat Anthony and Balsamo. The old man grinned that evil grin of his and Vinny tried to concentrate on his teeth. The brown lines fascinated him. He thought of brown heroin. The kind they used to bring up from Mexico. It was never as good as the white lady. The white lady could get him out of this trick bag. Vinny began to mumble, "Saint Jude sucks, Alex sucks, the feds suck. Oh, Ba-Ba, you're a dumbo, a dumbo."

Matty Musca said, "You figure you got a shot here kid, or what?"

Vinny shook his head, once. He looked over at Toto and smiled. He knew he was going to die in the next few minutes, the question was how.

Matty held the tape recorder. He walked over to Vinny and tapped him on the head with it.

"What is it with this gismo here?" he asked.

Vinny shrugged, he was as wet as if he'd just stepped from a shower, and the sweat caused a fire in his shoulder that made him feel dizzy, nauseated.

"You're going to tell me what this is about, understand? Or

I'm gonna blow your kneecaps off. Then I'm gonna cut off your prick and stick it in your mouth. Then I'm gonna, I'm gonna . . ."

Vinny nodded. "Yeah," he said, "but you can't eat me. It's against the law."

Everyone laughed, and Vinny smiled. Balsamo said, "Geez, what a dumbo."

Matty Musca looked at him for a long time as if trying to make up his mind.

Chapter Fifteen

The sound was Latin, easy to follow. It was lively. It moved. Alex felt it was a rumba or maybe a mambo. The floor was large with plenty of room. Under crystal chandeliers that hung from a mirrored ceiling, there were, it seemed to Alex, at least one hundred people dancing. Boys and girls in Beatle haircuts, children really, edged close to the bandstand. Oldtimers, hefty silver- and golden-haired matrons twirled around the edge of the floor. The center was crowded with couples of indeterminate years. Some nineteen—others could be forty.

> *You kiss me once*
> *I kiss you twice*
> *la, la, la, la,*
> *It's Pa-ra-dise . . .*

There were women in leather pants, boots, and puffy silk blouses, dancing with men in suits or in jeans and open shirts. Many women wore outfits of dazzling color. Some wore gowns.

Alex had never seen the likes of it. It made a wedding in the land of the golden community centers look drab. Fingers snapped.

> *You kiss me once*
> *I kiss you twice*
> *la, la, la, la,*
> *It's Pa-ra-dise . . .*

Long tables were set out banquet style, providing for parties of fifteen and twenty people. You had to have the eye of a bird to see a speck of tablecloth. Plates covered every inch of space. There were dishes on top of dishes that were on top of other dishes. Most of the food was a mystery to Alex. He did recognize orange caviar spread on black bread. And the lox and stuffed derma were familiar, as were the sliced egg in aspic. Beets and cabbage and ratatouille and white fish. But there were many other dishes he couldn't name.

In front of every fourth or fifth person was a roasted duck, and there were multi-tiered silver platters draped with grapes, holding oranges, pears, and apples. Slices of chocolate layer cake, creme puffs, and other pastries were on the bottom tiers.

Waiters and waitresses flew in and out of the kitchen carrying three-foot-long skewers of shish-kebab lamb, beef, and pork.

Each table was a banquet with specialities, from each Soviet state. There were bottles of Gordon's vodka and Hennessey brandy everywhere. Music filled the room, and Alex felt alone, a traveler in a foreign land, at a wedding of strangers.

Two guitars, a piano synthesizer, drums, and bongos made up the five-piece band. A black female singer belted out—

> *You kiss me once*
> *I kiss you twice*
> *la, la, la, la*
> *It's Pa-ra-dise*

The singer spun her tambourine, moved her arms over her head, then began to sing a Russian rock song. The change of pace made Alex jump. He missed his mouth, and vodka dripped from his chin onto his jacket. He sat back in his chair and watched, lost in the wonder of it all.

Vinny's message on his phone machine had sent him off. Most of the time Vinny left messages which made little sense. Short, childlike stories starting off with, "It's me, Ba-Ba," and ending with, "I'm on the job, partner."

This time he'd yelled into the telephone that he was on his way to kill a Russian in a cowboy hat.

Alex had found five messages in all.

The first message had been from Chief Ross, the second, from Delaney. Chief Ross was a policeman from the old school who never liked or trusted federal agents. In the past, he and Alex had disagreed about joint operations. "You'll make the case," Ross had said, "then the feds will steal your informant and take all the credit. That's their way. They can't help it. They think of local police as gofers, nothing more." Alex disagreed, the only way to beat organized crime was through joint task forces and strike forces. Alex had always believed that such operations gave law enforcement real punch and flexibility. He still believed it. Alex found Ross at home.

"Whatever you're doing, you're doing a good job," Ross said, his voice filled with pride. "You're making the bureau crazy. They're calling every half-hour looking for you."

Alex told him that he couldn't imagine why. Ross laughed and said, "Use finesse. Be careful. They can come at you twenty different ways."

Delaney's message was soft, almost soulful. "Alex, ol' buddy, where are you? We need to talk, friend, we really do. Call me at home."

There were two calls from the boys. Josh had thrown up on Frog Ass, and David was planning to run away from home. The usual stuff. Then there was Vinny.

By mir bis du Schoen,
please let me explain.
By mir bis du Schoen
means that you're grand . . .

The black female singer was strutting her stuff. The band was playing easy, and Alex poured himself another vodka. He was sitting alone at what seemed to be the only small table in the nightclub.

When he'd arrived, he'd spoken English to the waiter, who shook his head, mumbled a bit, and shrugged. Alex tried Yiddish. It was uneven, not his best. The waiter wrinkled his nose and walked off. A waitress appeared. She was plump, with beautifully made-up eyes. That seemed to be the common denominator, Alex decided. All Russian women had beautiful eyes.

He went straight to Yiddish, and asked for something to eat, asked to see a menu. The waitress nodded, rearranged his table setting, then left without saying a word. After several minutes she returned placing a fifth of Gordon's vodka and two bottles of soda on the table. Then she smiled pleasantly, and walked off.

"Food," Alex called out after her.

Vinny's message had left Alex with two choices. One, he could call Delaney. Maybe Delaney would tell him what was happening with Vinny. Had they wired him up and sent him out? Chances were Delaney would tell him nothing and, instead, get all over him about the bugs and wiretap. No, he didn't want to talk to Delaney.

Two, he could try and find the Russian in the cowboy hat. Alex was an intelligence officer, it was his talent to find people. A Russian street hood, in a cowboy hat and feather, playing street games, should be known to local precinct detectives.

Alex couldn't predict if he'd know anyone at the precinct, or even if they'd be helpful, but that was the place to go.

The 62nd Precinct station house was the old, large variety, with holding cells and a muster room the size of a small gymnasium. The desk sergeant, a small black, told Alex he'd have to wait; the squad was out doing real police work. To a precinct desk sergeant, no matter what his age or experience, the only real police work occurred at the precinct level. There were times when Alex was inclined to agree.

Alex was beginning to feel funny. His throat was dry, and he felt wired, like he did after too many strong coffees. His inability to talk to cops, cop to cop, was always a disappointment to him. He didn't have the knack. He believed that Vinny was somewhere within the confines of this precinct. And, if he was, he'd be with that Russian in the cowboy hat, probably nose to nose right now.

The desk sergeant, who introduced himself as Sergeant Williams, asked Alex if he knew of any openings at the Intelligence Division. He was tired of precinct work. Three years of aided cases, loonies, and Internal Affairs inspections took their toll. It had become an effort to come to work. "And this around-the-clock shit, well . . ." the sergeant had had enough. Alex told him that he was always on special assignment and he didn't know too much about the unit's needs.

"Let's talk about that," the sergeant had said. "Do you really need a hook to get into Intelligence—a rabbi, a connection?"

Alex answered that he'd never been able to figure out why, but he'd gone to Intelligence right from the academy.

The sergeant was almost dreamy when he said, "You mean you never worked the street? Were never on patrol?"

Alex admitted that no, he hadn't and that he was real sorry, too, because he thought he'd like patrol. That buddy-buddy stuff. Your own sector car, bowling teams, and precinct picnics, car pools, and all—he'd never had a chance to do any of that. Didn't even know who the PBA president was.

Sergeant Williams asked what grade detective he was. Alex told him he was first grade. The sergeant's voice went up an octave or two, and a pink tint came to the tips of his ears. He was a light-skinned black, still, Alex thought, his eyes were playing tricks on him.

"That's lieutenant's pay," Sergeant Williams said. Alex told him it was. As far as he knew, a first grade detective received the same pay as a patrol lieutenant.

Sergeant Williams mumbled and asked him to wait in the clerical office until the squad came in from the field.

It was already eight o'clock. Vinny's call, at best, must have been around four or five. Whatever was going to happen has happened, he thought. But he'd stay at it until he found Vinny, or that Russian cowboy.

The squad arrived an hour later; two detectives, both younger than Alex, and both talking that television-cop crap that made Alex twitch. They went on about him being a downtown cop. "A guy from Intelligence, a real downtown boy." And sure, they knew every dirtbag in the precinct. "A Russian in a cowboy hat and feather? You're kidding," they said at first.

Then the one who said his name was Harold something-or-other said, "I think I know him. He does a little coke from a nightclub on Brighton Avenue and Sixteenth. In fact, I dropped a dime on the guy to Narcotics a few months back.

"The name of the club is Moscow Nights, and if you don't speak Russian, forget it," Detective Harold said. "They won't talk to you. They'll pretend they don't understand a word you're saying. They'll just smile and shrug, smile and shrug. A bunch of phonies, a bad crew."

Now Alex sat watching a gypsy violinist. Half the patrons were in tears, but the little guy in the cowboy hat was nowhere to be seen.

* * *

"Are you religious?" Paul Malatesta asked.

Niki threw him a questioning glance, then shook his head and looked at his watch.

"It's eight o'clock," Niki said softly. "I should be going."

He could hear John Reno moving quietly about the apartment turning on lights. They'd talked for more than two hours, and Paul Malatesta had lost not a bit of concentration. It was unnerving. Malatesta drank as much as he did, but barely blinked.

"John will drive you wherever you need to go. He'll get you there in no time."

"We open the club at nine," Niki said, "but we start seating people at eight, eight thirty." He waited for Malatesta's reaction. He wanted to leave, but Don Paul Malatesta was not ready to excuse him.

"You wouldn't hesitate to tell me the information I need to know, would you, Niki?"

Niki was stung. "Why would I?"

"Please, don't do anything silly. Help yourself, Niki," Malatesta advised.

There were compartments in Malatesta's mind, and like all his kind, lights were on in some. In the others, there was nothing but darkness.

If Niki believed in God, then, of course, he'd have to acknowledge the existence of the other side, the dark side. If there was a God, then a force for pure goodness existed in the world. But the other side would also be real, wouldn't it? And, if pure evil existed in the form of a devil, a demon, Niki believed that one would be walking in Malatesta's shadow.

"Do you believe in God?" Malatesta asked again, from his carved wooden chair. "It doesn't have to be the God of the Jews. Any God will do."

Niki continued to shake his head. He was getting nervous, really anxious and was beginning to wonder if the man sitting across from him was sane.

"How can you not believe in something?"

"I have no roots," Niki said. He managed a laugh, a small one, but a laugh nevertheless. "Why do you ask me about religion? I never think about it. You learn about these things as a child. I was born a Jew, but I've never been in a temple or a synagogue. There was no one to bring me, or teach me. So I have no interest. In my country those things are not important. I have nothing but myself, my wife, and my friends. And right now, none of these are secure. I think more about that than about religion."

"I believe in God," Malatesta said. He paused and poured himself another brandy, looking at Niki as though he expected to see disbelief.

Niki lowered his head so as not to look into those brown eyes.

"I don't doubt it," Niki said.

There was silence between them, and the longer the silence lasted, the more anxious Niki became. He had nothing more to say to this man. So he sat and waited. He heard the telephone ring. He heard bits and pieces of John Reno's muffled conversation. He heard the word *fuck*, alone, not part of a sentence, but as a response to a statement.

John Reno came into the room and whispered in his don's ear. Niki saw Paul Malatesta's blood drain, and his face tighten. He flashed a look at Niki, then grabbed John Reno by the back of the neck. Niki heard him say something about a dwarf. "Get the dwarf," he hissed. "Tonight! I want it done tonight!" A coldness came over Paul Malatesta, the likes of which Niki had never seen before. He felt a quick stab of terror. Whatever was happening between Paul Malatesta and John Reno had to do with him, because Malatesta stared at him a long while before he spoke.

"Your man Yuri is dead. Matty killed him. I'm sorry, I don't know how this could have happened."

* * *

178

Alex had no sense of time passing. He was caught up in the music, and the food, and the looking. It seemed as though he'd been staring at a particular group for quite a while. There were four of them, all men, seated at a table in the far corner near the band. He noticed that two of the men were weight lifters, body builders for sure. One had red hair combed in a fifties-style pompadour.

When everyone else in the place laughed in response to a song lyric, they didn't crack a smile.

There were more people in the club now. He would have to pay close attention if he was going to pick up on the guy in the cowboy hat. Was he big, like the weight lifters, or small and dark like some of the others? He realized, dimly, that he'd met and passed his limit of drink. More than three vodkas and he was scratching his nose and his chin. "Cut it out," he told himself. "You'd better clear your head." The music was sounding better and better. He hadn't noticed before, but the mirrored ceiling was now reflecting colored lights. And there were women seated alone. Some, quite beautiful. One or two smiled at him. He scratched his nose and sipped a little more vodka.

Alex had used the retriever on his phone machine twice. No Vinny, but two more messages from Delaney asking for telephone calls he didn't plan to make.

When he came through the door, Alex made him immediately. He moved by stages, nothing hasty, nodding to people as he came.

Detective Harold what's-his-name, from the precinct, had told him that the owner of Moscow Nights was a man named Niki Zoracoff. The guy in the cowboy hat was known as his right-hand man.

"This Niki is a piece of work and a half," he'd said. "A big, good-looking guy if ya like the type. He reminds me of a

179

German U-boat commander. And the cute piece of work never talks English, just shrugs and smiles, shrugs and smiles."

Well, this *was* Niki Zoracoff, no doubt. He looked like he'd just stepped off the set of a Bergman film. He had blond curly hair, and was wearing a knee-length black leather coat with a long white scarf hanging from his shoulders like vestmentory.

He walked close to where Alex was sitting. Their eyes met. Niki held on and Alex turned away. "A piece of work and a half," Detective Harold had said, and Alex believed him. The guy looked solemn, ominous.

"Who is the American at the corner table?" Niki asked, joining Petra, Vasily, and Yuri's two friends from Tashkent.

"He's been here a few hours. He sits and drinks and looks," said Vasily.

"Find out who he is," Niki snapped.

"And Yuri?" Petra asked.

"Do what I tell you to do, do you hear me? Yuri is dead, and you two are responsible. As responsible as that pig Musca. Now go and find out what a lone American is doing here listening to music he doesn't understand, and not eating our food. Send one of the girls."

"Yuri is dead? Killed?" asked Petra.

A fury took hold of Niki, and he let loose with abandon. Everyone at the table became very still. The guitarist looked down from the bandstand. They all heard Niki out in silence as he said good-by to Yuri, and then they all flushed away half-full water glasses of vodka.

She nodded and showed white teeth, one trimmed in gold. She asked if he wanted to dance. It was a beautiful, slow ballad.

Alex said, "Not right now," but asked her to sit and share

a drink with him. "Yes, indeed," he thought, "these Russians are amateurs, sending a woman to dance with me, to feel me up. I could do with a rub, God knew it had been a while, but not a back rub on a dance floor." He grinned at her. And the undercover agent's rush came to him, the pleasure of the game when it's your park, your ball, your bat.

"I'm Tanya," she said. "You like Russian music?"

"Love it. I'm Alex," he felt confident, in this place he could rule with the minimum of effort. Amateurs.

"Not Alex. Alexander," she said softly. "Alexander is Sasha." Her eyes were beautiful and sly, the tip of her tongue appeared.

"Fine, I like that. My grandmother called me Sasha."

Alex never knew his grandmother. She'd died long before he'd been born, but this blond woman, with a face that reminded him of a Persian cat, and lips that made his knees wobble, certainly could care less. She was here to probe, to make conversation, to find out what he was all about.

"Oh," she exclaimed, "your family is from Russia?"

"Actually they're from Queens," he said with a smile, "via Williamsburg, via someplace in the Ukraine."

She tried to laugh while sipping her vodka, and was forced to cover her face. She dabbed at her lips with a napkin.

"You're an American. A Yankee Doodle Dandy," she giggled.

Her voice reminded him of a movie star, an old movie star, whose name he'd never be able to remember.

"If there's anything I'm not," he said to her, "it's a Yankee Doodle Dandy."

Alex looked at the table where Niki Zoracoff was sitting. The two body builders glanced in his direction, then turned away.

"You like Moscow Nights?" she asked again.

"I'd like it a whole lot more if I could find what I want."

She looked puzzled. "And what do you want?" she asked. Then she said, "If you don't see what you want, you should ask."

Her English was accented, and although she spoke slowly, she made few errors. Alex was impressed. He had no real plan; still, that was the way the game always began. It was the moves that counted, not the preparation.

"I bought coke here a few times, from a guy in a cowboy hat," Alex said sharply.

Set the bait, he thought, move crime onto the field of play.

There was a very thin, very tense smile on her face.

"A cowboy? Here?"

"C'mon," he said, "let's dance."

The music was beautiful, the vodka made him feel warm and sexy, and he wanted to get on with whatever was going down. He'd let her feel his gun butt. That's what she wanted. Probably half the men in this place were heeled, he thought. Another gun won't be a surprise. As they danced Tanya ran her hand from his shoulder across his neck and down his side, then around his waist in an exquisite move that was pure professional. Alex loved it. He preferred dealing with pros. Tanya didn't flinch when she ran her hand over the PPK in the pit of his back. And Alex never felt her tap his rear pocket, she did it so lightly.

After a while she excused herself and went to the ladies' room. He watched her go and as she went he saw her glance about the room. One of the body builders, the one with the red pompadour, followed her out.

Alex checked his impulse to follow them both. That would not be smart. That was the vodka. So he drank another and waited.

Tanya didn't return.

"He's carrying a gun," Petra whispered to Niki, "and probably a badge. But a gun for sure."

Everywhere he turned there were problems, and Niki was

beginning to feel that they were impossible to solve. His instinct was to forget the man with the gun, and do what he'd originally planned. That was to find Matty Musca and kill him. But Petra also told him that the man had asked for Yuri, had said he'd bought cocaine from Yuri in the past.

Niki knew it was a lie, a sloppy, fumbling move to draw him out. Yuri never sold to anyone that wasn't from home. The man seated across the room was a policeman, or a spy for the police. This could get beyond his managing. Were the American police after him too?

He sat puffing a cigarette, thinking, looking at the band, not hearing the music, wondering about this man, who sat in his nightclub. Niki felt eyes burning somewhere near the center of his back, and it made him angry.

How would Viktor Vosk, with his mountains of ego, deal with all this, he wondered? He desperately needed the old policeman's counsel. "Okay, move a pawn," he thought.

"My name is Nikolai Zoracoff. I own this place. This is my restaurant. Can I help you?"

To Alex, Niki looked as though he were about to smile; he didn't. And there was a cocky self-assuredness in the air about the guy. It made Alex twitch. He extended his hand and Niki took it.

"A nice club you have here," he said.

There was a glint, just a trace of a smile. Niki Zoracoff shrugged, nodded his head, and sat.

That Niki was the most important man in the place was clear enough. Even people seated at tables furthest from them were watching. And band members' eyes darted from sheet music to their table.

"I'm looking for someone," Alex said, smiling broadly.

"So I understand."

"He wears a cowboy hat and he is here all the time."

"Really? A cowboy hat you say?" Niki laughed, then turned away.

Vodka can be warm, soothing, salve for the aches and pains of the heart and spirit. It can also put a fire in the stomach, and shorten the fuse. Alex could feel his toes curl. Niki was now looking toward the bandstand.

"Well," continued Alex easily, "I've been here three or four times. I met this guy, the one with the cowboy hat, but I've forgotten his name. You know him. He's a friend of yours, isn't he?"

Niki shifted nervously in his seat. The man spoke as if he were reading the words, an actor, a dangerous actor. Viktor always said a good policeman is known by his ability to act.

Niki took a long breath and said, "You are a policeman, and I think you came here to make trouble for me. I don't understand why. I do nothing illegal here. Nothing that would interest the police. I serve food, good food. You should try some. There is music, dancing, once in a while a little too much drinking. But that is the worst of it."

The lighting had dimmed. The band played a ballad. Alex felt the slightest touch of anxiousness, yet a curious pride (some would say arrogance) swelled his chest. He grinned and said, "Well, so you think I'm a cop. Why would you think that?"

Niki looked at him closely, wrinkled his nose, then brought his head two inches from Alex's. It was a very threatening gesture.

"You have a badge in your back pocket, and a gun on your waist," he whispered. "You are a policeman, or someone pretending to be a policeman. In either case, you are trouble, and I don't want any trouble here."

Alex looked at him thoughtfully. Niki held his eyes, but Alex went right on staring.

"Well?" Niki said.

"Well, what?"

"You are a policeman, aren't you? And you are trouble."

Alex folded his arms and leaned back in his chair.

"Zoracoff," he said, "you don't know what trouble is."

"You are wrong again, Mister Policeman. But it doesn't matter to me, not at all."

Niki got up from the table, he seemed to have not a care in the world. He looked around the room, shrugged, and said, "Your city is full of liars. I've met all kinds since I've been here. You, Mister Policeman, are another one."

Alex raised his eyes toward Niki, who was glancing around the room.

"Sit down," he said.

Niki's smile disappeared. His light blue eyes stared at Alex. Alex leaned forward as if to attack him.

"*Sit down!* . . . All right," said Alex, "let's really talk, Zoracoff. You're right, I am a policeman."

Niki smiled and shrugged, again.

"The worst mistake you can make right now is to think that you're not in serious trouble," Alex said in a voice so low that he wasn't sure Niki understood him.

"I'm here looking for someone. I didn't just drop in to try the stuffed derma."

Niki looked at Alex and nodded his head. "You're not here looking for me though, are you?"

Alex glanced at his watch, it was past midnight, but time had lost all meaning. If he checked his machine again, and Vinny still hadn't called . . . He could feel inside him, the beginning of fear. Allowing Vinny to wear a wire was like sending him to his own suicide. He'd known it all along. Another victim in a hopeless war. But this smart-ass Russian could help—he knew that as well.

He stared at Niki a long time, then he said, slowly, clearly, "You're exactly who I'm looking for."

"And your friend in the cowboy hat? Was that another lie, Mister Policeman?"

To Alex, the Russian sounded less sure of himself than he was trying to appear. He seemed unable to grasp the meaning of what Alex said. He moved nervously, then lit a cigarette. "Go at him," Alex thought, then he said, "Not my friend, Zoracoff, yours. Like the Muscas are your friends, and Paul Malatesta. You have a lot of friends, Niki, a lot of good friends."

Niki sat straight up in his seat, he moved his shoulders and neck like a great hitter coming to bat. He looked across the room to Tanya, who smiled at him, her gold-edged tooth all a-sparkle in that beautiful Persian-cat face of hers. He waved her over and when she arrived he told her to get some vodka. Alex understood the word *vodka* and guessed at the rest.

The crowd was beginning to thin. Fewer people were dancing, but the music went on and on, never a break, not even a pause.

"Would you like something to eat?" Niki asked.

Alex shook his head.

"You shouldn't drink vodka without eating. It's not smart."

"But you're smart, hah?" Alex said evenly.

Niki didn't answer him, just pinched his bottom lip and turned away.

"You know what you are, Niki? You're just another asshole walking along a highway going nofuckin'where."

"You talk a lot, Mister Policeman. The trouble is you don't say much."

Niki smiled at his own remark, and Alex smiled back.

Then Alex got up from the table and told Niki he had to make a call. He asked Niki not to leave.

"This is my restaurant, my club. I'm not going anywhere, I belong here," Niki said emphatically.

"Maybe," Alex said. Then he walked from the room to the foyer, where a wall pay phone hung beneath a print of a boy standing on newly cut timbers floating in an azure lake. The boy was fishing for frogs with a long cane pole and net. Somewhere Near Khartov was the inscription on the print. Khartov, in the Ukraine, Alex's maternal grandmother was born in the

Ukraine. As he dialed his home number he wondered if his grandmother would have known that lake. It was an idle thought, he'd never met his grandmother. Still, his mother talked of her often, spoke of how brave she was, how courageous. His mother believed all immigrants were heroic.

This policeman on one side, Paul Malatesta on the other, Matty Musca coming from he didn't know where. Niki felt as though he were living at ground zero, and the clock was ticking.

He looked across the room, into the foyer. Alex was dialing the pay telephone on the wall. Police methods, he thought, were little different here in America from those in the Union; thinly veiled and with few surprises. He was afraid, clearly this policeman had information. He knew about Paul Malatesta; and Matty Musca. How much he knew, he hadn't let on. Still, if the policeman had enough to arrest him, he would have. When they have you, they come for you. He'd made a simulated attack, not a real one, and there was a terrific element of bullshit in his tone. Niki poured himself a drink, and decided that he wouldn't say much, let the policeman talk and watch. But then what? He saw himself as he was, alone, vulnerable, without power, without real friends or connections.

Alex's disappointment was visible, and Niki took notice. He'd hung up the telephone and slapped the wall with the palm of his hand. Then he dialed again. Now he spoke, single words—parts of sentences—nodding and wagging his head. Niki watched him carefully.

Alex's telephone conversation went on, and Niki watched as he waved his hand in the air. At one point Niki thought that he'd hit the telephone. He talked for a long while. This man was a fresh voice, and a whole new set of problems.

When Alex finished his call, he walked back toward the table. His demeanor was that of a man with total confidence. The serious look on his face jerked Niki.

"What else do you think I've done?" Niki asked moodily as Alex once again joined him at the table.

Niki felt as though they were both preparing for war. He opened a fresh bottle of vodka, poured Alex two fingers, and himself four. This slightly built American would soon play on his field, a field where he was master. The room was thick with smoke, the music wailed on, Niki sucked away the vodka, then tapped Alex's glass with the bottle, a challenge.

Chapter Sixteen

Carl Marx Syracusa got the call around nine o'clock. He had his nephew Philly drive him to Paul Malatesta's apartment building on East Seventy-fifth Street and park in the garage, but he went by himself to meet his don.

The parking attendants stared, self-consciously. Carl had grown used to such attention. When he was young it depressed him. Now, it no longer bothered him. Still, he was not deceived by the stupid smiles of people who looked at him as if he were entertainment. In his mind's eye, he saw himself as a giant of a man, quick as a jungle cat, and more deadly. Carl Marx was a dwarf. A killer dwarf.

In the real crime business of New York, people believe that you must be connected to one of the five families in order to survive.

But Carl Marx was the exception that made the rule, or so it seemed. Everyone that mattered believed that he owed allegiance to no one, that he operated on his own; therefore, he wasn't a threat. He dealt with everyone. Carl Marx had access.

His business was small-time loan sharking: neighborhood

people and small businesses. He also booked sports bets. His nephew Philly had a thriving heroin business in North Harlem.

As a young man, Carl collected his outstanding bills with a hammer and sickle. It was a statement. It earned him a lifelong nickname. People said he enjoyed it, that he liked being called Carl Marx.

Three people knew that Carl Marx was Paul Malatesta's personal killer. It was a lonely and dangerous business. Carl stayed outside the family so no one, other than the don, his driver John Reno, and Philly, Carl Marx's nephew, knew he was a member.

Like Paul Malatesta, Carl was a believer, committed emotionally, passionately, totally to the *via vecchia*—the Old Way.

A religious passion burned in Carl unknown to modern members. He considered himself one of the few true brothers of the Honorable Society. The new generation promised all sorts of things, but they dissolved in the face of real pressure.

Carl Marx's heart raced when John Reno brought him into the room where his don waited.

He started to say something, but the look on Don Paul's face quieted him. The dwarf felt as though he were in the presence of a man touched by spirits, a man truly born to lead. He lowered his head and waited for instructions.

"Matty, his driver Carlo, the old man Balsamo, and Fat Anthony who owns that junkyard on Staten Island."

The don gave him the address of Matty's girlfriend in Queens. Carl Marx was stunned. There was no one, he thought, more important to the don than Matty Musca. But the don must have his reasons, and his reasons were his own. Carl Marx asked no questions, and though he was ten years older than Paul Malatesta, he spoke to him as if he were speaking to his father.

Their conversation was in Sicilian, and it was a short one. It was getting late and Carl Marx did not have a lot of time.

The don wanted the business with Matty taken care of immediately, tonight, if possible. The others could wait a day or two, no more.

There had been no word from Vinny. But Alex's message machine recorded concerned words from Delaney, and a soft urging from Chief Ross asking for a call. Alex telephoned Ross. The inspector confirmed that the feds had wired Vinny and sent him out. He also told him that the two agents Alex had met, Corso and Rivera, were *hummers*. "Ringers sent from Washington," Ross said, "not organized crime types." They were part of a unit sent to New York specifically to infiltrate the Russian émigré community. They believed Vinny had access, through Balsamo, to Musca. The bureau knew of Musca's dealings in Brighton Beach. Ross told Alex he'd gotten his information from the AIC, Agent In Charge, of the New York office. He told Alex to be warned, that he was fishing in uncharted waters.

Alex knew that Niki Zoracoff was the linchpin. Niki struck Alex as the kind of guy that watched the world explode around him, then somehow slid out. "Not this time, Mr. Slick," he thought. "This time I yank the life line."

Alex had been drinking for a couple of hours, and his brain was starting to complain. Nevertheless he sat confidently across from Niki and poured himself another.

He'd had no food and was beginning to feel slightly frozen, a little lost. Even so, he was a cop, and cops can exert constant pressure when a target's liberty is at stake. Alex sipped more vodka. It was all part of the game. Another sip, then another. He finished all of what was in his glass. Then he shook his head. He soon discovered that the vodka was Niki's ally, certainly not his.

One feeble attempt to get up from his chair so shocked and embarrassed Alex that he immediately sat back down and waited for the tide to shift. It didn't. If anything it rose. And Niki seemed to be just hitting his stride.

"Anyway you slice it, Zoracoff, you have problems," he whispered.

Alex's voice, however, quivered a bit, a signal to Niki, so he poured him another drink.

The more Niki thought about it, the darker his prospects appeared. He had to deal with the facts, and the facts were that this policeman knew more than Niki thought possible.

"You continue to speak to me in riddles," he protested mildly.

Even in the dim light of the club, Niki could tell that Alex was feeling the bite of the vodka.

"Why don't you tell me about my serious trouble?" he suggested.

Alex made a delicate move with his finger. He pointed directly at Niki's heart.

"Killing people," he said, "has always proven to be the most effective way your friends, Malatesta and Musca, have found to keep the peace. Let's drink to killing people. Whadaya say, Niki, bottoms up to exploding heads?"

"America is a hard-hearted land," Niki said, then he downed the vodka in his glass with pride.

Niki knew from experience that physical intensity will win out across a table just as sure as the first sure shot thrown in an alley.

Alex sipped another drink. "I don't know too many Russians," he said, "but from what I understand, the Soviet Union is not exactly Disneyland. You probably had trouble there. I know you have problems here. You'd better start thinking about where to look for help."

"C'mon," Niki said, "I don't want to think about problems. How about you and I get drunk. Then maybe I can forget my problems for a while, and you, Sasha, can stop thinking about how to make me trouble."

They were at the icy-slope part of their conversation. Alex

thought he could lean harder, or pull back for a time, but then he'd come again. He'd twist this Russian's head off before he was through.

"Okay," Alex said, "let's drink to a budding friendship."

"To my newest best friend," Niki said, then he poured Alex a full four fingers.

"Before we go on with this," Alex said, "I should make something very clear to you."

He paused a long time before he spoke. Alex wanted this to come out just right; he wanted Niki to be positive that there was not a shot that he could be safe.

"I'm in Brighton Beach now," he said, "and, Niki, I'll stay here till I find out what it is I need to know. When I'm gone the FBI will be around, and when we're both through with you, your playmates, Musca and Malatesta, will be oiling their guns for you. You're floating, Niki, and any second you're going to sink beneath the waves without a sound. Zoracoff, you're a walking, burning disaster. But drink up, new friend, because behind one of these doors there's a light, and I got my finger on the switch." Then Alex smiled. It was a dirty smile, meant to be.

Niki Zoracoff shrugged, then shrugged again, and then he laughed.

"To light," he said, and then what seemed to Alex a magical move, his head and glass and hand moved as one. There was terror in Niki's heart, though Alex was unable to tell. The smile that had made Niki Zoracoff famous remained etched on his face. No one had ever been able to checkmate the Prince of Pushkin Square. He'd lived with the knowledge of that. For Niki there could be no other way.

Carlo parked the car near the telephone booth on the corner. Not a light shone from the apartment building. Carlo didn't like that. There was always a light in the building's foyer.

"Boss," he said, "whyn't you hang on a minute. I wanna check the building."

Carlo was afraid, and Matty found his fear annoying.

"What for?" he snapped.

"I don't see no lights."

"So what. That spic super lets the bulbs burn out all the time."

"Well, I don't like it," Carlo said, pulling on his ear lobe. "I got one a those feelings that I use'ta get in Vietnam. Like them little fuckers are all over the place, 'cept you can't see 'em."

Matty got out of the car, stood in the street and stretched. It was two o'clock in the morning. Lynn would be sleeping, but that was tough shit, he thought. He'd had a good day. He felt great. Better than he'd felt in weeks. He wanted a topper, and the topper would be Lynn's legs wrapped around his neck.

"Look, Carlo, you go check out the building, and I'll call Lynn."

Matty always telephoned before he went anywhere. And he had codes. Signals in case there was trouble. If Lynn said, "Hurry home, baby, I'm wet and waiting," Matty would be gone like a big bird, not looking back. If Lynn's sweet voice said, "Drop dead, you big sonofabitch," he'd go right up, pulling at his clothes, rubbing his crotch before he got off the elevator.

He dialed Lynn's number thinking that Kid Vinny went down hard, spitting and kicking and motherfuckering all over the place. The kid had heart.

Carlo started for the apartment house door; he was not confident that Matty was right. True, the super of the building did let the foyer lights burn out. This wasn't the first time.

But in the past, both lights had never burnt out together. "What are the odds on that?" Carlo thought, as he walked toward the building.

He advanced slowly, carefully. The pistol in his jacket pocket felt good in his hand, it gave him instant courage. There was a sound in the darkness on his right. In 'Nam he would have blown it away.

Now he moved with apprehension. His shotgun was under the front seat of the car. What if someone were hiding in the hedge? They'd get first shot.

"Fuck it, everyone dies sooner or later," he said to himself.

That was an old Vietnam line. It worked in the jungle, wasn't worth shit here in Queens. In the jungle death was random, almost accidental. Here in the street, death waited for you, just for you. It let others pass. Once in the foyer he felt stronger, the bulbs were out but there was no one around. He tapped once, then again. It flickered, light danced. He turned the bulb and the light came on.

"Beautiful," he thought, "what a beautiful light." Then a scream in his head: Someone had loosened the bulb—he could feel it. "This is the fuckin' end."

When Matty heard "Drop dead, you big sonofabitch," and then a childlike giggle from Lynn, he began to rub his crotch.

When he heard, *"Questo e ciao de Don Malatesta,"* he looked around and at first didn't see anything. But then he felt a presence, and looked down. A three-foot, five-inch dwarf wearing a stocking mask was pointing a double-barreled sawed-off shotgun at his head.

There was just a tiny fraction of a moment of physical weakness. Then Matty Musca brought his head back as if to spit. *Boom-boom.* A ball of fire, from a twelve-gauge, loaded with "double o" buck, took Matty's head clean off.

As had happened in 'Nam, shots from nowhere brought superstrength to the legs of Carlo. He ran right through the foyer door. Large fragments of glass crashed down and went through him like lashes from a whip. His knees trembled. A loud scream came from deep inside him, as he slammed head first into the wall. Then he fell to the floor. He was conscious, but sliding fast.

There was glass in his hair, and blood was running from his scalp, down his forehead, and into his eyes. He tried to wipe his eyes free of blood and shards of glass.

"Breathe deeply," he thought. "It's over, you're alive."

Seconds passed.

He tensed his legs to get up, and wiggled his eyebrows so he could see. He heard the sound of someone running, saw the flash of moving feet, tiny feet, like a child's. He watched, astonished, as a grotesque little thing came through the shattered door, came all the way, right at him, and there was nothing he could do about it.

Carlo bit right through his tongue. His heart quit, stopped dead. The dwarf swung a straight-edged razor once, then again.

Alex walked, or he tried to. There was a misty rain, and it brought with it a smell of the sea. He'd forgotten how close Brighton Avenue was to the ocean. He stumbled in front of a bookstore with posters, photos, and paperback books, all in Russian. The vodka had moved from his stomach and was now lighting a small fire in his chest.

He passed one shop, then another. A boutique, a delicatessen, a record shop, another delicatessen. He was walking in circles. Niki took hold of his shoulders and leaned him against a building. "Just stand here," he said. "Don't move, Tanya's coming with a taxi."

Alex took a deep breath and tried to arrange the pieces that were falling apart inside his head. When a picture became clear in his mind he'd reach for the drunkenness. It made things all right. Eased his conscience, clouded the memory of the stupid drinking bout with Niki; helped him forget about Vinny.

He was depressed and way too drunk for his own good. Gratefully he took hold of Niki's shoulder as he led him to the cab.

"We'll talk more in the morning," Niki said. "Tonight Tanya will care for you, you'll be fine."

"And you, Niki, how will you be?"

"The only thing I'm sure of is that, in the morning, I will feel better than you. Good night, Sasha."

When Niki moved away from him, Alex could not hear him walk. The man stepped lightly. But he watched the way Niki moved. To Alex he was a man without fear, a man with authority. He had presence, starlike presence. With all his macho bullshit and posturing, there was a very basic friendliness. Alex couldn't help but like him. Then, again, Alex was very drunk.

The smell in the lobby of the building was brutal. It tickled Alex's guilt, made him come awake.

"Dogs," Tanya said. "Everyone in the building has dogs."

"Where are we?"

"You should not drink without eating. Russians eat a lot when they drink."

"Never mind that. Where are we?" he asked again.

They walked up the first flight of stairs. Alex was forced to climb the second one holding on to the banister, one shaky step after the other. He couldn't believe he was this zonked.

"Believe it or not," he said, "I don't drink much."

"Oh, I believe it," she said. Then Tanya reached into her shoulder bag for her keys.

On the floor landing, Alex gathered himself for the walk to the apartment. It was at the far end of a long, dark hallway. When she slid her key in the lock, he asked again, "Where are we?"

"My apartment."

"I figured that one out. Where is your apartment? What city, country, state? You know what I mean."

"Silly. I live in Brighton Beach with all the other Russians. You like Russians, no?"

He was in a bedroom. Once out of his clothes he got quickly beneath a set of covers, sheets, and blankets that were so heavy he couldn't move.

Tanya was gone. He had no idea where she'd disappeared to.

Suddenly she was in the doorway laughing.

Silhouetted in the light from the kitchen, she made Alex realize for the first time that she had a magnificent body.

"I'm making some tea. Would you like some tea?"

"Oh, sure, great, wonderful. Anything. Tea, coffee, cognac, vodka, whatever you have. It'll be great."

He was aware of nothing other than the sense that he was riding a long, rolling wave. He traveled a great distance, and as he traveled, the wave settled into an easy sway, as if he were on a hammock being pushed by a very small, very weak child. Deep, glorious, velvet sleep, warm, like water from a tropical pool, came on and on, covering his legs, his stomach, his chest. The warm feeling came to rest on a satin sheet, just below his chin. A sweet-scented breeze crossed his cheek lightly. It was Tanya's breath.

"Sleep," she whispered. "You've drank enough. In the morning there'll be tea."

He smiled. She kissed him full on the lips and gently tweaked his nose.

SATURDAY MORNING

Sitting alone by the telephone Niki waited for the call from Vika. Dazed from lack of sleep, he stared at Katya in wonder.

As she had done in Moscow, Katya had managed to remove herself from his business life, which was his whole life.

Within a month of their arrival, Katya had found work with the Board of Education.

In the eighteen months, she'd come to Moscow Nights twice. Once for the grand opening, and once for Niki's birthday party.

He'd known from the beginning that Katya objected to his friends and his lifestyle. They never talked about it. In truth, over the past several months they rarely talked. Katya was totally caught up with "her kids," as she described them.

Katya's English was perfect. She had been a teacher of languages. In America, she thought she'd be teaching Russian.

The Board of Education had assigned her to a ghetto school in Brooklyn. After her first day, she came home full of elation and terror. She would not be teaching languages; instead, she would be more or less a babysitter for a small group of learning-impaired crazies. That was what the principal of the school called them, *crazies*.

All the children were black. The principal told her to be careful. They were out of control, unteachable, crazies.

Katya explained to Niki that they were not crazy, just poor and in need of help to learn. She told him a story about one boy the others called Bat.

On the morning of her first day with the class, Katya had been taking attendance. Bat was not in the room, but his books and things were piled on his desk. When Katya asked the others if they'd seen Bat, they all turned toward the wardrobe.

Katya opened the wardrobe door. There hung Bat, his sneakers in the coat hooks, his arms folded, his head one inch from the floor.

She asked Bat why he was hanging upside down in the closet. He said he liked it. It cleared his head. Katya told him he could hang for as long as he liked, and that he could join the class whenever he was ready. In time Bat came down.

Katya struck a deal with him. He could hang in the closet every day, but only at a specified time. Bat said he preferred hanging in the afternoon. In the days that followed, at one o'clock, Katya reminded Bat it was time for his hanging. She placed a timer in the closet, set it on the half-hour, and when the timer buzzed, Bat would come down and rejoin the group. In a week he gave up his hanging.

Katya's relationship with her kids blossomed. Each joined together in the wonder of new discovery. The exotic Katya and the ghetto street-life kids explored New York City, its museums, zoos, parks, and the Statue of Liberty. Only the park administrators asked them to come back. Two of the bigger boys assigned themselves as her bodyguards, and saw her home daily. They called the apartment at strange hours of the day and night. She brought excitement into their existence, and things foreign. They delivered to her a sense of worth, of value. They gave her love. Niki found himself walled out of her life more and more. The mad world he lived in, with its terror and double-dealing, was as alien to Katya here as it had been in Moscow. So he protected her from it. He refused to bring her into his forest where the wild men he dealt with lived.

The telephone in Niki's apartment rang. When he answered it and heard Vika, he made himself comfortable on a chair and lit a cigarette.

"So, Vika, another week."

"Yes, Niki, another week."

Her voice was unclear. She sounded tired.

"Vika, it's two o'clock in the afternoon there. You sound exhausted. What have you been up to? Wearing out another lover, I bet."

There was silence, as if she were giving her answer some

thought. Niki had meant to be funny. They always began their conversations with a laugh.

"Oh, Niki," she said at last. "To be in love with a married man is like spending your life with a pillow covering your face. You can't breathe."

"You, Vika, in love?"

"Yes, Niki. All things are possible in this land of sun and sea." There was a moment when Niki thought he heard a sob.

"I get so lonely, Niki. There are times . . ."

"What of your young lover? The one you chase from your bed in the morning. The one that crawls home to his mother."

"When I look at his beautiful brown eyes, free of grief, but full of bewilderment, I think of John Carlo, the man I want, sitting with his fat wife and six children. Six, Niki. I think God is cruel."

"There is no God, Vika."

"Oh, yes there is, Niki, and he uses his power to make jokes of foolish people. There is a God. He is a man, and like all men, he is mean and enjoys the torment of women."

Niki's instinct was to hang up. Vika was in pain. He was too far away to be of any help. And the questions he needed to ask would not bring her any joy.

"I'm a man, Vika, and I don't enjoy the torment of anyone."

"I loved you once, you know," she said softly.

"No, I never knew that you loved me, Vika. I swear to you, I never knew."

There was a long silence. At last, Vika said, "I have some good news and some not-so-good news."

Niki considered that a moment. "Start with the bad."

"John Carlo is leaving Rome. He's taking that Sicilian Mafia chief to his family's farm outside of Calabria. The man has begun to tell him things that frighten even John Carlo. These Mafia people are insane, Niki. Do you know they killed his entire family? Practically everyone he's ever known. They

201

poisoned the guests at a wedding party. Killed twenty people."

Niki didn't say anything. He just sat there holding the telephone. A farm, a family farm near Calabria, how difficult would that be for Paul Malatesta to find?

Vika kept talking, and Niki kept holding the phone . . . thinking. Then Vika's voice dropped. She began talking quietly, soberly.

"John Carlo will stay with this man. The man trusts him. John Carlo is a wonderfully understanding man. He understands everybody," she said with a laugh, and it was the laugh that brought Niki back.

"So you will be without your John Carlo," he said.

"It seems I am always without my John Carlo. No matter who my John Carlo is. But did you get my point? Do you understand what I said? The man is talking, Niki, telling them everything. And from what I've heard of these people . . . thank God."

He didn't hear her.

"Do you know where the farm is, Vika?"

"Yes I do," she said gently.

"And the good news, Vika? You said you had good news."

"Yes, very good news. A message for you from home. Do you remember Mikail Yagoda, the jeweler?"

"Of course, Yuri's brother."

"He's here in Rome, and he brought a message to me for you."

"From who?" Niki said laughing.

"Viktor Vosk."

Lights went on inside him, making him feel warm and airy. It was a feeling he remembered he sometimes experienced as a child when he thought there must be another Zoracoff somewhere. But then the lights would dim and he knew he would be alone, more lonely than ever before. Those were hard times—then came Viktor.

"You're kidding."

"No, Viktor wants to meet you at the Esperanza Hotel in San Diego, California. You should be there this Sunday."

"San Diego, tomorrow? Vika, San Diego is at the other end of the country. My God, it's a half a world away."

"Really, Niki. You are in America, not the Union. You get on an airplane and go. You are a free man, Niki. All you need is the airfare."

Niki Zoracoff became aware of the inexplicable twisting of his nerve endings beginning their frantic dance in his stomach, chest, and throat. The old feeling.

"Well, Niki, will you go?"

"I would go to Siberia to see that old policeman."

"San Diego is hardly Siberia. Niki, you are so melodramatic."

"I'm a Russian, Vika."

"That you are. And you know, it's true."

"What's true?"

"I really did love you once."

"Long ago in another world, I suppose I loved you too."

"Men are such liars, such beautiful liars. *Ciao*, my Niki."

Chapter Seventeen

Alex felt as though his teeth were on fire and he covered his face with his hands. Tanya's mouth was on him and the sound that came from her was that of a mourning dove. Though the curtains were drawn, Alex could see it was full daylight. Her head moved with the quickening rhythm of a sea bird. He pushed his head deeper into the pillow and thought of Marsha and her infamous line.

"If you lose control of yourself you should die. Don't let those things loose in my mouth. They're alive. You should die in this bed if you do."

What a sex life. Once he'd vowed to abstain for a month, then get her high and drown her in semen.

Suddenly Tanya was off him as if she'd been hit by an electric shock. All the iron dispersed in him, as a result of the quart of vodka, came together now. Tanya bent over him and worked him as if there were a fire stick between his legs.

"Now, my Yankee Doodle Dandy, you can wake me." Her breasts danced across his chest as she drew her face near to him. The tips of her fingers traced small circles on his cheeks, round his lips, and over his chin.

Then she pleaded to be satisfied. "Go in deeper, Sasha. You're a fine lover. The best."

It seemed as though there were scores of doves in the room.

"Go in deeper. You're a fine lover, Sasha. The best."

"Niki Zoracoff, you are right," Alex thought. "It's a city full of liars."

Tanya rode on.

The mourning doves flew off and were replaced by bluejay barks.

She continued to ride, rolling as if they'd made love for years and this was their song. Her head moved side to side keeping the beat.

Her eyes were quite beautiful. Alex connected with a tiny tear of sweat that was building between them.

He was thinking of Vinny, a Russian cowboy, and Niki Zoracoff.

For Tanya this could be a long, long ride.

The clock on the dresser said it was nine thirty.

Maybe, Alex thought, Marsha is telling Frog Ass to go in deeper, telling him he is the best.

Alex tried to concentrate on the bead of sweat on Tanya's swaying breasts.

"Concentrate, concentrate," he told himself. "Let it be, let it come." He didn't feel anything.

And Tanya rode on.

Finally he bit into his bottom lip, and raised his head in the way that he did when it was real.

A city of liars, a nation of cheats, a world of phonies.

He reached up and took hold of Tanya's breasts that were now all but splashing off her skin, and let loose a liar's moan that shamed all liars' moans ever made.

Tanya grabbed the back of his neck and held him.

"I'm here, Sasha," she yelled. "I'm here. I've got you. You're fine. You're safe. You're the best ever."

After a moment of silence, Tanya whispered to him in Russian something gentle and sweet. So lyrical it could have been a lullaby.

Streams of vodka fog ran through Alex's brain. His eyes were out of focus. He shut them, held them closed, then opened them slowly. He'd dreamed that Kid Vinny had been with him at Moscow Nights. That they'd danced together to the music of the fiddle, and laughed the way the Russian men did. He'd been happy in his dream, and wanted to return, quickly.

> *You kiss me once,*
> *I kiss you twice*
> *La, la, la, la,*
> *It's Paradise.*

Daylight, filtered through yellow shades, shone on the naked Tanya. She breathed gently, and lay motionless next to him on the bed. The exertions of Tanya's ride, the vodka's residue, and the cry of the fiddle lulled him.

"Nothing is so important that I have to get up now," he thought.

His eyes went to the clock on the night table. It was 10:00 A.M. Alex saw his gun, his badge case, and papers he'd used to take notes, and he wondered, in a casual way, how they'd ended up neatly layed out on top of the dresser.

Tanya sighed. It was an erotic sound and it sent a small tickle into his groin.

Alex slipped back into his own deep sleep.

Fat Anthony parked the car and walked the muddy path to the junkyard. He opened the lock, pushed a button, and the electrified gate rolled on steel wheels crushing dirt and tiny pebbles. He liked that noise. Fat Anthony was raising the curtain to his junkyard world. He stood still for a moment and looked around.

The Russian's tan Mercedes had been crushed.

The two corpses, together with the leather and steel of the car, soon would begin to ripen. The grease, and oil, gasoline, kerosene, benzine, and filth of the yard, would never conceal the stench.

Fat Anthony knew. There had been other times. In a matter of hours the stink would rise like a protest. He wished he could dig a hole and bury the whole package. Get it out of sight until the truck with its powerful magnet arrived.

Fat Anthony sipped coffee from a styrofoam container, then bit the heel from a fresh loaf of Italian bread smeared with butter.

There was nothing to panic about. Soon all traces of yesterday would be gone. The truck from the metal recycling plant in New Jersey was on its way.

The Russian, that dumbo Vinny, and the Mercedes would be cremated, leaving only ashes.

Fat Anthony felt terrible. His junkman's heart was broken with the thought that a beautiful Blaupunkt radio had been smashed. Had he stayed calm, cool, he could have saved the radio. Those things go for six hundred wholesale! What a shame, what a crime, he thought.

He took another bite of bread, almost choked, and swallowed a mouthful of the sweet coffee.

For a moment Fat Anthony stood looking down at the lump of steel. He sighed and wagged his head. "A six-hundred-dollar Blaupunkt, what a crime."

Fifty yards away, Carl Marx walked through the open gate. Fat Anthony lit a cigarette and smoked. When he turned he saw the dwarf walking toward him. He flicked the butt into the mud.

His heart began to race.

What is this? He was confused. He knew the dwarf. Why was he coming this way like a shooter?

He was connected, known to be. Nervously he bit off another piece of bread. Where the hell was this little nobody coming from?

"Yeah?" he wanted to yell.

He was a capable guy. It was known. Nobody fucked with him. He was connected. A made man.

Maybe he was hallucinating. The little sonofabitch had a gun.

He stepped back, one step, then another. The dwarf kept coming.

Fat Anthony brought the container of coffee to his lips, a terrible cramp attacked his fingers and he dropped it. Coffee splashed and stained his two-hundred-dollar Bartocelli boots.

And the dwarf kept coming.

"What are you doing? At least tell me what you're doing. Tell me the truth, will ya? Wait!" he screamed. Bits of partly chewed semolina flew in the air.

Fat Anthony moved backward, faster now.

"What'd I do, Carl? Will you wait, goddamn it?"

Fat Anthony tripped over the axle from a late-model Chevy that had been chopped. He fell backward into the mud, and rolled around like a battered seal.

"*Police*," he screamed. "*Police*."

He yelled as loud as he'd ever yelled.

Carl Marx was amused. He smiled and said, "From Don Malatesta."

The dwarf spoke in English. Fat Anthony was one of the new breed. He didn't understand Sicilian.

Fat Anthony rolled to his knees.

"Why, for chrissake?"

Carl Marx shrugged, "You gotta know better than me."

He looked Fat Anthony in the eye and fired.

It was a clean shot, an inch above the bridge of the nose. Still Carl Marx left nothing to chance. He removed the razor from his pocket, unfolded it slowly, and walked to where Fat Anthony lay in the mud, grease, and partly chewed semolina.

To him this was a religious experience. Carl Marx crossed himself before he sliced Fat Anthony's throat.

When Alex woke the room was in full daylight. The shades were up, music played on the kitchen radio, and Nikolai Zoracoff sat at the foot of the bed.

Tanya, carrying a steaming mug, walked into the room. "Here, drink this. It's good, strong tea," she said.

"Good morning," Niki said. "How do you feel?"

"I've felt worse," Alex lied. He sat up and sipped the tea.

"You must eat when you drink vodka. It's most important," Niki said.

"I heard, I heard. Russians eat a lot, I know."

Alex's eyes went to the dresser. His gun and badge were still there, but his notes were gone.

"So, my friend, Detective Alexander Simon, you write my name on a piece of paper, then come to my restaurant and try to trap me. You tried to make me do something illegal. Something I would never do. That is not fair, Alexander Simon, not fair at all."

Alex took a big gulp of the tea. He could see clearly now. He looked at the clock. It was 11:00 A.M.

Alex didn't answer, but did his best to stare back at Niki, who sat grinning at the foot of the bed, one leg crossed over the other. His hands were folded in his lap. He looked like a fox, comfortable on the crest of a hill as the hounds ran in circles beneath him.

"You're feeling pretty good, huh, Zoracoff?"

"Call me Niki. I feel better than you right now, I bet."

Self-consciously, Alex rolled from the bed and dressed. He

put his badge in his pocket, and clipped the PPK on to his belt.

"Nice gun," Niki said. "Everyone in New York has a gun."

"We have a lot of home-grown criminals. And a few too many new arrivals, if you know what I mean, Zoracoff."

Niki smiled and put up his hands—surrender.

Alex walked from the bedroom into the kitchen, looking for Tanya. He didn't know if he should be anxious or not, but Tanya was gone. "She's shopping," Niki said. "Wouldn't be back for an hour."

"A nice woman," Alex said.

"Oh, a wonderful woman. Very kind. She had a tough time at home and an even tougher one here."

"How long have you been in the States?"

"Two years, a little less."

"Your English is very good."

"Thank you."

Alex stood in the bedroom doorway and looked at Niki, who continued to sit on the bed. He remembered the night with Tanya. She *had* been kind to him, and one helluva lover.

"A very nice lady. You're right, Zoracoff, kind is a good word for Tanya."

"She thinks of herself as a poet. All poets are kind," Niki said, smiling.

"And all Russians are poets, I suppose."

"Poets from an evil empire, hah, Detective Simon?"

"Call me Alex."

"I'll call you Sasha. You like Sasha? It's a nice name."

"Whatever makes you happy, Zoracoff. But I'm going to tell you something. I think you're full of shit."

Niki felt as though he'd been slapped. Still Niki smiled. It was his way.

"I am?" he asked.

Alex looked as if he were pleased with what he'd just said. Then he continued, "I have a flash for you, Zoracoff. You're a fuckin' criminal. I figure you're involved in at least three killings. You walk around that restaurant like you're some kind of tsar. And you serve cocaine for dessert."

"Anything else?" Niki asked.

"Yeah, you're from out of town."

Niki was surprised by Alex's display of temper. He'd thought that their night of shared drinking had warmed Alex. Apparently not. He was disappointed. He wanted Alex's friendship. There was something of Viktor Vosk in Alex. More than the fact that they were both policemen. Spirit, he thought. Viktor had courage and spirit, and so did this American detective. To come alone into his club, to confront him the way he did. The man had courage, Niki respected that.

"Listen," Niki said. "There's only the two of us here, just us. We should try to understand one another. First of all, I am not a criminal, not a murderer, not a dealer in drugs. Your information about me is wrong. But how do I convince you of that?"

Alex looked at him in wonder.

"You can answer the question I asked last night, and try the truth this time."

"Last night you asked me to get cocaine for you. Nothing's changed. I have nothing to do with drugs."

"What about your friend in the cowboy hat?"

"And I told you I fired him. That he was gone."

"What's his name?"

"If he is so important, how is it you don't know his name?" Niki tried to smile.

"Damn you, Zoracoff! You said you'd be straight with me. You're starting that Russian toe dance again."

"I think you are guessing about him, and you are guessing about me. You should tell me what it is you want to find out," Niki offered. "You said something about murder, what murder? And what about this Musca and Malatesta?"

Alex was looking at him with suspicion. Police were the same all over.

"Tell me the name of the man in the cowboy hat. Let's start with that."

"His name is Yuri."

"Good, good. You see, it isn't hard. The truth comes easy when your heart is in the right place."

Alex switched off the radio, then joined Niki on the bed.

"Where does he live?"

"In Brighton Beach."

"Where in Brighton Beach?" Alex asked, matter of factly.

"I don't know the address," Niki lied. The truth, like vodka, can be easily overdone, he thought.

"Call him. He worked for you. If you want me to believe a word you say, call him."

Niki tried to make this come out right in his mind. He liked Alex, but there was no reason to trust him. The idea of telephoning a dead man was far worse than the reality of it. Yuri was dead. Why was this detective so interested in finding him? He didn't like playing a game when he couldn't plan ahead.

"Okay, you think about calling your friend. In the meantime, I need to make a call of my own," Alex said.

"I don't have to think about it. I'll call him if you like."

"I like. But give me a minute. It's later than I thought. I need to call someone."

When he dialed his apartment number something inside Alex told him he'd hear Vinny's silly, lovable voice on his machine.

With a certain amount of ceremony, Alex took the retriever from his pocket, and buzzed into the phone. It made a sound like a cricket. He heard the tape whirr; there was either one very long message, or many short ones. It was a long process, and Alex grew anxious.

Finally . . . Delaney. Screw Delaney, he thought. He chirped the machine for the next message. It was Chief Ross.

A sick feeling settled in Alex's stomach. He didn't like the sound of Chief Ross's voice. Didn't like it at all.

"I'm calling from the 113th Precinct in Queens," Ross said. "It's 10:00 A.M., I'll be here for awhile."

Alex hung up and quickly dialed the precinct. He asked the officer on switchboard duty to connect him to the squad.

A detective came on. Alex asked for Chief Ross.

"Where are you?"

"In Brooklyn. What's up, boss?"

"Somebody took out Matty Musca. Blew his head off."

Alex looked into the bedroom. Niki was still on the bed. He had a magazine and was fingering it.

"When?" he asked.

"We have a witness. Well, not a witness exactly. He didn't see anything. But he heard the shots. This morning, two o'clock in the morning exactly."

At two o'clock in the morning he was with Niki. Yuri, the cowboy-hat-wearing Russian, was not around.

"And, Alex," Ross said, "Musca had a wire in his jacket pocket."

"Musca was wearing a wire?"

"No."

"Well?"

"He had a Nagra in his pocket. One of those body recorders, self-contained. You know?"

"Yeah, so?"

"It had your guy Vinny Esposito all over it. *He* was wearing the wire. There was adhesive. It had light brown hair stuck to it."

"Christ."

Silence on the other end of the telephone, then Chief Ross said, "Right."

"Maybe I should call Delaney?" Alex said, to himself as much as he did to Chief Ross.

He decided to wait. Instead he called his home phone again and listened to all the messages. No Vinny.

"Okay," he said to Niki, "I'm through. Call your friend Yuri."

Niki walked into the kitchen, sighed, and shook his head.

If fear and madness lived in people's eyes, as Viktor said they did, then anger lived there as well. And Niki saw anger in Alex's eyes.

Alex was standing with his arms crossed, leaning against the wall near the telephone. His head was cocked to one side, and he seemed to be biting the inside of his cheek.

"You continue to be angry with me. You think I'm a criminal, a major gangster or something."

"Stop pulling my chain, and make the call, huh, Niki."

"Pulling your what?" Niki asked.

Niki picked up the telephone and dialed Yuri's number.

"No luck," he said, "there is no answer."

"Fancy that, I never would have guessed."

Alex took a deep breath and exhaled slowly.

"Listen, I have some bad news for you, Niki. During that last telephone call I made, I found out that a close and dear friend of yours passed away unexpectedly during the night."

"So he *knows* about Yuri," Niki thought.

"He died of a disease called holes. Affected his head. Took it right off. I figure it must be genetic. There is a family history. His nephew died of the same affliction just a month or two ago. And the way I see it, you're a carrier, a regular fuckin' plague."

Niki didn't answer him.

"Aren't you the least bit curious?"

"I am sorry, Detective Simon, but I find it very difficult to understand you."

"What happened to Alex, to Sasha. Are we going to get formal again, Zoracoff?"

"Okay, Alex, are you making jokes with me?"

"What kind of jokes? I tell you that I have news of a tragic death, and you don't even ask the name? You Russians are a cold breed, Niki."

"All right . . . so who?"

"Early this morning, Matty Musca, your dear friend and protector, was sadly taken from us."

"Good," Niki said with a defiant smile.

"Well, that's phenomenal. Niki Zoracoff finally tells the truth."

Alex winked and a grin began to spread.

They laughed together. Niki had a sly laugh that started slowly, then exploded. A Russian laugh.

Alex's was free and open like a teenager's.

"You are something, Niki. But I am the master of fucka-round. So no more lies, hah. Trust me, be straight with me and I'll help you."

Alex said this laughing but he meant it.

Alex stopped laughing and looked over at the telephone that sat silent on the kitchen wall. A thought that had been resting came up again.

The tension between them had been smashed. Niki felt as though he'd been through a storm. Maybe he'd found a new friend, someone he could truly trust, a comrade.

"New York is an evil place, isn't it, Sasha?"

"There really is no evil place, Niki, just heartless, mindless, fucked-up people."

"Do you still believe that I am a gangster, a murderer, a dope dealer?" Niki asked as if Alex's answer were important to him.

"Maybe yes, maybe no. I don't understand you, Niki."

Niki laughed. "Who knows? Maybe someday soon I will understand me."

"Well," Alex said, getting up and walking to the telephone. "I do understand why you have such a following. You're quite a guy, Niki."

Niki grinned, scratched his head, and shrugged his shoulders.

"Just remember that prisons and graveyards all over the world are full of people that other people described as 'quite a guy.'"

Then Alex dialed his phone, chirped his retriever, and said a quick prayer, hoping he'd hear, "It's me, Ba-Ba."

Chapter Eighteen

Sector David, of the 122nd Precinct, bounced through spine-rattling holes. It swerved just in time to miss illegally dumped, worn-out washing machines, refrigerators, television sets, three-legged chairs, topless tables, and green garbage bags containing rotten melons, tomatoes, used cat litter, crappy pampers, and an old Kotex.

"*Ohh*, you wanna slow down to maybe fifty, dear heart, before you wreck this car?" Sergeant Kurt Mueller told his driver, Police Officer Mary Ann Scott.

"They said murder, sarge, murder. You can't blame me for being a little excited."

"They said body, Scott, body. And turn off the goddamn whoopper, it's giving me a headache."

Suddenly Sergeant Mueller bounced from the seat, banging his head off the cruiser's ceiling. Police Officer Scott pulled a hard left and slid the cruiser into Fat Anthony's junkyard.

Sergeant Mueller had come into the department before Vietnam, before they burned down Harlem and the South Bronx.

He was on his way to his four hundredth D.O.A. This was Police Officer Mary Ann Scott's first.

Police Officer Scott was out of the car, nightstick in hand, in world-class time. Before Sergeant Mueller stopped rubbing the top of his head, she was back behind the wheel.

"Oh, he's dead all right. Shot, stabbed, and maybe poisoned. There's white gooey stuff coming out of his mouth."

"I don't want to seem grouchy, Scott, but don't you think you should maybe take a look around?"

Police Officer Scott ran a trembling hand across her chin.

"*Wellll*," she said.

"Go look around, Scott. I'll be with you in a minute, soon as my stomach lands."

"*Wellll*, how about I wait for you, sarge. I mean it's not as if he's going to run off."

"If you can stop your hand from shaking, take the clipboard and follow me. The lieutenant and maybe the captain will be here in a few minutes. Let's see if we can con 'em into thinking we know what the hell we're doing."

"*Wellll*."

"Scott, let's go."

Five minutes later, Police Officer Mary Ann Scott let loose a scream that sent two junkyard dogs three blocks away, scurrying for cover.

"Ohmigod! Ohmigod! Ohmigod! . . . *Yuccch*!"

If Sergeant Kurt Mueller stayed in the police department for thirty years, he'd never stop talking about his four hundredth D.O.A.

Dripping from a square tangle of steel the size of a footlocker came the essence of life, kitetails of flesh, and shards of bone. When Sergeant Mueller crouched so as to get a better view, vines of intestine clung to chrome, plastic, and leather.

There was more. For years, Sergeant Mueller would attempt to explain the feelings he'd experienced at the sight of a severed hand clutching a cowboy hat.

Nino Balsamo told Junior that he was going up for a nap. Balsamo lived on the fourth floor of a four-story walk-up on Fourth Street. He owned the building, and the one next door, and a pizza parlor on Fort Hamilton Parkway, managed by three brothers who'd arrived from Palermo the year before, and who'd purchased, one after the other, three two-family brick houses on Staten Island.

Every six weeks, along with twenty gallons of imported, second-rate olive oil, the brothers received ten half-kilograms of ninety-seven-percent-pure heroin, processed the old French way, by German chemists, till it was white as ivory.

"I'm going up for a nap," Balsamo said. "Remind me when I come down that I promised the old guys I'd play seven and a half at the club later."

Junior asked him if it was okay if he picked up Toto and ran to the O.T.B.

Balsamo said, "Wa sure. Just you be back in an hour. I gotta play cards."

Nino Balsamo was seventy years old. Before his teeth had gone to streaky brown, he'd bewitched women with his genteel old-country ways and rolled fifty-dollar bills.

Angelina Molina, a sixty-four-year-old widow, lived rent free on the first floor of Balsamo's building. She had one of those large commercial-sized jars of Hellman's mayonnaise filled with rolled fifty-dollar bills.

Every afternoon, except Sunday, Balsamo sat in her kitchen, smoked and sipped heavy Burgundy, while Angelina made magic at the stove.

They'd eat a *frittata* together, Balsamo would drink two glasses of wine, then stretch out on the couch, just like he'd done for thirty years.

He'd sleep for an hour. Sometimes he'd wake with an erection. Angelina could tell by the tenting of his pants. Balsamo always slept on his back.

She'd whistle softly in his ear, as a thousand years of machismo bubbled into his prick. Then Angelina, with a certain pride, would make herself ready with vaseline—just a dab, the tip of a finger, more or less.

He'd smile that evil grin of his and undo his trousers. She'd mount him, and Balsamo would slide home to the whispers and purrs of dear Angelina.

When they were through, they'd reminisce about the times when Balsamo came for his nap three, sometimes four, times a day.

"You're a saint, Angelina," he'd say.

And she'd answer, "You're the best, Nino Balsamo."

For years, Balsamo's wife sat in her window upstairs. She'd watch him come, then see him go. Never once did she dare hint that she knew what was happening beneath her feet.

One day the moment of truth would come. Balsamo's wife knew it. One day the horns she flashed through the window into his back would take root in his black heart. Then Nino Balsamo would pay for the years of humiliation and the red-colored nightmares that haunted her sleep.

The street door was open, but for the foyer door, Balsamo used his key. He stood still in the hallway, waiting to get a whiff of Angelina's *frittata*. He glanced up the stairway. The building was quiet, and the aroma of the *frittata* came stronger now.

Under the staircase was an alcove with a door that led to the basement. The hallway was in half-darkness there, and as Balsamo walked past the alcove, the dwarf stepped out, and fired. He shot Balsamo neat and quick with a nine-millimeter Baretta fitted with a silencer. He shot him with his arms outstretched, both his hands wrapped around the gun. Balsamo fell and the razor flashed in the twilight of the hallway.

Once out on the stoop, something made Carl Marx turn and

look up. A woman sat in the fourth-floor window. It seemed to Carl she was smiling. The dwarf ran his little hand across the large golden horn that he wore, and, just in case, crossed himself twice, then kissed his thumb, and raised it to the woman in the window.

They were sitting in one of the booths along the wall under a large print of "The Doors of Dublin."

Delaney had first suggested they meet at the Federal Building in Foley Square. "Not on your life," Alex told him, and suggested Police Headquarters.

They settled on the Emerald Isle, a quiet, out-of-the-way West Side pub.

Steeped as it was in the misty green history of the NYPD, in this pub Alex could be strong. In this place, where he'd taken more than one policeman's vow, he could tell Delancy what he thought of the FBI.

"They'll take your case and steal your informant," was what Ross preached.

"And we shall learn from our mistakes," had been said by someone once.

It was two o'clock in the afternoon. As Alex approached the booth where the feds sat, their conversation died. Alex told himself, "Be warned, most of the thinking world is smarter than you. Though you are the master of fuckaround, be warned."

Agents Corso and Rivera, that Russian-speaking fed who looked like the head of a death squad, so slick and smooth, sat still.

Delaney stood and reached out his hand. Alex took it and winked. Delaney grinned. They had a history and it was good. It would overcome all recent bullshit. Alex felt better.

"You look godawful," Delaney said. "What have you been up to? I've had a helluva time reaching you."

"Busy. I've been busy," Alex said.

221

And then, as if to test the waters of the other two, he quipped, "You two look great. J. Edgar would be proud."

A counterattack: Rivera smiled and shook his head, then said, "Sit down, will ya Simon? We're not agents of the devil, ya know. Some people even think we do a helluva job."

"I *used* to be your biggest fan," Alex replied.

Alex took a seat next to Delaney, opposite Rivera. Corso sat still and quiet, and just stared.

"Do you ever think of yourself as a team player?" Rivera asked.

"Him?" Delaney chuckled.

"Listen, I'm here because Tom Delaney asked me to be. I'll be glad to work with you guys. We'll be a team, a joint task force brought together to root out the evil of this city. Let's get started. But first, someone tell me where my informant is. We'll need his help." Alex scanned their faces, and each of them, in turn, looked away.

Agent Corso said he wanted a beer. Delaney did too. Rivera, who sat at the end of the booth, nearest the bar, got up. Corso slid past him and went for the drinks.

"We haven't seen him since late yesterday morning," Delaney said softly.

"And where was that?" asked Alex.

"In Brooklyn. We wired him up and sent him out. I told him to wear a transmitter. I told him to use the Nagra only as a backup. We could have covered him if he'd worn a transmitter. But no, not him, not Vinny Ba-Ba. He said they'd pick us up in the street in a minute. So he wouldn't wear a transmitter."

By the time Delaney finished his explanation, Corso had returned with the beers. He set one in front of Delaney and one in front of Rivera. Alex asked, "Where's mine?"

Corso said, "Sorry," and went back to the bar.

"They found Musca with the Nagra, you know."

Alex's voice quivered enough so that Rivera sighed and said, "You're not going to blame us for that, are you?"

Alex shrugged. "There's no blame. I'd like to know where he is, is all."

Corso brought Alex's beer, then moved into the booth next to Rivera.

Corso's hand reached as if from reflex of a thought he was considering.

"Look, Simon," he said, and he made a move with his hands again, this time with both hands.

"Look, Simon," he began again, "Frank Rivera and I are not from O.C., we're not from the Organized Crime section, and I'm about to push my luck here. I am going to bend, to the screaming point, every fucking rule of the bureau. Tom Delaney swears by you, and Frank and I swear by Delaney."

Corso took a draw from his beer, wiped his lips on the back of his hand, then said, "You insist on misunderstanding us. We're not here to screw up your case, fuck around your informant, or anything like that. Everything we know about you, we like. We know you're a better technician than some of the people we have. We found that out in Queens."

"I don't know what you're talking about. What about Queens?"

Delaney laughed.

"Hold on, Tom, hold on," Corso said, and continued. As he spoke, he looked into Alex's eyes, as if what he was about to do was dangerous, and Alex should understand.

Agent Corso cleared his throat and turned to Agent Rivera, who got up from the booth saying, "Look, I'm going to get myself a drink. You guys want another round?"

No one answered him, and he left.

Corso explained that he and Rivera were from Washington. They were part of a headquarters unit in New York on a special recruiting assignment. They were looking for agents.

Well not agents, an agent. And not an agent really, an informant would be more precise.

"Did you know we turned Musca?" Corso asked.

Alex didn't answer, he remained quiet, wondering.

"But we're not interested in Musca, or Balsamo. We'd like to help drop Paul Malatesta, who wouldn't? And Musca was our man. I think in time he would have given us Malatesta. I believe that, but then again, I don't know a whole lot about organized crime. I defer to Delaney in that area.

"Alex," he said, "I hope and pray you understand we're in a war, a shooting war. Wherever you look they're making progress, inroads, subverting, converting, moving toward our throats."

Alex turned to Tom Delaney and asked, "Who's he talking about?"

Delaney said, "Alex, just listen."

Corso went on. "For years we've been safe in our own hemisphere. No longer, Alex, uh-uh." Corso looked down at his hands as if they held the last sword at the last post on the barricade.

"This is a joke, right?" Alex whispered to Delaney. "This guy's putting me on. Huh, Tom? This is some kind of FBI April Fool's party."

"Other agencies concern themselves with what happens outside the continental U.S. It's our job, people in my section, my unit, to protect home base."

Alex put his chin on his hand, and rocked forward just a bit, not so you'd notice.

"There are people who think this is a joke, Alex, but believe me, it's not. Do you have any idea how many Cubans, Haitians, Vietnamese, and Russians we've let into this country over the past five years?"

Corso grabbed his wrist. "The Cubans fucked us to here, Alex." He moved his hand up his arm and took hold of his elbow. "The Haitians, to here." Then he reached across the

224

table and slapped Alex's shoulder. "If we let them, the Soviets will fuck us right to the shoulder. There's close to one hundred thousand of them here now. All recent arrivals. How many of these people are agents planted here? Do you know?"

Alex wagged his head and rolled his eyes. Delaney turned away and took a deep breath.

"No one knows," Corso said. "No one knows except our counterparts in the Kremlin. And they know because they sent them here."

Corso finished his drink and looked very sad.

"The Russians are paranoid," said Rivera, "always have been."

"So I hear, and paranoia is contagious," Alex said softly, so softly that Delaney, who sat next to him, shoulder to shoulder, barely heard him.

Alex shrugged and asked what all this political stuff had to do with him and his informant Vinny.

"We're in a war, Alex. There are casualties in war. Did you know that Arafat was in Managua, and Castro too? They both *said*, in Managua, Alex, 'Your enemies are our enemies.' These people are coming together, Alex, and who do you think the common enemy is?"

Corso leaned across the booth. He pointed a finger at Alex's chest.

"Do you know how many Jews are left in Managua, Alex?"

"Don't patronize me, Corso, I read the newspaper. You want to tell me what anything you've just said has to do with Matty Musca, Paul Malatesta, or Vinny Esposito?"

Agent Corso sat back in the booth, he laughed and shook his head.

"You're hopeless. Don't you see they're climbing over the walls? They're coming up from the sewers, they're dropping out of the sky, they're landing on our beaches, and you're worrying about the fucking Mafia. We know the Mafia, Alex. We have charts, flow charts, and more flow charts. We know

225

every time one of the bosses shits, for chrissake. We know everything there is to know about them, Alex. There's nothing new or different in Mafialand. But we don't know squat about the real enemy. And that's where these people fit in. That Musca crew—Balsamo, Malatesta, that whole bunch—have been dealing with a sharp bunch of Russians, Alex, and we need to be in there. We need to know what's happening in that community. We need information, Alex. We need a good intelligent informant. We want this guy Zoracoff. But we need a case, some leverage. We could use your help."

"You want my personal opinion?" Alex asked.

"Of course," Delaney said.

"I think you guys have gone round the bend. Now don't get tense, I'm not jumping on your patriotism. I'm not calling you right-wing wackos. If you believe that the communist menace is on the Verrazano Bridge, then go get 'em. As an American taxpayer, in good standing, you have my support. As for me, the Mafia is more than I can handle. As far as any international threat is concerned, let me tell you something, Corso. As a direct result of organized crime in this country, more of our young people have died than have been killed in all the wars we, as a nation, have ever been involved in. Drugs, in my humble opinion, are a far greater threat than all the Marxist, Leninist, international revolutionaries combined. Communism is a fraud, a tragic fraud, and anyone with half a brain can see it hasn't worked. It is the major most singular catastrophe of the twentieth century. I'm not afraid of the communist threat. It's drugs, heroin and cocaine, in particular, that scare the shit out of me. Those drugs, and the politics of those drugs, are the real threat."

Alex heard the bar phone ring, he heard the bartender answer, and he heard him call out, "Alex Simon, is there an Alex Simon here?"

"I told Chief Ross where to reach me."

"Simon," Agent Rivera said, "there is no one here that

would disagree with a thing you've said, but the issue is more complex than you think."

Alex got up from the table, shrugged his shoulders, and said, "Maybe."

He took his call and returned to the booth, but didn't sit down. He stood and looked at Delaney for a long time. Finally he reached for his beer and finished it. To Delaney he looked pained.

"Something wrong, Alex?" Delaney asked.

Alex nodded his head and exhaled slowly. He let his shoulders sag. Rivera and Corso looked at him without expression.

"You know," he said, tapping his temple, "I'm a smart man, way above average, I've been told. I know that when you force someone to do something that is foreign to their nature you court disaster. I knew from the very beginning that Vinny couldn't pull this off. I knew it, and I did nothing to stop him. The truth is, I didn't want to jeopardize my relationship with you, Tom. And Vinny? He went ahead and did this thing to please me."

Agents Rivera and Corso sat as if they were deaf.

"They found him?" Delaney asked.

Alex nodded and said, "Yes, they did."

"He was a stupid guy, Alex, a real stupid guy," Rivera said. "Now, what about this Niki Zoracoff? Can you help us bag him?" Rivera said.

Alex didn't answer Rivera. He took a deep breath, turned away, and slowly walked toward the door. When Delaney called his name, he stopped, looked back over his shoulder, and said, "You guys are going to find out that Zoracoff is no Vinny."

"What the hell does that mean?" Corso shouted.

"He understands," Alex said. "He understands it all."

It was late afternoon when Niki saw Alex spin an illegal U-turn and park.

"Do you ride on the Sabbath, or are you planning to stand there until you take root?" Alex called from the car.

No one he'd met gave Niki more difficulty with the language. Alex spoke so quickly. Even the Italians with their codes and half-sentences were easier to follow. Alex had told him it was Queens English.

If Niki didn't pay close attention he'd miss half the words. He told Alex that his car was filthy as he slapped the seat with his hand. Alex didn't say anything, just gave him a blind stare. After three attempts the engine decided to turn over. Alex blew his horn and drove off. A dozen or so pigeons, ugly things, jumped into the air, as Alex, without signaling, flew into an illegal turn. Miraculously he missed running down an old man and two small boys. The man, dressed as Jakob Grossman had been, froze in the middle of the street and pulled the two boys to him.

"Careful," Niki shouted.

"Careful, my ass. They should cross at the corner. These people think their magic can stop cars. I'm amazed that more of them aren't run down."

Niki turned in his seat and looked through the rear window. The old man remained frozen, afraid to move. The boys covered their faces with their free hands.

"You frightened those people. You really did. You are a policeman. Why do you drive like a crazy man?" Niki shouted.

"Because I'm a policeman. Relax, Niki, I didn't hit them. And, besides, I told you they believe in magic. They're not afraid of automobiles. If you don't believe me, try driving in their neighborhood on a Saturday and see what happens."

Niki shook his head and lit a cigarette.

"Jews *are* strange," he said.

"We certainly are. It's part of our charm."

"Alexander Simon? Of course. *You* are Jewish!"

"Isn't everyone?" Alex laughed. It was a small, short laugh. He was not in a good mood, Niki could tell. He hardly knew

Alex; nevertheless, there was an understanding, a kinship. He liked this man he called Sasha.

"It certainly seems that way in New York, doesn't it?" Niki said.

"There are more Jews in New York than there are in Tel Aviv," Alex said.

"And more Italians than there are in Rome. I heard that," said Niki, looking out the window and wondering why they were speeding so.

As they neared the parkway entrance, Alex looked flatly at the road and said, "If we're not careful, soon there'll be more Russians than there are in Afghanistan."

"No, no, no," Niki said, "there are many more Russians in Afghanistan than there will ever be in New York."

"No shit."

"Excuse me?" Niki said, with a great deal of frustration. Then he sighed and said, "You're making a joke, right?"

"Right, but not a good one, I suppose."

"No, no, no, a very good one. It was funny. It was my fault. The language, you know, it's difficult."

"My grandfather was here for sixty-five years, and compared to him, you sound like Alistair Cooke."

"Who?"

"Never mind."

"Where are we going, Alex? You told me to wait for you. I waited. You haven't told me where we are going. Not to jail, I hope."

"No, Niki, not to jail. We're going to see your friend Yuri."

In fifteen minutes they were at the Verrazano Bridge toll plaza. Alex seemed deeply troubled, and Niki smoked cigarette after cigarette.

Paul Malatesta had told him that Yuri was dead, killed by Matty Musca. So where was Alex taking him? None of this made any sense. But he was afraid to ask questions. While crossing the bridge, he tried one. He asked Alex why, why were they going to see Yuri? But Alex stared back at him, stone-faced, and didn't answer.

They turned into a rutted road strewn with trash. He supposed that Alex was taking him to Yuri's body. What would that prove?

There were police cars parked on both sides of the road. Several men and a woman in uniform. There were others in civilian clothes; Niki believed that they, too, were policemen.

The police stood near the entrance to an enormous yard that was piled high with car parts and parts of cars.

"Is Yuri here?" Niki whispered.

Alex shrugged. "You'll have to tell me, mister."

Alex did not stop the car at the entrance, but drove directly into the yard and parked. Niki thought there was no point in leaving the car, so he sat. Alex had practically jumped out and was now talking to a group of three men. They were all dressed in suits, and each, in his turn, glanced at Niki.

Niki thought, "Of course I can get out and walk around." Alex hadn't told him to wait. It just seemed to be understood. But nothing special was happening. The police talked with hands in their pockets. Every so often Alex would nod, and another would shrug. Niki sat still and waited.

Finally, after ten minutes, Alex walked back to the car, opened Niki's door, and said, "C'mon, I want to show you something."

It was a bright day, the beginning of April. There was a hint of summer in the air. But there was something terrible here. Niki felt it, could almost smell it. He sensed that everyone in the yard had their eyes on him. He half expected to be given a cigarette and blindfold.

He followed Alex a short way, near to where the three men in suits stood. One, who had the face of a farmer, deeply creased and tired looking, moved away from the group and said, "Zoracoff, let me warn you, you'd better have a strong stomach."

Niki's answer was silence, but he breathed deeply and called to Alex, who walked ahead of him as if he were beginning a long march.

"Sasha," he called out, "wait a minute. Please tell me what we are doing here."

Alex stopped next to a greasy puddle, and turned to him.

"Do you see that thing?" he pointed to a boxlike tangle of steel off to his right. There were others. They'd once been cars, that was not difficult to see. But the one Alex pointed to was separate, apart, by itself. A piece of ugly modernistic sculpture, lying in grease and mud.

"There are two bodies in there."

By now everyone that was in the yard had moved closer. They began to ring Niki, and he began to panic.

"I have no need to see dead people, Sasha," Niki said gloomily.

Alex walked toward him, took him by the elbow, and led him to the crate of steel. It was Yuri's car, Niki had no doubt. It was easy to identify.

He tried to put some anger in his voice when he asked the next question, but that old feeling was ripping holes through him, and he felt his English sliding away.

"May I ask why you are doing this?"

"To show you how the people you've chosen for friends play."

"I don't have much choice, hah?"

"No."

Niki felt weak, his legs began to tremble. Alex put his hand on his back and forced him to bend.

"Look," he said, "see your friend."

It was hard for him not to look, still he resisted.

Normally when cars are crushed for junk, the seats and engine are removed. The thin steel and plastic are easily compressed to a size no larger than a standard television cabinet.

The seats had not been removed from Yuri's Mercedes, and the engine was still there. There was space, and inside that space was light. Niki had no trouble identifying his mangled friend from Tashkent. There was another body as well, and that one was even more gruesome. The face was intact, the horror still alive in wide-open eyes.

Niki fell back and sat in the mud. He felt sick and afraid. Then he got angry.

"My God, you're a bastard," he said.

"God had nothing to do with this," Alex answered. There was anger and revulsion in his voice.

Niki turned and looked into Alex's eyes. They were loaded with tears, and his cheeks were wet.

"Someone I've known is sharing that tomb with your friend," Alex hissed.

"Poor Yuri," Niki said.

"Yes," Alex said, and stood up. "Now, my Russian friend, you are going to tell me why your partner got himself crushed. And what the hell you got going with Musca and Malatesta."

To Niki's astonishment, Alex reached and grabbed a handful of his shirt, and twisted. Niki slapped his arm away.

"Face it, Niki, you're through. Next time it's you in there," Alex shouted.

Niki shrugged in mock despair.

"I should have these cops break out the gym set on you. I oughtta let them really kick your ass. Maybe wake you up."

"Don't threaten me, Sasha, it doesn't work. I've lived too long to scare so easy."

"What a character," Alex thought, stepping back so Niki could move out of the mud. "But he has balls, without a doubt." It seemed to Alex that Niki could operate in midair.

They nodded good-by to the policemen, got into Alex's car, and drove back toward Brooklyn.

Alex told him that within the past twenty-four hours, six

232

people had been murdered. And, if he included Frankie Musca, and the other two, that made a total of nine. Nine lives, and all of them connected, in one way or another, to Niki.

"Look there," Niki said, "pull in there."

It was a parking area just over the bridge, at the very toe of Brooklyn. Alex parked the car and shut the engine. "Well?" he said softly.

"There are three others," Niki said. "That makes twelve."

"What three others?"

"The Ippolito family. Two brothers and the uncle. Frankie Musca killed them. They were trying to help me with something, some business thing. It made the Muscas angry and they killed them. The Muscas are shit people."

"You think Paul Malatesta is any better, for chrissake?"

"Of course not," Niki said. "Paul Malatesta is far worse than Musca. He is intelligent, a very smart man, and I think insane."

Niki tried one last attempt to persuade himself to go easy. Never say too much, Viktor had always warned, there's always tomorrow. But he failed.

He told Alex the entire story, from Viktor to the nightclub, to Paul Malatesta. It was simple, it rolled from him. Once or twice he got sidetracked and mentioned Katya and his life in Moscow. How different things were here. How much more violent the life was. With a force of tremendous pride he spoke of how much he was respected in Moscow. How he could do things for people and that he never in his life did a violent thing.

Only eighteen months in New York, and could it be he was responsible for a dozen deaths?

"You responsible?" Alex said. "Don't give yourself so much credit."

When he saw a hardness settle on Alex's face, Niki hoped he hadn't said too much. He was at ease with this policeman, and that could be fatal. He'd put his entire future in the hands of a stranger. Finally he said, "I am not evil. I may have, in some way, been responsible for all this madness, but I am not evil."

Alex started the car and began to drive, and as he drove he considered his options. For a moment he considered calling Delaney. It was possible they could turn Niki now. Make him a full-time working informant. It was possible.

He was relieved, pleased with himself when he decided against that option. He no longer trusted the feds.

Still, if what Niki told him was true, and Alex had no reason to doubt it, he could arrest him for acting in concert to a murder, a triple-murder. His story of self-defense, and the rest, were problems for a jury, not him. No. He'd decided. He'd use Niki, not arrest him.

He could wire him up and send him back to Malatesta. Make one helluva case. Delaney would give a month's pay for that one.

"Would Malatesta talk to you again?" he asked. "Would he tell you about his plans for the guy in Italy?"

"I suppose so. Why do you ask?"

"Just thinking out loud." What a case, he thought.

Traffic was light. Alex moved quickly past Coney Island, past Sheepshead Bay. Ocean Parkway, Niki's exit, was directly ahead. He glanced across at his companion Niki and smiled. Niki smiled back and shook his head.

He thought he understood him, at last he believed he had a handle on this Russian. But he no longer saw Niki. What he saw was Vinny's eyes wide, full of fear and understanding. Maybe, at the very last moment, at the final fraction of a fraction of a second before it ends, there is understanding, knowledge, even for someone like Vinny. Then he thought, especially for someone like Vinny.

Alex eased the car to the curb, into a no parking zone in front of a synagogue. Stragglers, men, late for services, held onto their hats as they ran toward the temple steps. Niki's apartment building was on the corner.

"Tell me more about this woman in Rome," Alex said.

"Not much to tell," Niki said quickly. "Vika is a woman I knew at home. She was always a bit of a cat, you know what I mean. Smart, very smart, and very beautiful. She moved carefully. Well, anyway, she now lives in Rome and is involved with an Italian magistrate. And as luck would have it, this man is interviewing an important Mafia informant. This is obviously information Malatesta would give a great deal to know about. And it is information I can get from Vika."

"Obviously, and you told Malatesta," Alex asked him.

"Well, I told him something. If I hadn't maybe I wouldn't be here now. Maybe I'd be with Yuri and your friend."

"It's possible you can come out of this in one piece," Alex said, not because he believed it, but because he wanted it to be true. "Malatesta needs that information, and you're the one that has it. He'll wait. He won't come for you till he has it," Alex explained.

Niki became aware that Alex was listening closely, his eyes had softened. Maybe at last he'd found someone he could trust.

"How did you get yourself involved with these people?" Alex asked wearily. "You're in the country eighteen months and dealing with the worst kind of people imaginable. Then again," he sighed, "maybe they're no worse than you are." Alex said this without bitterness.

He turned from Niki and looked into the street, thinking, wondering. He thought, I have the biggest case of my career, of any police career, sitting here in my car. Niki Zoracoff is talking about the head of the most powerful Mafia family in the country, and he talks about him so easily. The man has courage . . . balls. As far as Alex was concerned, courage was a virtue; rare and special. Vinny ("Ba-Ba") Esposito, to Alex, was a virtuous man. And, like Vinny, what were Niki's chances of survival? He'd failed Vinny miserably, he remembered sadly. What was that Delaney had said? "An amateur falls in love with his informant. It's stupid."

Niki felt that he would have to explain himself simply. Still, Alex was a policeman. He very well may refuse to understand.

"It just happened," Niki said, and after he said it, he regretted it immediately.

Alex laughed.

"Look, Sasha," he said, "for me to open the restaurant I needed money, a lot of money. I accepted a loan, a secret agreement. I thought it would be okay. Soon, I found that I would need another loan, just to make the interest payments on the first. It was stupid. The information from Vika gave me room. I didn't know what was said, or by whom. The next thing I knew, they came to assassinate me."

"You were a victim," Alex said, smiling. "Trouble is that now it's hard to figure who is the victim of whom."

They sat in the car and stared at each other for a long time.

Finally Niki asked, "What do I do now, Sasha?"

"Well, for one thing, you don't give Malatesta any information."

"I decided that awhile ago. He'll not get any information from me. And then. . . ?"

Alex turned the ignition key and started the car.

"I need some time to think about this, Niki. Give me a day or two. I'll be back in touch with you. In the meantime, take my number. If anything comes up, and you want to talk to me, just call. Anytime, day or night. I'll be there. If not, leave a message on my machine, okay?"

Niki nodded.

Alex handed him his card and wrote his home phone number on the back.

Niki considered telling Alex about his plans to fly to San Diego. He decided no. He'd already said far too much.

"I really do appreciate your thinking about helping me," Niki said.

"There's always a price tag," Alex said quietly.

"I don't have much money." Niki laughed.

"I don't want your money," Alex said. "I'm not you, looking for the easy way. I get paid for what I do. No, Niki, there'll be a price all right, but it won't be payable in cash."

"If not money, what is it you want from me?"

"Information, Niki, a lot of good information."

"No, Sasha, you misunderstand. I'm not an informant. That could not be part of my life."

"No, Niki, you misunderstand. You're already an informant. The next step will be easy."

"Impossible. For me, impossible. I am no one's informant."

"Niki, you have no options. You'll call me in a few days and we'll talk. I can't believe you feel any loyalty to Malatesta."

"I don't. But it's your job to catch him, not mine."

Niki opened the car door slowly. For awhile he stood on the sidewalk and stared at Alex. When he turned to go, Alex called to him.

"You're an informant or a dead man, Niki," Alex said. Then after a short pause he added, "It's your move."

"An informant has no room to live, Sasha," Niki said sharply, "I'd rather be dead than to live for a pat on the head."

Chapter Nineteen

The 747 broke through dense clouds. Niki peered through the window hoping to get a glimpse of the world's greatest skyline. But the clouds were thick and gloomy. There was nothing to see.

Suddenly the cabin was filled with bright sunlight, so bright he shielded his eyes. Katya let out the sweetest moan, and, for a moment, Niki almost believed there was a God.

Niki was both tired and anxious. He knew that sleep would not be easy to find. Ten milligrams of Valium, and a triple vodka, encouraged him. Somewhere over Ohio, Niki drifted away.

There had been no discussion. He'd told Katya that he was flying to San Diego to meet with Viktor Vosk. It would be only for a day or two. Katya thought it sounded wonderful, and she packed her bag.

The combination of vodka and Valium negates dreams. Niki slept as though he were in the front yard of the house of death, a deep, unhealthy sleep.

Katya poked him once . . . then again. She patted his cheek.

"Up, Niki, look, it's beautiful."

There were miles of dark blue ocean, and mighty waves that left a milky trail in the sea. The waves rolled onto a narrow strip of beach that formed a neat curlicue at its farthest end. Beyond the beach, green rolling hills and a sprawling city. In that city was the Esperanza Hotel and Viktor.

"It is beautiful," he said.

"And warm," Katya smiled.

They stepped off the airplane into glorious early summer. A cloudless blue sky and a fragrance in the air that Niki believed he could taste.

At first he thought it was the Valium. Then he believed it was the combination of Valium and vodka. He felt odd, strange, almost high. Maybe he'd contracted a weird variety of air-sickness, or was it simply jet lag? They walked through the glass doors of the terminal and the feeling intensified. Finally, totally mystified and anxious, he stood still.

"Katya, I feel strange. Not ill, but strange. As if something is seriously wrong, but not wrong . . . different, strange."

"You look wonderful," Katya said. "Listen and look around you, Niki. It's the quiet."

It was true. The world moved in quarter-time. And people were smiling. Wherever he looked people seemed happy. It made him dizzy.

They had one bag, and Niki held it. Still the taxi driver insisted, so Niki let him take it from him.

He was a young man with blond, shoulder-length hair. He wore a blue T-shirt, and white pants that were cut off just above the knees. In his sandals, and soft smile, he made Niki marvel at how much he resembled the picture Niki'd always had of the typical American.

The driver held the door for Katya. Niki hesitated before getting into the rear seat, Moscow residue, he'd probably never lose it. It was ironic, taxicabs made him think of home.

"Where to, folks?"

"In San Diego, the Esperanza Hotel," Niki said.

"Right-o. You did say the Esperanza Hotel?"

"Yes, the Esperanza Hotel in San Diego."

The driver reached into the car's glove compartment and removed a small, green book.

"I thought I knew every hotel in the city," he said, "but this must be a new one. New hotels are popping around here like mushrooms after a rain. Not that we get any rain," he said.

"Is the weather always like this?" asked Katya.

"Boring, isn't it?"

"Terrible." Katya laughed.

"I detect an accent." The driver smiled and glanced at them, then fingered his book. "Where ya from?"

"New York," Katya said, and Niki said "Moscow," on top of her New York. They all laughed.

"Now, now, let's get this straight," the driver said.

"My husband is right. We're from Moscow. We just happen to live in New York now."

"The old Big Apple." Then the driver added, "There's no Esperanza Hotel in San Diego. It's in Encinitas, about twenty miles south of the city on the coast road. It's right on the ocean. A beautiful little town, you're going to love it."

Within seconds they were out of the airport. The driver whistled at the road and Katya rested her head on Niki's shoulder. Her hand made small circles on his thigh, and Niki fell in love all over again.

The coast highway took them past green rolling hills. The Pacific Ocean, on their left, sparkled to the horizon, just beyond graceful bright valleys.

Three hundred feet below their terrace a couple were beach walking, each with an arm over the other's shoulder. They were in slow love, Niki thought. The carefree, wondrous time.

He watched them for what seemed a long while. The couple stopped beneath him in front of great brown rocks that rose from the sea like the backs of primeval monsters. The woman turned, faced Niki, and waved. Then the man extended his arm. Surprised, Niki stepped backward, then forward, gripping the balcony rail. He gave a half-hearted wave, saw their smiles, and raised both his arms.

Back in the apartment, Katya was already in shorts and sneakers.

"Niki, let's run on the beach," she said quietly.

Within the hour they sat on a rock and watched the sea.

The strolling couple Niki had seen earlier was gone. A single sailboat drifted in a light breeze one hundred meters offshore. Katya screamed, "There, in the water, Niki! Quick, Niki! Just behind that last rock."

Niki scanned the beach, then he looked out to sea. He put his hands across his forehead to shade his eyes and looked alongside the rocks.

Katya shrieked, "There, Niki! See them there?"

He felt panicked. Was someone coming out of the ocean to get him? Mafia terrorists rising from the sea to come for him? They'd take him off, crush him, like they did Yuri. He moved quickly, lost his footing, and slid from the rock.

"They look like people. My God, Niki, they're beautiful."

"What?" he screamed.

He fixed his concentration on Katya's finger, and in the direction she pointed. Then he saw one leap, then another, and another. A big one on its back moved across the surface like a torpedo.

Spinning, dancing, idling in the water not fifty feet from him, a group of sea lions were doing business with the Pacific Ocean.

After a time Niki looked over to Katya who seemed lost in some private emotion.

"What are you thinking?" Niki asked.

"That we are so far from home, my Niki, so far."

"Maybe not," he said, and Katya smiled.

Walking quietly, not speaking, they made their way along the beach. After a while they stopped at a spot that put them directly in front of the hotel. A boulder, like the top of a squat, brown volcano, jutted waist high through the sand.

"Should I be afraid?" Katya asked, leaning on the volcano.

"Of what?" Niki asked. Then he added, "It really is paradise here, isn't it?"

"Will the Mafia kill you like they did Yuri?"

"I have nothing to do with the Mafia, Katya. Why do you ask such questions?"

"Because I'm your wife, and I have a right to know."

"Because you're my wife?"

"No, because I love you."

He watched Katya try to smile. She nodded, then shrugged her shoulders as though his nonanswers were the best she could hope for.

"Kayta, please, I don't want you to worry about such things. I have nothing to do with the Mafia. Yuri was involved with God knows what. His business was his own. It had nothing to do with me."

"I see," she said. "Then can you tell me what we are doing here in San Diego, California?"

"To see Viktor Vosk, my old friend. My colleague from Moscow. I told you, he sent word to me through Vika. He wants me to meet him here at this hotel."

"But why San Diego, Niki? Why not New York?"

Niki turned toward the hotel and saw Viktor standing with his arms crossed. He stood on Niki's balcony. A passing jogger stopped his run to look and see what Niki was staring at. "Viktor," he said softly to himself. Then Niki began to walk. He walked toward the sheer steps that led to the hotel. Viktor waved, and Niki broke into an even trot, then he was running,

running flat out, running as he did when he was a teenager and ran from the Militia in Pushkin Square.

Two boys, dark as Indians, moved aside. He took the steps two at a time. He ran as a son did to a father, to a father that had been taken from him, to a father who now returned, came home at a time when the son needed him most. Niki's eyes were wet, he felt embarrassed, but then he decided there was nothing wrong with that, nothing wrong with tears. Sons cry for their fathers. Sons the world over cry for their fathers all the time.

Viktor met him at the top of the stairs and they embraced.

Dizzy with joy, Niki stared at the old policeman in wonder. An ancient feeling surged through him, a feeling older than the brown rocks on the beach beneath them. Son for father, student for teacher, novice for mentor, and Niki revelled in the feeling, delighted in it. He held Viktor's face in his hands, and listened wide-eyed to the voice from home.

Katya came up behind him, and touched his shoulder. Niki turned to her and said, "Look, Katya, look at Viktor."

"You look wonderful," she said. "You look ten years younger than you did when we left the Union."

She was right. Niki couldn't believe it. Viktor's face was firm, not puffy and yellow. His eyes were clear and bright. He'd lost weight, he was clean shaven. The tufts of hair that Niki remembered sprouting from Viktor's nose and ears were gone.

Viktor Vosk was a new man, a healthy new man.

"I've been watching you two from the balcony for quite some time. You look like teenage lovers in Gorky Park, not an old married couple."

They stood together on the balcony for a long time, looking into each other's eyes, and smiling.

Katya brought chairs from their room, vodka, and two glasses.

"We have much to talk about," Niki said.

Viktor looked at Katya in silence for a moment. He smiled and said, "Come join us, Katya. I have news from home, and you can tell me about your adventures in the shining city."

Even to Niki, Viktor did not sound convincing. He spoke to Katya as if she were a schoolgirl.

Katya smiled sadly, looked at Niki, and slowly shook her head.

"No," she said, "I think I should go. I'll go watch the sea lions."

"Stay here, Katya. Don't you want to hear news from home, from Moscow?" Niki asked.

Katya walked to the head of the stairs that led to the beach and Niki walked with her.

"You can stay," he whispered.

"I don't trust that man, Niki, I never have."

Niki was stung.

"Katya, Viktor is like my father. He *is* my father."

"Remember that *I* love you, Niki." Katya stood a step beneath him, and neither moved.

"Come, Niki," Viktor called. "Come and tell me about the Western Wonderland."

Katya said, "I'll be back in an hour or so, Niki. I'll be here when you need me."

By the time Katya was on the beach, Niki and Viktor were laughing, squeezing each other's shoulders. Katya walked to the edge of the water. Niki glanced down at her. She had her back to the sea and was looking at them.

"So," Niki began, "tell me, I'm dying to know what brings you to America. Have you emigrated? Did you defect? How did you get here, you old bull?"

Viktor reached out his hand. "I drink less now, but I drink," he said.

"How about a toast to old friends and adventures."

They both laughed outrageously, and Niki poured the vodka.

"You first, Niki," Viktor said. "Tell me how you have done? How is your life here? You have been here for almost two years, so . . . what has it been like?"

"Eighteen months and two weeks," Niki said, then he drank his vodka. It was cold. Katya had left it in the small refrigerator in their hotel room. It tasted wonderful. Vodka, like fine wine, Niki thought, improves geometrically when it's drunk in the company of good friends.

Niki looked at Viktor and then at his vodka glass. Viktor was smiling.

"I needed you here, Viktor, God did I need you."

Niki talked for two hours. Viktor only interrupted with a grunt, a nod, a shake of the head. Niki was so lost in his story that he never noticed Katya walk from the beach, come halfway up the stairs, turn around, and return to the beach.

"Isn't it tragic," Viktor said at last, "that a country this enormous, this powerful, is incapable of policing itself? And still it insists on trying to police the world. To reshape the world in its own image. To spread this madness you describe from one corner of the earth to the other. Men who look like women, women who behave like men, teenagers who fall somewhere in between. All of them crazy from drugs. When I see America, do you know what I see, Niki? I see comfort and dirt. Dirty people living comfortably. I don't mean filthy streets, and unwashed people, though they seem to have much of both. You should see Los Angeles, Niki, San Francisco. No morality, no order, the people in this country behave like in a wild cowboy movie. The police don't matter, Niki. It doesn't seem as if the police here do anything. It's a madhouse with the windows and doors wide open and no guards. The single most tragic nightmare of the twentieth century is the United States of America."

Quite a speech, Niki thought, then he laughed. "Well," he said, "since when have you become so political? This change in you, Viktor, is very dramatic."

Niki got up from his seat and stretched. They'd been talking for hours. Where was Katya, he wondered. It was dusk, the sea seemed very quiet, ghostlike, beneath them. Niki stretched over the balcony and looked along the beach for Katya. She was nowhere to be seen.

"It is not a joke, Niki, this is not at all funny," Viktor said from behind him.

"Where's Katya?" Niki asked, concerned. "Have you seen her?"

According to his watch, Katya had been gone for almost three hours.

"She's sitting on those rocks," Viktor said, "off there to your left."

"Katya!" Niki shouted. There was no response, but he did see a figure. That was no comfort, so he called again.

Niki realized that it was Katya, and she was sitting alone. It was getting dark, and she was some distance off. Finally, after he called a third time, she raised her hand. Niki waved, then turned back to Viktor.

"It really isn't so bad, you know," he said.

"What isn't?" Viktor asked.

"The States, America."

Viktor grunted. "Don't kid yourself, Niki. They'd like to spread this poison you see everywhere around you."

"C'mon, Viktor, since when have you become so political? At home, in the Union, you weren't a revolutionary. Is it this decadence, this delicious decadence you see, that's raised your consciousness?"

Niki laughed. He refused to take Viktor seriously. The man never had a political thought. He was wondering what the joke was. Why was Viktor performing for him?

Viktor got up from his chair and walked to the balcony railing.

"I've always been a loyal supporter of the revolution. And I've always been political. You just never noticed. You never paid attention."

"Please, Viktor," Niki said sharply, "I've known you for ten years. You're talking to me, not some KGB interrogator. You're a revolutionary, all right. You were fighting the system the day I met you. And you were fighting it the day I left the Union. You and I are not political. Remember, we served the people of Moscow together. We had spirit. It was all a game, just a game. Please don't get political on me now, Viktor."

"You're a fool, Niki," Viktor snorted.

"Viktor, what the hell has gotten into you?"

"You have been here for two years!" Viktor said.

"Eighteen months, two weeks," Niki corrected.

"Damn it, everything is not a joke. Come on, Niki, look around you. Is this the world you want for your children?"

Niki began to laugh, and as he laughed he grabbed his old friend by the shoulders and shook him. He pulled Viktor to him and embraced him.

"I think you've lost your mind, Niki."

Niki laughed harder.

"I really do, Niki, something has gone out in your head. You could use a rest in a sanitarium."

Niki began to cough. It was from the smoking. The look on his face was that of acute physical pain. Still he continued to laugh.

Viktor had returned to his chair, though not before going into the hotel room and coming out with a water glass, which he half-filled with vodka.

"So," Niki said, opening his arms the way he did when he felt relaxed, untroubled, at peace. "So I should look around me and see if this is a place I would want to raise my children.

You've come to the wrong city for that speech, Viktor. In Brighton Beach I would not have laughed."

Niki leaned his back against the terrace railing. He stood directly in front of Viktor.

"Tell me, Viktor Vosk, my old friend, my comrade, where does all this anti-American, up-with-the-revolution bullshit come from? When I left, and there was no one to look after you, someone turned you into a reborn communist. They made you stop drinking, cleaned your ears and nose, gave you horseshit to eat and you thought it was chocolate. I never should have left. You see, you old bull, you needed me."

"Try to be serious, Niki."

"Serious? I couldn't be more serious. Do you want to tell me what you are doing here?"

"I'm on a mission for the government," he said, and neatly finished the water glass of vodka.

Niki again began to laugh.

"Please, Niki," Viktor shouted, "will you laugh at my funeral? Will you laugh when they take me to Lubyanka and I disappear in the fucking snow?"

"What happened, Viktor, will you please tell me what happened?" Niki asked quietly. "Birds don't become elephants in eighteen months."

"I got my fingers burned."

"Well, that's not hard to believe. How?"

"Labor books. You weren't the only one in Moscow with a forged labor book. It was just too bad they weren't all Jews. I could have gotten rid of the evidence if they were."

Viktor got up from his chair and walked into the room. He returned with still another vodka. But this time there was something of the old Viktor in him. His trousers were undone, and his shirttail had popped from his pants.

"Well?" Niki asked.

"You don't understand what it is like in Lubyanka. I was charged, tried, and sentenced in six weeks. Twenty years,

Niki. They wanted to send me to prison for twenty years."

"What kind of hell is Lubyanka? You certainly came out trim and fit. And speaking of getting out . . ."

"I was about to get to that. Twenty years, Niki, is a long, long time. Are you paying attention?"

"Go on, twenty years is a long time . . . and . . ."

"Well, I became somewhat friendly with one of the interrogators."

"That's not unusual," Niki said. "It's part of his job."

"Hers." Viktor smiled.

"All the better, then what?"

"Well, we were talking about Jews one day, you know the usual stuff, *blah, blah, blah*. I told Natalie, that was her name, Natalie. I told her I had friends in the émigré community, and you know, *blah, blah, blah*."

"Viktor, fill in the *blahs*, could you? Why do I get a feeling that you were *blahing* about me?"

Niki then went into the room and poured himself a drink. He walked to the edge of the terrace, made sure Katya had not been washed from the rocks, and sat back down.

"Well, I told Natalie that I knew one émigré in particular, that did not want to leave the Union, but felt he had to, for reasons that were a complicated family matter."

"And she believed you?"

"Yes, of course. You see, I am here. They made me a proposition, *blah, blah*."

"Viktor!"

"And part of their proposition was for me to make you a proposition. Do you want to hear it?"

"Why not?"

"They told me that they needed intelligence inside the émigré community in America. And that, furthermore, many of the émigrés are skilled technicians and so on. And from their point of view someone that would be willing to undertake . . . you know what I mean."

"Spying on their fellow émigrés."

"Yes. Well, that person could receive substantial gain. And someone he thinks of as a father would be paroled from prison. Given an opportunity to start a new life. All debts paid."

"And that's what they told you?"

"Yes."

"That's all of it?"

"Yes."

Niki sat in thought.

"You know, Viktor," he began, "during the past eighteen months I have found myself in situations, forced to make decisions that would make your head swim. And all during that time, I suffered, because I didn't have you with me. My counselor. I believed that I needed your advice desperately."

Viktor bowed his head, took a sip of vodka and smiled. "We were a good team, Niki. Pushkin Square will never see the likes of us again."

"But, while I was running on the beach," Niki continued, "after I saw you standing on the balcony with your arms crossed in that way of yours, I remembered."

"Remembered what?"

"I remembered that you gave plenty of advice all right, but that I never took it."

"You were always impatient, Niki."

Viktor's eyes began to shine. Soon they would fill. Soon, he would look like the old Viktor.

"That's not the point," Niki said. "The point is that I've always made up my own mind, did what I thought was right. But that doesn't mean I love you less or need you less. You, Viktor, and Katya, are my only family. And you are a family *I* choose . . . me . . . another good decision."

"And the proposition, Niki? What about the proposition?"

"What proposition?"

There was a dull smile on Viktor's face.

"*Niki.*"

"Oh, *that* proposition. Tell them, thank you for their interest, but I decline. In other words, Viktor, tell them they can go piss off."

Viktor did not think that was funny, not funny at all, and he told Niki so.

"You don't fool with the KGB, Niki. No, not with them. You, my Pushkin Square playmate, have never met such people. No sense of humor. They won't laugh at your jokes. People that make you sweat when you're freezing are not people to laugh at."

Viktor stared at Niki and there was something in those eyes of his that said you have to learn, you need to be taught. Niki was reminded of Paul Malatesta . . . and it made him shake with rage.

"And you carry messages from such people?" Niki said.

He got up, walked to the railing, and kept his back to Viktor.

"I'd hoped that you would help me solve my problems, not bring me a list of new ones," he said sharply.

"Do you know what their plans are for me?" Viktor replied.

Niki turned and faced his old friend and comrade.

"No," he said, "and I'm past caring. I'm tired, Viktor. Tired of being used, tired of being twisted into something I'm not. I'm good and fucking tired, Viktor. You got yourself in trouble, you're not going to use me to get you out. People are coming at me from everywhere, the cosmos lives with shit people out for my head. They're coming up out of the earth for me. Viktor, I don't care anymore—I'm done. You're on your own."

The last phrase floated from Niki's mouth and stood in midair between them. Viktor's whole body tensed. A tremor ran through his hands and vodka spilled from his glass. It dripped and stained the new suit the KGB had bought for him.

"You're an ungrateful bastard," Viktor said, then he sighed audibly. He ran his hand across his lips, swallowed hard, then walked to the railing.

The dying light that fell on Viktor's face revealed a very frightened man. And age, with its lines and sagging skin, skin with a sheen of soft yellow, returned to Viktor's face. All that Viktor was, not three short hours before, drained from him.

Niki watched his old friend standing helpless like a stricken child.

"I need your help," Viktor moaned.

Niki wagged his head. Then he said as gently as he could, "I can't help you, Viktor. I'm no one's informant, you, most of all, should know that."

"So it's not that you can't help me, it's that you won't?"

"Have it your way."

"I suppose I should not have expected more from a fucking, selfish Jew," Viktor hissed, then he finished the contents of his glass and smiled. It was almost the old Viktor smile, kind of loose and jaunty. But this time Niki saw evil there . . . and it made him sad, sadder than he'd ever been.

"You know, of course," he said, "that that last stupid statement doesn't do much for your case." Niki sighed and continued. "I think you'd better go."

"Goddamn you, Niki," Viktor said evenly. And there was something in the way he stood, holding on to the railing, that told Niki not to answer him. A door to his past had just been quietly shut, somewhere deep inside him a light had gone off.

Daylight had become sunset, and now the sky was full of color. The Pacific Ocean beneath them seemed as quiet and as gentle as a lake.

Katya stood in semidarkness at the end of the balcony. Niki looked at her for a long time and she stared back at him until he felt foolish. She looked at Viktor with eyes like stones, then made her way across the balcony and now stood with Niki at the railing. Niki had never loved her more.

"Go away, Viktor," she said, "go away before I call the police."

The following night Niki and Katya boarded the plane to New York. Petra and Vasily were waiting at Kennedy Airport. And Niki and Katya were greeted as they had been greeted when they first arrived from Europe, with flowers and champagne and a rented limousine.

It was early morning and the parkway allowed the limo to move easy.

"So," Petra said, in his quickly improving English, "you survived California. Many blond people, no? Many crazy people? Motorcycles, hah? Disneyland, hah?"

Petra was driving, glancing in the rearview, laughing. Vasily handed glasses to Niki and Katya. Niki answered Petra in Russian, and he spoke with authority.

"Slow down," he said, "and why the celebration?" he added.

"I don't know," said Petra cheerfully. "It seemed like a good idea."

"It is," Katya said, "thank you both."

Vasily carefully poured champagne into tumbler glasses that were already half full of orange juice.

"How was your friend?" he asked Niki softly.

Petra eased the limo into the right lane. They were approaching the access for the Belt Parkway, to Brooklyn.

"Go straight ahead," Niki said. "I want to go into Manhattan."

Petra almost asked why, but when he saw the expression on Niki's face, he nodded, moved to the center lane, then roared off to the Grand Central Parkway, and the Triborough Bridge.

"My old friend," Niki said, "is dead, Vasily." Vasily raised his eyebrows.

Niki turned away and looked out of the window. "Viktor died and was reborn a Stalinist."

Vasily roared. Petra broke into a silly, confused grin. Katya smiled and sipped her drink.

"Ah, but California," Katya said. "There are sea lions in the water, and the air smells like gardenias."

"I heard that the air is green," said Petra seriously.

"Where did you hear that?" asked Vassily. "On radio Moscow?"

"No, from an Israeli cab driver that lives in New Jersey."

Niki turned around in his seat. He didn't want to, but he laughed nevertheless.

"There's an apartment building on Seventy-fifth Street and Second. You can pull directly into the garage under the building, Petra," Niki said.

Katya tugged at his sleeve. "It's all right," Niki whispered. "I'll just be a minute. I need to speak to someone."

Niki left Vasily in the limo with Katya, and told Petra to come along.

They walked up a short flight of steps to a door that led to the building's lobby. Niki glanced up at the TV cameras. They passed the elevators, and went to a desk, where a man in a blue and gold uniform sat in front of four TV screens.

"Can I help you?" the man asked. He looked past Niki to Petra whose red head, on his six-foot-three-inch frame, spun as if on a swivel, his mouth open, his gold tooth shining, his eyes stretched wide, as he took in the dazzle of the crystal chandeliers and the mirrored walls.

"My name is Niki Zoracoff. I'm here to see Mister Malatesta."

The doorman, looking sharp in his blue cap and golden epaulets, stood up.

"We have no Malatesta here," he said.

"I was here, just a few days ago," Niki said evenly. "I was right here, and I went to Mister Malatesta's apartment. It was on the sixth floor."

"Check your book," Petra said. Niki turned to Petra and smiled.

"I know there is no Malatesta here. Are you sure it was this building?" the doorman asked calmly.

"Let me see the book," Niki said.

"I will not. No one looks at that book 'cept me, and people that work here."

Petra picked up the black leather-covered, loose leaf book, and handed it to Niki.

"How would you like me to call the police?" said the doorman, sitting back down.

There was, in fact, no one named Malatesta listed. Under the R's Niki found the name Reno, John Reno, apartment 6-A.

He handed the doorman back his book and told him to ring apartment 6-A.

"That is not Malatesta. That is Mister John Reno," the doorman said with a superior throw of his head.

"Call him," Niki said.

The elevator door opened and John Reno stepped out, his arms crossed, a half-smile on his face. He glanced at Niki. When his eyes fell on Petra he seemed to take a step back.

Niki walked to John Reno and took his hand.

"Whadaya say, Niki? What brings you here?"

"I'd like to see Mister Malatesta for a minute."

"Don't read the newspapers, do you?" John Reno asked.

Then he walked over to the doorman's desk, opened the top drawer, and took out a copy of the *Daily News*. The doorman whispered something to him. John Reno smiled and patted his head. He then handed Niki the newspaper.

Niki read the front page headline, turned to the second page, and scanned the story. It was full of drama, quite an event had taken place. Niki had to struggle to keep from smiling. This was serious, not something John Reno would find amusing.

255

The headline read Under Attack: The Mob. The story went on to detail that Italian authorities in Rome had announced plans to arrest Mafia chieftains throughout Italy. Federal prosecutors in America, it said, were cooperating with their Italian counterparts. U.S. officials announced they were ready to mount the most sweeping attack on the Mafia since the days of Elliot Ness!

"Who was Elliot Ness?" Niki asked John Reno.

John Reno shrugged, took the newspaper from Niki and returned it to the doorman. Then he said, "Mister Malatesta won't be around for awhile. He's taking a vacation. And believe me, the poor guy needs it."

"Good for him," Niki said softly. Then he added, "Can you get a message to him for me?"

John Reno sniffed. "Don't see any problem."

"Tell him that I'm going to arrange to pay back the money I owe. And that is all I can do."

John Reno sniffed again.

"Will you tell him that?"

John Reno, Niki assumed, understood the meaning of what he'd just said, because he closed his eyes and nodded.

Chapter Twenty

The phone, it seemed, rang at dawn, and Alex listened to Niki more asleep than awake. And so, with false brightness he said, "I'll meet you whenever, wherever, however you want."

Niki told him they'd meet after he closed the club. Alex was to go to the Brighton Beach boardwalk at Eighteenth Street. "That's around four o'clock in the morning," Alex said.

"No, more like five o'clock," answered Niki.

To Alex, five o'clock the following morning, when it was now just 9 A.M., seemed like a century away.

He'd hung up the telephone, rolled back into bed thinking that there had been a real long pause on the line when he told Niki that yes, he'd seen the newspaper. He'd seen it the night before, and yes, he did believe him now.

Alex had discussed possible options for Niki with Chief Ross. They'd both agreed, the smiling Russian had none. He'd cooperate or go to jail. Alex had him under his thumb. Niki had been foolish. He'd told him too much, he'd gone too far. For Niki Zoracoff the match was over.

Vasily and Petra listened to Niki's plans with far less joy than had Katya.

She'd leaped from the floor, thrown her legs around his waist, circled his neck with her arms, and shrieked, "I was hoping, oh, Niki, I was hoping so hard. And I prayed, Niki, I prayed. When do we leave?" Soon, he'd told her, as soon as I can arrange it.

Vasily and Petra glanced back and forth at each other when Niki told them they could have the club. They'd buy him out with notes, pay him on time, the American way.

As for Malatesta, and the money he owed the Italians, he'd handle it somehow.

Hadn't they once told him that the bill was paid? Didn't they say he was free and clear? He'd work it out. Niki believed that he could work anything out. After all, he was the Prince of Pushkin Square.

Still, there was Alexander Simon, Sasha, and his little tricks. Niki believed that he'd taken the first steps toward climbing out of the hole he was in. He believed that he was in control now, yesterday, and he would be tomorrow.

Alex had a miserable day and spent most of it trying to think of the right words that would trigger Niki, get him gently to roll over.

He felt regret; wished it could be different. However, this time around he'd not fall in love with his informant. Niki would not haunt his nights, like Vinny. He did not handle Vinny the right way. He wondered if there was a right way.

Alex decided to spend the night, the waiting time, with a Chilean woman he knew in South Brooklyn.

She lived in a four-story walk-up on Degraw Street across from a Pentecostal church. He could make out the rhythmic sounds of tambourines. The melody was from the old country song "Red River Valley." The lyrics were in Spanish. They sang about Christ, but the melody was definitely "Red River Valley."

She made pastellas and rice with beans. They ate and made love on the floor. Afterward he watched as she polished her fingernails, and he listened to her describe, in the minutest detail, a haircut she was considering.

In the shower he counted thirty different kinds of shampoos. Before he left she made him strong Latin coffee.

It was four in the morning when he drove off. He thought, why would I want to live any other way.

As Alex drove in silence on the Gowanus Expressway, the lamps at Moscow Nights grew dark.

Petra seemed neither tired nor ill, but in the dim light of a street lamp, he asked Niki if Vasily could drive him home. He said he wasn't well. Vasily did not talk at all. Niki was puzzled. He felt very tired. He studied Petra's face, then shrugged.

It would be okay. Tonight he could be alone.

He walked from the restaurant, past the men's club, two short blocks to the steps that led to the boardwalk. He then walked straight to his favorite bench and sat. He flicked a cigarette between the boardwalk railings and watched the glow die in the sand.

Niki had decided that for a chance at a new life with Katya in San Diego, he'd give serious consideration to Alex's proposition. But he wanted to hear the details. He wanted to know what he was letting himself in for. For now, he put the thought of being an informant out of his mind. Belonging, he thought, was the most important thing. He wanted to fit in somewhere.

And it was not as if he hadn't tried. He had. It just never seemed to work out.

The Brighton Beach boardwalk, unlike San Diego, was pale, without color. But the ocean smells were strong here. He lit another cigarette and breathed in the smell of the sea.

Niki tried to see somehow through the darkness to the ocean. He saw nothing but blackness compounded by darkness. Niki always felt a strange elation here on the boardwalk waiting for sunrise. He'd sit, and wonder if there was a God out there. And if there was, why was it only for other people, not for him?

He leaned back against the bench and stretched. He was tired. He was lonely. He missed Katya, and suddenly he felt chilled.

To his right he heard the sound of footfalls on the steps that came up to the boardwalk. He was glad that Alex had decided to arrive early. He put on the smile that was now famous from Pushkin Square to Brighton Beach. A pale line of light touched the horizon. Niki blinked. It wasn't Alex coming to meet him, but a child, or maybe a dwarf. He was too weary to tell.